The
ANTIQUE STORE
Detective

BOOKS BY CLARE CHASE

Tara Thorpe Mystery series

Murder on the Marshes

Death on the River

Death Comes to Call

Murder in the Fens

Eve Mallow Mystery series

Mystery on Hidden Lane

Mystery at Apple Tree Cottage

Mystery at Seagrave Hall

Mystery at the Old Mill

Mystery at the Abbey Hotel

Mystery at the Church

Mystery at Magpie Lodge

Mystery at Lovelace Manor

Mystery at Southwood School

Mystery at Farfield Castle

Mystery at Saltwater Cottages

Mystery on Meadowsweet Grove

CLARE CHASE

The ANTIQUE STORE Detective

Bookouture

Published by Bookouture in 2024

An imprint of Storyfire Ltd.
Carmelite House
50 Victoria Embankment
London EC4Y 0DZ

www.bookouture.com

ISBN: 978-1-83790-196-8
eBook ISBN: 978-1-83790-195-1

For David and Pat, with much love

ONE

A LITTLE DOMESTIC DIFFICULTY

Late in the afternoon on Sunday, Bella Winter was standing under a blissfully hot shower, feeling more human by the minute. Her shower gel filled the cubicle with the most glorious scent of honeysuckle and she smiled, closing her eyes. She had just started singing when the water went freezing. Her words changed abruptly in pitch and content. The shower had a sunflower head – you couldn't just duck out of the way.

Ice-cold jets poured down her face as she grabbed for the controls to switch it off.

Blasted thing. After a horribly early start to her day, its behaviour felt treacherous. She'd been up at four, and in her electric ex-London taxi by quarter to five, travelling to an antiques fair in a neighbouring county. She'd come back laden with stock for her shop, and had spent the hour before the shower unloading it all. She'd only bought small pieces this time and had crammed them onto shelves in her study-cum-storeroom.

Bella had moved to the flat six months earlier, but she'd known it long before that. As she stepped out of the shower and wrapped herself in a thick towel, she thought back to lounging in that same bathroom, surrounded by bubbles, as her policeman father sat in his study, pondering a case. Bella had visited him there often from the age of six, after her parents split up.

The flat, nestled in the Shropshire Hills in the town of Hope Eaton, had spelled sanctuary. A warm, calm oasis in contrast to her mum's commune-like run-down house in London.

Standing safely outside the cubicle, Bella turned the shower on again and waited for it to behave itself. As she stood there shivering, she surveyed the room and felt she'd come home. Except home had changed. Been overwritten by two owners since her father's day. He'd died twelve years ago, when Bella was twenty-nine, but there were echoes of him everywhere. His calm smile and gentle voice. Her heart still contracted at the memories, but the sense of his presence was comforting too.

The flat's interim owners had introduced some luxury that her practical father would never have considered, including the walk-in shower and a claw-foot bath. It was a ridiculously spacious bathroom for a flat, but Bella loved it. If you were going to bathe, you might as well do it in style. Her mum's old house, with its rising damp, meant she appreciated life's luxuries.

Bella stuck her hand under the shower and withdrew it immediately. Even colder than before. The weather outside was bitter and the boiler was clearly doing nothing. She sighed and switched the water off.

The flat was a ground-floor conversion in seventeenth-century Southwell Hall, with views over the River Kite on one side, and the town of Hope Eaton, rising out of the valley, on the other. The estate agent had sung the praises of the period features, of course. When she'd bought the place, she hadn't appreciated the boiler might be one of them.

She dragged on the 1940s swing trousers she had ready,

with their four-button side fastening – a period detail that gave her great pleasure – then layered up in figure-hugging sweaters.

A moment later, she was standing on a chair in her flat's kitchen-diner, resetting the boiler, which looked dead as a doornail.

No joy.

She checked the troubleshooting section of the manual. It wasn't her preferred weekend entertainment – the sofa was calling to her loudly.

Fix after fix failed to produce a result. This wasn't the time to keep flogging a dead horse. She picked up her phone to google a professional. She called a local outfit with a 4.7-star rating, feeling a rush of relief that was quickly dashed. They couldn't help until five the following day. After cordially pursuing the matter, just to make certain they couldn't squeeze her in, she eyed a guy who'd achieved 2.7 stars. Looking at the lifeless boiler and the frost-covered trees outside, she decided he had to be better than nothing and dialled. No one picked up.

She called the first lot back and booked. They continued to be terribly apologetic that they couldn't help sooner and she continued to be gushingly understanding. By the end of the conversation, she'd heard about their daughter's upcoming wedding and told them about her shop, Vintage Winter. Before she rang off, the call handler eagerly agreed that an antique would beat any modern mass-produced wedding present. Bella hung up feeling warm and fuzzy; there was nothing like a friendly conversation topped off with the prospect of a sale. She made a note of the woman's details. She could pick up where they'd left off if they met in real life.

As she went back to the manual, willing one of the fixes to work, the fuzzy feeling wore off. Tomorrow during the day would be okay. Vintage Winter was closed on Mondays but the auction houses she planned to visit would be crowded, warm and welcoming. Between now and then, she'd be stuck in her rapidly cooling flat. Her mind flicked to her neighbour, Matt. She could see if he had an electric heater or a hot water bottle he could lend her. But she barely knew him. She was better acquainted with his cat, who sidled into her flat at every opportunity. She had a certain respect for the creature: it seemed sure of its goals and appeared to like her teal armchair almost as much as she did.

She regretted giving her own heater to one of her sisters now. They'd seemed more in need at the time. They usually did.

She shook her head. She wouldn't bother Matt. He was probably too impractical to have anything as mundane as a heater anyway. He kept odd hours and had a constant stream of girlfriends sashaying in and out.

She'd rather sort things out herself. Besides, Matt was the brother of John, the assistant manager at her shop. Word might get back and John would feel obliged to offer help. Invite her to stay the night or something. He was too kind not to. It would be awkward all round. And the last thing she wanted was to come across as a helpless no-hoper.

She abandoned the boiler manual a second time and called the Blue Boar, but their rooms were fully booked. She'd been outside to check the boiler's condensing pipe when her mobile rang. She answered without looking, hoping it might be tomorrow's plumber offering a cancellation.

It was her mother, Amanda. She'd abandoned the title of 'Mum' when Bella was around four. She'd said it made her feel old.

'You take so long to pick up, darling. Anyone would think you didn't want to speak to me.'

Perish the thought. 'I was doing battle with my boiler.'

'I beg your pardon?'

Bella explained. It hurt to admit she was failing to tackle the problem. It had always been borderline chaos at Amanda's, growing up. Bella had dealt with lots of domestic issues, especially after her three half-sisters were born. She'd often felt older than her mum.

'Oh, dear. Have you thought of calling an engineer? Anyway, darling, I rang to tell you Thea's news. The clever thing's only got herself shortlisted for best newcomer at the Randall Awards.'

Bella's youngest half-sister. She was in a band and most often to be found lurching from one crisis to another. When she was in trouble, she called Bella. When it was good news, it was their mother who heard. Thea was the one who had Bella's heater. Bella gazed at the lack of pilot light and thought dark thoughts as Amanda filled her in.

Her mother had scratched together a living writing literary short stories when Bella was a child, supplemented by income from their boarders. She got critical acclaim but precious little cash. She was better off these days, thanks to some successful novels, and Amanda deVere had become a known name. Her mother loved the fact that Thea was exploring her artistic side, and Bella's second-to-youngest sister got kudos for her patchy acting career too. (She did an awful lot of waiting tables.) Bella and her nearest sibling, an academic, didn't come in for the same admiration. And Bella was the odd one out. The other offspring were all deVeres, like their mother. She was the only Winter – her father's sole child – but she was proud of that.

She loved her career too. All the more now she'd left the antiques shop she was managing in London and set up her own business.

She'd admitted defeat with the boiler and was assessing a Kilner jar as a possible hot water bottle when her mother rang again.

'I've solved your boiler problem,' she said. 'I should have thought of it immediately, only I was so distracted by Thea's news. You remember the poet I told you about in Hope Eaton?'

Bella did remember. Her mother had met the woman at a literary festival and had encouraged Bella to look her up.

'*I can't believe you haven't made contact yet,*' Amanda continued. '*I assumed you would have when I called her.*'

'You did what?' Bella treated all her mother's acquaintances with extreme caution.

'*Called her. I knew she'd have you to stay. She and her husband have a huge pile just up the hill as you head east out of the valley. I was surprised that you hadn't met yet, but it makes no odds.*' No odds to whom? Bella couldn't believe Amanda had landed her and this unsuspecting contact with a fait accompli. '*She's happy to put you up. Why freeze when you don't have to?*'

Having let Bella run wild for her entire childhood, Amanda's sudden impulse to interfere came as an unwelcome surprise. A woman in her forties ought to control her own destiny. Bella took a deep breath and tried to relax her shoulder muscles. 'I refuse to land myself on total strangers.'

'*Nonsense,*' her mother said. '*Alexis is expecting you.*'

TWO

A DISTURBANCE IN THE NIGHT

Dinner at Raven House was just as awkward as Bella had predicted.

Random visitors had traipsed in and out of her mother's place while she was growing up and Amanda had loved it. True to form, she assumed everyone else must too.

But sitting opposite Alexis and Harvey Howard in their formal dining room, Bella could tell they were cut from a different cloth. She had a feeling they'd rowed before she'd turned up and that she might be the cause. Alexis had probably agreed to invite her under duress, before passing on the good news to her husband. Bella had already apologised on her own and her mother's account. Thanks to her upbringing, she was used to tackling all kinds of situations, but all the same, she wished she'd put her foot down and not come.

After dinner, they moved to a large reception room. The furniture was a feast for the eyes, but although there were some standout pieces, Bella would never furnish her home like that. The place wasn't comfortable. The chairs forced their occupants to be horribly stiff and upright and there wasn't a book or ornament out of place.

As she and Alexis got to the small-talk-before-we-can-all-decently-go-to-bed stage, Harvey disappeared into the kitchen.

'I'm sorry we haven't met before, Bella.' Alexis tucked strands of her wavy dark bob behind her ear. She was pretty, with delicate features and a tip-tilt nose. 'I've been meaning to come to your shop.'

Amanda had probably told her to do that, too.

'It would be lovely to see you.' Bella smiled brightly.

But the contents of Raven House suggested that Vintage Winter would be superfluous to the Howards' requirements. Just behind Alexis in the bookshelf, Bella eyed a couple of Agatha Christies which she suspected were first editions. They'd sell for tens of thousands if they were in good condition.

She asked and Alexis nodded enthusiastically. 'I love them. So beautifully bound, and such classics. Perfectly plotted. They were presents from Harvey, though he's not keen. Non-fiction's his thing.'

Perhaps he couldn't let go and relax into a story. At least he'd given Alexis the books, though. Treasures for a treasured wife?

Harvey reappeared, carrying coffee on a tray. He struck Bella as rather stiff. She was getting his public face of course, but she couldn't help wondering if that's what Alexis got too. It was hard to imagine him giving her a spontaneous hug or roaring with laughter.

He poured for his wife, brushing her hand as he passed her the cup. She took the drink quickly and didn't meet his eye. She was glancing at Bella, as though he should have served her first, but Bella wasn't offended. She was an interloper, not a visitor.

She thanked Harvey as he poured hers, then picked up her cup and turned to Alexis. 'My mother told me about your poetry.'

She blushed. 'I wasn't sure what she thought of it. I haven't made my name the way she has.'

'It took her ages. I gather you teach, alongside your writing?'

She nodded. 'I've even given some lecture tours. I travelled around the States for three months a few years back.'

Harvey puffed out his chest. 'I missed you, while you were gone.' He took her hand and she flinched slightly. If he was holding out an olive branch, he'd gone in too soon. They were an interesting match. Harvey must be around twenty years Alexis's senior, maybe sixty to her forty. He looked conventional and moneyed in his dark trousers and crisp white shirt. Possibly not lively enough for her.

Alexis sighed. She was holding her wedding ring, twisting it round and round. 'I didn't like being away so long.'

But her eyes had sparkled when she'd talked about the tour.

The atmosphere was tense, and Bella decided to move the conversation on.

'I gather you run a classic car business,' she said to Harvey.

He smiled briefly. 'That's right. It's based down the valley towards Upper Bewley. I set it up a few years ago after I wound up my wine business. I got hooked on motors when I was a boy. Cars and fishing were my passions, then and now. I don't manage the showroom day-to-day any more, but I'm often over there.'

She'd noticed a Jaguar in their garage as she'd come up the drive. She'd wondered if they'd been out in it, or if the door had been open so she could admire the view. Bella liked beautiful things too, but if they were used as status symbols their owners were generally compensating for something. Perhaps Harvey's ego needed bolstering.

She mentioned the Jaguar and he nodded. 'It's a beauty. I intended to sell it on, but it was too late. I'd fallen in love with it.'

He must be doing well if he could afford to hang on to an expensive Jaguar on a whim. Or maybe he relied on family money. Hanging on to things was a professional hazard in Bella's business too.

They got on to Bella's move from London, and her reasons for leaving the antiques shop where she'd worked. She gave them her standard spiel: that she'd always wanted to run her own business. It was true, but the scandal which had catapulted her move filled her head. She'd intervened to prevent a woman being defrauded. It had made her a heroine in the woman's eyes but persona non grata elsewhere. Her boss hadn't liked her making waves. Her fury at his attitude meant she'd walked out just before he'd sacked her.

Harvey was producing an occasional yawn and stretching in his chair. It was only nine fifty, but Bella seized her moment.

'Thank you again,' she said, standing up. 'If you won't think me rude, I'll turn in now. I'm not much of a night owl.' That was a lie. Considering her circadian rhythm, antiques was a crazy choice of profession. The early starts were horrendous. Tomorrow's would be mild by comparison. 'I'll be out of your hair by eight thirty. I'm due at an auction down the valley.' Bella had had pinpricks of anticipation about it all evening. She'd been to the viewing on Friday and wanted one last look before the bidding started.

'You're welcome to stay as long as you like.' Harvey smiled the smile of someone who knows they won't be taken up on their offer.

Bella sympathised. What had her mother been thinking? But they were through the worst.

Upstairs in her room, she could hear the television burbling down below. If they were going to clear the air, they were clearly waiting until she'd left. She was glad they'd got back to their Sunday-evening routine, and grateful for the central heating, now she was alone. For a moment she looked out of her window, over the extension below and into the dark woods beyond, but then she went to bed. Hours of peace stretched ahead of her.

The following morning, Bella was dragged from sleep by her alarm. She resisted the urge to press snooze, her thoughts turning to the auction. She could hear movement downstairs already, and across the landing, Alexis was singing in the shower. How did people get that cheerful before their first cup of coffee?

Through a massive effort of will she pushed herself out of the comfortable bed with its gloriously warm, soft duvet and enjoyed a piping hot shower in the en suite. After that, she dressed and repacked her overnight bag, then sat at the nineteenth-century mahogany dressing table. She brushed her dark hair until it shone. You couldn't use a table like that and not do as the Victorians did. It would seem rude.

She stripped her bed before she went to join Alexis and Harvey in the breakfast room. Alexis rose to pour her coffee.

'Please, don't trouble.'

She let Bella take over. 'Do help yourself to toast or cereal.' It was laid out ready. Multiple pots of marmalade and jam, upmarket muesli and orange juice as well as the coffee.

'This is wonderful.' Bella pasted on her morning-face-for-public-consumption. 'Thanks so much.' She took some toast, butter and marmalade and sat down, her coffee cup brimming. As the smell and first sips did their work, she made a mental note to buy the Howards a nice thank-you present. Being in debt made her twitchy.

'Were you disturbed in the night?' Alexis asked, after glancing at her husband in a way that told her they had been.

'No, not at all.' She normally slept like a log.

'It's just as well we gave you one of the back rooms.'

'Why, what happened?'

'A crash woke me in the middle of the night,' Alexis said. 'Something falling over in the garden.'

'It didn't disturb me.' Harvey patted his wife's arm. 'You did!'

'I'm sorry, but you know what a light sleeper I am. It jolted me awake. Really set my heart hammering – you know the way it can when you come to suddenly?'

He nodded. 'I'm sorry I wasn't more receptive.' He got up. 'It was probably a fox. I'll go and have a look. Make sure the bins are all right.'

He left the room and, as Bella ate, Alexis asked her about the auction and admired the 1950s suit she was wearing. Bella had always liked it. Neat and nipped in at the waist. She'd loved clothes ever since a fashion-student lodger of her mother's had used her as a dressmaker's dummy.

Alexis had already finished eating, so the moment Bella had swallowed her toast and coffee, they stood up. Bella helped her clear away. She didn't want to be remembered as high mainte-nance. Through the kitchen window she saw Harvey pick up a metal ladder. He was well down the lawn, beyond a trellis, a fledgling clematis at its base. He paused to talk to the postman. The Hope Eaton squire, mixing with the locals. Getting his hands dirty.

'What's the ladder doing there?' Alexis frowned. 'It belongs in the shed.'

Harvey moved off, carrying it back to its home. His breath plumed in the bitter January air, dank and misty, as the postman walked towards the door, stamping his feet.

Everything in the kitchen was shipshape. Bella went to gather her bags and fetch her faux astrakhan coat from the hall stand. Another treasured item. It had a wonderful, extravagant collar. 'Thanks so much again.' Almost free.

'Don't mention it.' Alexis walked with her to the hall and picked up the post. 'I'm sorry we weren't more—'

But Harvey opened the front door at that moment. Alexis stepped back as he shut out the frigid air which caught at Bella's throat. His brow was furrowed. 'The shed lock's broken and the ladder was out.'

Not a fox, then.

Alexis was frowning too. 'I thought the crash sounded like something metal. Have any of the tools been stolen?'

'No. Everything else is in its place. Maybe it was kids, mucking around.' Harvey turned to Bella. 'We get a few like that. They climb over the wall and clamber on the ruins even though it's dangerous. It'll be all the more tempting at the moment because the security lights are out. Vandals broke them a couple of weeks back.' He sighed heavily.

Bella had known the basic history of the ruins since childhood, thanks to her dad. They were stone – all that was left of Raven Hall, the grand house that had once stood in the grounds. It had been built in the Baroque style in the early 1700s. The place had gradually crumbled. Lost its roof, and some of its walls. Those that remained varied in height from near ground level to six foot. Asset-strippers had got at the place before it was protected by law and sold off bits as architectural salvage. It was a terrible shame.

She thanked the Howards again and left the house to find Thomasina. The black cab had acres of space. Perfect for ferrying purchases back from sales. For the most part, Bella walked. There was more time to take in the world. But Thomasina appealed to her; she was fun.

Bella trundled down the drive, past the trellis that marked the end of Alexis and Harvey's garden. The ruins were on their land too and sat just beyond.

She glanced at them, remembering plans her father had shown her of the building. She was imagining how the hall's kitchens must have looked when she spotted a dark shape, close to a bit of wall around four feet high. It looked like something covered in cloth. Out of place and unmoving. The talk of intruders was enough to make her pull to a halt and get out.

As she moved closer, she realised she was looking at a figure. She caught her breath, her legs turning wobbly.

The person was crouched. She could only see part of their back. A thick jacket. A man's.

She walked closer, pulled forwards, needing to know what she was looking at. But at the same time, she had a horrible feeling she knew already. If this was to do with the commotion in the night and a man was *still* here, then maybe he wasn't crouched, but slumped...

Sudden death. She thought back to when she'd heard her father had died. That feeling of disbelief as a page turned which could never be turned back. It always seemed so impossible.

As she walked over the cold, hard ground, the freezing air still, as it had been for days, the entire scene came into view. Bella didn't look at the man directly at first. She was scared of what she might see. Her gaze circled him.

He was surrounded by holes, a trowel close to his right hand, a metal detector off to one side.

A notice nearby. *Danger. No climbing.*

At last, she made herself focus on the man himself.

Above his shoulders lay a large stone.

His head was crushed underneath.

THREE

POLICE, BOILERS AND CANDLES

Bella was interviewed in Harvey Howard's study by Detective Sergeant Barry Dixon. Thoughts of the auction and her plans for the day seemed very far away – like something from a different world. She'd never seen a dead body before. It hadn't been a gentle introduction to the experience. She wished her stomach would settle; it felt skippy, and full of a breakfast that now made her nauseous.

Dixon looked incredibly young, but as he got nearer, she modified her estimate. Early thirties perhaps. Around ten years younger than her.

He sat on the edge of his chair and rubbed his elastic-looking face with both hands. His hair was all over the place and his eyes rather bloodshot. 'We— I mean, you need coffee. I've asked a constable to bring some. For the shock.'

Wasn't that meant to be hot sweet tea?

It arrived a moment later. Dixon tried to swig his immediately and looked as though he might spit it out again. 'Let's start with how you came to be at Raven House overnight.' He blew on the surface of his drink and had another go, wincing.

Hangover? She hoped he was up to the job. She explained

everything from the broken boiler to seeing the man whose head had been crushed.

Dixon took notes, sighing at regular intervals. Every other second his phone flashed with a message. He looked at it and flinched. Bella pulled her chair nearer and only responded to each question when he'd made eye contact. As the interview wore on, he slumped further in his seat. Distractingly, he had what looked like straw in the turn-ups of his trousers.

'Did you get all that down?' she asked at last. It came out rather sharply, thanks to her suppressing it for so long.

He looked affronted. 'Yes. Thank you for your time.'

He stifled a yawn as he got up to see her out.

As Bella exited Raven House, she heard one of Dixon's colleagues refer to 'the accident'. Alexis Howard was pale, her husband ashen. Bella somehow felt responsible. Not only had she got them to make up a spare bed, she'd found a body in their grounds.

Bella dropped her luggage back at the now-arctic flat and took a moment to collect herself, staring into space in her living room, another coffee at her elbow. In the end, she went to the second auction she had scheduled that day and caught the later lots. It made no sense to sit at home and at least she could avoid hypothermia. She forced down thoughts of the dead man as she drove, focusing on the empty lane and stark winter trees.

Once she was in the crowded room, the buzz hit and instinct took over. She came back with several pieces she was pleased with, including a beautiful cold-painted bronze lizard. She was slightly ashamed that she'd enjoyed herself after seeing something so horrific. The dead man was back on her mind as she pottered round her flat that evening, putting on lamps that gave it a friendly glow. It somehow helped compensate for the lack of heat. In the background she could hear ominous clanks as the plumber worked on the boiler.

She lined up the stock she wanted to take to the shop the following day. As she cleaned a pair of eighteenth-century brass candlesticks, she wondered about the dead man. Who was he? One of those nighthawkers: a would-be thief who used his metal detector to search for ancient artefacts without permission? It was an awful end to his career.

Later that evening, as the flat approached an acceptable temperature, she browsed the news, sitting at the desk in her study, cocooned by its dark-red walls, curtains closed against the night. Her vintage captain's chair made her feel in control. She thought of her dad, sitting in that room years earlier, imagined him with her now.

Reports of the accident were still sketchy. The man hadn't been named yet. She leaned back and looked at the ceiling. Why had he needed the Howards' ladder if he'd been digging?

The following morning, she drove her stock up the hill to St Giles's Close, pulling up in the car park to one side of the Hope Eaton Antiques Centre. It was an early seventeenth-century timber-framed building containing four antiques shops, including hers. She'd known it would be a good arrangement. Four outlets attracted dedicated visitors as well as passers-by. The centre was next to the Hope Eaton Playhouse and beyond that there was a café – the Steps. The three buildings were perched at the top of the hill, looking down on the valley, the river flowing far below them.

Facing the antiques centre was St Giles's Church. The imposing building with its twelfth-century origins sat in the middle of a ring of houses. The area was secluded and peaceful, almost like a cathedral close.

Bella accessed the centre via the trade entrance and walked

through to Vintage Winter. As the shop bell jangled, she was met with the smell of brewing coffee.

Her mind had been on the day before. On sharing the news about the dead man. But focusing on normality and blocking it out felt a lot more comfortable.

John Jenks, quiet, smart and neat in his dark grey suit, turned in her direction, peering at her through his glasses. 'I saw your car draw up.'

He'd been her assistant manager for three months. She already regarded him as indispensable. 'I could kiss you, John.'

He gave her an austere look.

'Don't worry, I won't. I know Gareth wouldn't like it. And I'm sure you're more discerning anyway. But all the same, you have my undying gratitude.' She hung her coat on the rack in their office, then went to fetch her boxes from Thomasina, waving away John's offer of help.

She loved her shop. She'd got a whole, good-sized room at the front, with a window onto the close, and a smaller room at the back. The place had plenty of alcoves, nooks and crannies. Placing her stock was like setting a stage, one of her favourite parts of the job. Along with attending auctions and fairs. And sizing up dealers and customers. She loved working out what clients might like, what might convince them to buy, the added extras that would make a difference.

As she drank her coffee, she added labels with information and prices to each of the pieces she'd bought.

John smiled as she prepared a pair of Regency bookends. 'Nice buy.'

His words made her smile too. That was effusive for John.

She designed the spaces at Vintage Winter to mimic the most appealing rooms she could imagine. Currently, she had a Victorian leather library chair drawn up at a beautifully inlaid desk in the main room. A metal lamp, some vintage books and a paperweight sat on top. Now she added the candlesticks to a mantelpiece and the bronze lizard to the softly lit shelves in an alcove. She was half hoping no one bought the lizard. She'd love it for her study.

As Bella made sure none of her stock was dusty (a dead giveaway that an item had been hanging around), John disappeared into their office-cum-workroom. It was in the centre of the shop, next to a loo and kitchenette, to one side of a corridor which led from the front room to the back. He reappeared a moment later with the teak gentleman's travelling box she'd got for a song the previous week. It had been locked, with no key, when she'd bought it. He'd told her to leave it with him and the lid was now open.

'You're brilliant! Thank you! You found a key that fitted?'

He shook his head. 'Not yet, but I will. I picked the lock.' He frowned. 'You're not going to like what's inside.'

She went to peer. A pair of ancient false teeth. *Yuck.* 'At least I no longer want to take the case home.' She gave him a look. 'Would it be indelicate to ask where you acquired your lock-picking skills?'

'I learned when I was working for Mrs Hearst. It was a whole room that needed unlocking in her case. No one had been inside for years. The house was so huge, she hadn't worried about it. She couldn't remember what was in there.'

Bella tried to imagine being that incurious and failed. It counted as negligent in her book. 'What did you find?'

He smiled. 'Fifty-seven hats. Looks as though her mother had the same collector's bug she had.'

John had run Mrs Hearst's museum before he'd come to work for her. It was a Hope Eaton institution. Mrs Hearst had collected all manner of items over her long life and displayed them in her huge old house. But now she'd died and a nasty niece had inherited the place. Sienna Hearst was 'determined to put her stamp on it', and Bella was sure it would be an unpleasant one. She'd known John a little from visiting the

Hearst House Museum with her father. He was only five years
her senior, but it felt as though he'd worked there forever. When
she'd bumped into him a few months back, he'd indicated, very
subtly, that he might be looking for a change, now Sienna was
on the scene. He could communicate an awful lot with a raised
eyebrow. She'd offered him a job there and then.

Bella used a tissue to remove the teeth from the box,
wrapped them in it and walked to the bin.

She still got a huge buzz from having hired John Jenks.
She'd known he'd be perfect for the job. He was kind and
knowledgeable, helpful but not pushy. He knew just when to
take a step back and when to offer more information. Bella did
all this too, but her success was due to guile. John's was down to
a quiet, observant and open nature. She suspected he was one of
the nicest people she'd ever met.

He seemed quite unlike his brother, her neighbour Matt,
with his revolving door of girlfriends and erratic comings and
goings.

'Were the auctions busy?' John asked. 'Did you get the last
look you wanted before the first one?'

The time had come to face reality. She took a deep breath,
rallied herself and told him what had happened. Two minutes
later he knew all about her stay at Raven House and the dead
man with the metal detector and the smashed head.

She turned away quickly. Her eyes were pricking. She
wasn't going to let him see that. They were talking about a man
she'd never met. She pinched the skin between her thumb and
forefinger hard. Painful, but it usually worked. By the time she
turned back, she'd produced a smile and John had refilled her
coffee.

'Thanks.'

'I saw something about it on the local news,' he said, not
looking at her directly. The soul of tact. He must have spotted
her emotion despite her efforts. 'It struck me, because Carys

knows the Howards. Or the wife, at least. She goes to her poetry evenings. There's one coming up this week.'

Carys was John's sister-in-law, married to the middle Jenks brother who ran the Steps, the café on St Giles's Close. Bella wondered if the recital would go ahead. And whether she should attend, now she'd met Alexis, though going back didn't appeal.

They stopped talking as a customer entered the shop. She let the woman do a circuit to take in what was on offer. It provided enough time to judge how to approach her. Bella sighed inwardly. The woman was picking up item after item, then putting them down again without any real show of interest. The three ps of buyer behaviour – pick up, put down, then push off. They seldom bought.

'I'm here if you need me,' Bella said, then sat down behind the seventeenth-century oak refectory table they used as the cash desk.

The woman grunted, then made a beeline for the Sweet Agnes candles. John had insisted they stock them. All the Hope Eaton shops did, this time of year. They were like advent candles, decorated with hour markings. She remembered her dad having them. They'd burned down the hours until midnight one year when the eve of Sweet Agnes's Festival fell on a weekend. It had felt magical.

Sweet Agnes was a medieval mystic who'd lived in the town in the 1300s. Despite her renown, the candles only retailed at fifty pence.

At least the woman bought two. Bella mentioned a pair of affordable brass candlesticks as she took the candles. For a moment, the woman looked interested, but Bella could tell it was feigned. *Disappointing.* Just the same, she waved her off as though she'd spent a hundred pounds, not one. She might come back or tell her friends.

Bella had gone for a mix of antiques and vintage, some

cheap, some less so, but very few of the items were truly expensive. After working for years with pieces that cost thousands and were only ever valued if they were perfect, she wanted things almost anyone could buy. Stock to bring joy.

It was three hours later when the tone of the day changed. They'd closed for lunch and retreated to the office. John was eating a complicated meal very neatly. (It was a three-layer chicken salad, with special dressing from a bottle added in situ, and a bread roll. All carefully resting on a tray that protected the table.) As ever, she marvelled that he could be bothered. She was devouring a baguette she'd bought, crammed with turkey and chestnut stuffing.

They must have opened their phones to check the news at the same time. She stopped chewing and saw John's fork pause halfway to his mouth, some of his salad falling back into his Tupperware container.

A moment later he put it down altogether. 'I knew the man who died at the Raven Hall ruins.'

The weird thing was, Bella had just discovered she had too.

FOUR

NOT YOUR AVERAGE PROFESSOR

'Professor Oliver Barton.' She blinked and shook her head. She'd only met him once. She guessed that wasn't the case with John. He was rigid with shock. 'How did you know him?'

'He lives close to the museum. Lived.' He spoke slowly, his eyes wide.

She gave his shoulder a squeeze. She thought she could get away with it. He wasn't the sort to embrace embracing. 'He came in often?'

John nodded. 'We got chatting and after a while he used to invite me along for a beer at the Blue Boar.' The town's old coaching inn was run by John's parents. There were Jenkses everywhere in Hope Eaton. You couldn't walk ten paces without tripping over one. 'He was just... He was so full of life. Enjoyed everything to the full.'

It was her turn to supply the restorative coffee. She much preferred it that way round and got up to sort it out.

'He came in once, when you'd popped out.' She remembered him ambling into the shop, dapper but slightly dissolute. Handsome but rather ruddy. In his early seventies perhaps. 'He said he'd known my dad.' She swallowed down the lump in her throat. He'd implied he had some tales to tell. He was a lost link, but there was nothing she could do about it now.

If only she'd come to see her dad when he'd asked her that last time. She'd rushed off to Thea instead, to pick up the pieces after she'd broken up with a boyfriend. Bella had been planning to come to her father the weekend after, but by then he was dead. It had knocked her flat. She'd always wondered if he'd somehow known what was coming. She focused on pouring their drinks.

'What did you think of him?' John watched her over the table.

'He was charismatic.' He'd seemed like a loveable rogue, teasingly holding back information, hinting he might tell more. His eyes had danced as he'd surveyed her stock and she'd been gratified, and yet there'd been something about him which made her wonder. He'd looked covetous. It was a look shared with a certain sort of dealer: one who'd push the boundaries to get what they wanted. And he had, judging by his digging up at the ruins. Dealing with that sort could be all right, so long as you knew not to give an inch. She'd warmed to the professor in spite of herself. His laughter lines had told her he was full of fun.

She wondered if her dad might have come across him in a professional capacity. He'd loved his work in the police, watching over Hope Eaton. 'What's the professor's background? Any idea why he'd dig at the ruins without permission in the dead of night?'

'Not really. But archaeology was his subject.' John shook his head. 'He was a good sort. Still active at the university though he was past retirement age. Healthy, as far as I could tell – despite the whisky and cigarettes. Successful, I think, and fascinated by his work.'

She handed John his coffee and sat down at the table with her own, ready to read the article.

LOCAL MAN DIES IN TRAGIC ACCIDENT

Oliver Barton, professor of archaeology at Acton Thorpe University, Shropshire, was found dead on the morning of Monday 17 January in the town of Hope Eaton, where he lived. He was on the site of the ruins of Raven Hall and was crushed by falling masonry. It's believed Professor Barton had enjoyed an evening out before he made his way onto the site.

A polite way of saying he was drunk, Bella imagined.

It was not in character for him to trespass and the incident is thought to be the result of high spirits.

Another classic euphemism.

Friends and colleagues have been quick to pay tribute to Professor Barton. The police are not treating the death as suspicious.

The image of DS Barry Dixon with his straw-filled trouser turn-ups came to Bella's mind.

There was no mention of the digging or the metal detector. Maybe the police had left that out to minimise the suffering of surviving relatives.

Bella set her phone down. 'Did he have family?'

John put his head in his hands. 'Right here in town. A niece who works as a housekeeper at the Blue Boar and a great-nephew who's at the high school. I don't know how Nan's going to cope with this. She's had a bad time of it.'

'Nan?'

'The niece. It's a pet name for Anne, I think.'

'Why don't you go home? Take some time to get over the shock.'

His eyes were scrunched up, as though he could shut out what had happened. But he took a quick breath and shook his head. 'I'd rather stay.'

He got on with restoring a vintage document case, painstakingly gluing the leather cover down with starch paste. Bella served the first customer who came in, but an hour later, John was done with his work and had charmed someone into buying a 1930s wine stopper. He'd battened down his feelings. *No mean feat.* She got on with checking a proof of the flyer she'd had designed. She'd take them round herself as soon as they were printed, and chat to people as she went.

As she worked, she could hear John sighing between customers. Taking a breath as though he was about to say something. Then stopping again. Once she'd noticed it, she couldn't stop.

At last, she marched over at double-quick speed and perched on a handy stool. 'No offence, but you're driving me up the wall. Tell Auntie Bella.'

That produced the smallest of smiles, though his brow remained furrowed. After a moment, he pulled a wallet out of his back pocket and opened it up. He was tugging at something in an inner compartment. A second later, he had it: a worn silver coin decorated with a crowned head. It was pierced at the top so you could wear it as a pendant. He turned it over to reveal a bird sitting on top of a cross.

'Let's see.' Bella took it in her hand, feeling the thrill of connection with something from long ago. Coins weren't her area, but it looked ancient. She couldn't swear it was genuine, but she thought it might be.

'Oliver gave it to me as a present. I fed his cat while he was away.'

She handed the coin back, not wanting to seem Gollum-like in her interest. 'You fed his cat? Why didn't his niece do that?'

'He said she'd be all over his stuff, tidying up, rearranging his cupboards.'

He'd wanted someone who wouldn't pry. That was interesting.

'What do you think of it?' John held the coin as if it was burning his fingers, his eyes uneasy.

'It's not my field, but I could ask a contact. Medieval maybe? Adapted to make a pendant. You asked him where he got it?'

John nodded and looked even more uncomfortable. 'He tapped the side of his nose. I've wondered about it ever since. Only I didn't want to ask anyone official. We were friends.'

She dredged up memories. 'Single precious-metal coins don't count as treasure trove, but if they've been modified into objects, like this one, then I think they can do.' At the very least, Oliver Barton should have reported the find if he'd dug it up. Especially as a professor of archaeology. Presumably he'd been dedicated to extending public knowledge about the past.

'It makes me worry that the news reports are wrong,' John said. 'Perhaps he *was* in the habit of trespassing. Maybe he just never got caught.' He was chewing his cheek. 'The coin's not the only thing that makes me wonder.'

She raised an eyebrow.

'We were playing poker with some of the randomers he used to pick up last week.'

'Poker?' *John?* The lock picking had been surprising enough.

He gave her a dignified look. 'I won.'

'You're full of surprises.' But then she thought of the way he'd charmed the woman who'd bought the wine stopper. It had been impressive; you'd never have known he'd just had bad news. Perhaps she could see it after all. She wondered if she'd be any good at poker. She was good at spotting tells. You had to be, to deal in antiques. Reading your suppliers and your customers was crucial.

'I don't play for money,' John went on. 'Oliver explained that to the others before we started, as though it was rather quaint. After we'd finished, the friends went and I hoped to be off too, but he didn't want me to go. He kept restarting the conversation.' He frowned. 'I'd stopped drinking way earlier, but he'd carried on. It made him clumsy, and he knocked the playing cards onto the floor. Oliver stared down at them. The four queens had fallen next to each other. He shook his head, then picked them up. Hearts, spades and clubs first. "Three passionate women," he said. "One who loves too much, one who's full of fear, and one who's striving for immortality." Then he reached for the queen of diamonds and laid that down too and went on: "And a fourth, an enigma, but one who worries me."' John shook his head. 'I told Gareth about it that night and wrote it in my diary, it was so weird. After that, Oliver drank the last of his whisky, then he turned to me and clung on to my sleeve and said: "They're all people I know. I'm glad I made a friend of you."' John's face coloured sightly. '"You're steady. The others are precarious. And perhaps my life is too. Sometimes I look into the shadows and they're threatening."'

'Very melodramatic.'

'If you're not going to take this seriously...'

'No, no. I am. Go on.'

'I got as far as looking up the meanings of the cards in a book about fortune telling. Leo stocks them for the hippies that come to visit the stone circle.' Bella visualised the new and used books section of John's brother's café. A perilously tempting place. 'The descriptions don't quite align with what Oliver said. I think the people he was talking about were just in his mind when the cards fell, and the whisky led him to make the link.'

'You think he was genuinely scared?'

John let out a long breath. 'I think if someone could have

told him he'd die in such an unusual way within the week, he wouldn't have been surprised.'

Bella nodded. She suspected the alcohol had got the professor to the paranoid stage, but she didn't want to hurt John's feelings. Oliver Barton's relationships were intriguing, but her mind was on the rather more solid medieval coin. What else did he have in his house? Perhaps *that* was the reason he didn't want his niece poking around. Though, to be fair, she'd hate anyone messing about in her flat, despite it being free of stolen goods.

'Perhaps you should talk to the police,' she said at last. 'It can't hurt Oliver if you mention the coin now.'

But John was biting his lip. 'It could hurt his niece. Oliver died a horrible death; she must be devastated. I don't want to add to her pain. Maybe the coin was an isolated lucky find. And the police aren't like they were in your dad's day. They don't know the townsfolk.'

Bella still remembered her dad getting to know the locals, and how often he'd made himself quietly available at town events. No one had time to do that any more. As for Barry Dixon, he'd seemed barely conscious during their interview. Not likely to seize incisively on new information.

'Even if I told them about the coin,' John went on, 'imagine trying to recount the story of the playing cards.'

He had a point.

They were interrupted by a customer who'd come in for the wretched candles, and a couple more browsers who followed in their wake. The last one was present shopping, which was more promising. Bella was able to send him off with a thirty-pound jug. She smiled to herself as he left with her business card.

For the rest of the afternoon, John was distracted. He snapped into focus the moment they had company but between times, his gaze was somewhere out of the window. He was a pacer by nature, but he was pacing extra. He was worried, and unless she did something about it, the constant marching would wear out the carpet. To say nothing of her patience.

The professor was still on her mind too. And would continue to be, so long as John was in a state. She wondered how often Oliver had gone out with his metal detector.

She'd been looking forward to going back to her flat after work. Sitting in the friendly glow of the hall lamps to take off her boots, then putting her feet up on the sofa with a glass of red and a good book. The beguiling image faded. John's unease needed tackling.

She imagined talking it over with her dad. After a moment, she approached John, who was starting to lock up.

'You said you used to feed Oliver Barton's cat. Does that mean you have a key to his house?'

FIVE

TRESPASSING

'Remind me why I let you talk me into this.' It had been dark for a couple of hours and John was shivering in his wool overcoat.

They'd come to Oliver Barton's house after closing the shop.

She gave him a sidelong smile. 'It's logical, and you love logical. You won't stop worrying and you won't go to the police, so this is my solution. You want to know if Oliver had got himself involved in something dangerous, possibly relating to the ancient-looking coin he gave you. We can check his place to see if anything bears that out without bothering anyone. It's quite all right.' Perhaps not legally, but morally. She guessed they'd either find another artefact or two, or nothing at all. And afterwards, peace would be restored. Poor John could get back to mourning the professor in the standard way.

As they walked up Old Percy's Lane, quiet and deserted with its row of late-Georgian cottages on one side and worn red-brick wall on the other, she felt committed to the project. 'It should set your mind at rest. Even if Oliver dug regularly, it doesn't mean his death was sinister.' Bella thought of the professor's trowel and metal detector. They showed he'd planned his visit, but it might have been last-minute. Perhaps he'd gone to pick them up, his mood for exploration fuelled by alcohol. An impromptu hare-brained approach made sense. Why choose to dig now, otherwise? The weather was freezing, the ground rock hard. 'Whatever he was up to, he sounds like an adventurer to me. He was ignoring the warning signs about falling masonry and it looks as though he climbed as well as dug.' Why on earth had he taken the ladder?

She stopped talking as she realised John was looking over his shoulder instead of focusing on her arguments.

He regarded her from under his dark eyebrows, made prominent by his frown. 'A neighbour might see us. You're not very anonymous.'

'You say the nicest things. Is it the coat?'

She caught a momentary flash of smile under the street lamp. 'That and the hat.'

It was a bucket number. 1950s. Velvet. It had a couple of tassels, but it definitely wasn't ostentatious. It was black, for heaven's sake, and it was far too cold to do without.

'And the hair and lipstick, of course.'

He was exaggerating now. 'No one's watching.' Most of the houses were in darkness.

They were outside Oliver Barton's blue panelled front door now. John stood there hesitating as Bella cast her eyes over the red-brick frontage and sash windows. She shivered. His heating was probably off. Still, it was bound to be warmer inside than it was standing out there. 'We're more likely to get caught if you keep us waiting on the doorstep.'

John sighed, turned the key in the lock and shook his head. 'It's weird not to be greeted by Smudge.'

There was something incongruous about a trespassing, poker-playing history professor having a cat with such a homely name.

John looked pale in the moonlight as Bella closed the front door behind them. 'It smells just the same.'

Woodsmoke, cigarettes, ripe bananas and a hint of spirits. Bella used the torch app on her phone and John put his on too. It made the venture feel more nefarious, but it was good to be subtle. Having to explain their presence wasn't tempting.

'Shall I take next door while you give this room a once-over?' They'd come straight into a dining room, with a weathered oak table and dresser. It didn't look promising, though it gave an idea of Oliver's life, with its well-stocked wine rack, and the unopened jar of truffle butter on the sideboard. The wine looked upmarket. He'd liked the finer things in life.

John nodded and Bella walked through an archway to reach a sitting room with exposed beams and an inglenook fireplace. There was a saggy, comfortable-looking armchair and sofa, and side tables piled high with papers. Academic journals, newspapers, printouts relating to history and archaeology. The books on the shelves were a mix of non-fiction and classic thrillers. There were no ancient-looking trinkets that suggested Oliver had a nighthawking habit, which was a start. Though in his place, Bella wouldn't leave them on display.

It wasn't just stray treasure she was after. She wanted to reassure John and he was worried about the playing-card conversation too. That meant Bella wanted evidence of Oliver's personal situation, to show him there was nothing which rang alarm bells. It was where her father would have started.

What she needed was the place where Oliver put things to be actioned. His papers were all over the place. If he'd managed to function at all, he must have developed a method for dealing with the bits he didn't want to lose. Those items should be revealing.

She strode to the back of the house and found a spacious kitchen with a table at its centre. In that room, in the corner, she found what she was looking for. A small countertop with a stool next to it. Some recently opened post lay on top, and a cork board was mounted on the wall behind.

She moved closer and there, right in front of her, was a photograph of Oliver and her dad. What a gut kick, coming out of the blue. He and Oliver looked so carefree. They were in a meadow, strolling by a stream, with rolling hills beyond. Who had taken it? she wondered. The professor and her dad must have known each other quite well.

Bella couldn't help wondering if Oliver had left the picture out because he'd wanted to show her. She'd give a lot to know what he might have told her about her father. She photographed the picture, then pushed it to the back of her mind; she needed to focus on the matter in hand.

There was a bright red flyer, decorated with bees, tacked to Oliver's cork board. The bees were performing household chores: ironing, sweeping, dusting and so on. So far, so normal and reassuring. But it gave rise to a question.

John had entered the room and joined her, his eyes on the flyer too.

Meg Jones – busy bee household cleaning services, competitive rates and excellent references

Underneath there was a phone number, and a web address on Trusted Trader.

Someone – presumably Oliver – had put a question mark on the paper, and gone over it repeatedly, as though he'd been doodling. Pondering the merits of getting Meg Jones in.

'I went to school with Meg,' John said, 'though I haven't seen her for a bit.' He sounded guilty. 'I heard her husband died last year. They'd separated and he'd left the valley, but everyone says she was in bits over it. He was ill for a while beforehand apparently.'

'How sad. Do you know everyone in Hope Eaton?'

He considered the question seriously. 'Not as many as your dad did. What's special about the flyer?'

'Nothing, I don't suppose.'

'It made you frown.'

He watched people carefully, just like she did. 'It's nothing worrying; just interesting. You said Oliver didn't want his niece feeding Smudge because she'd mess with his things, yet he was considering getting an outsider to clean for him. Does that mean he didn't trust his niece?'

John's brow furrowed. 'I can't imagine that. Mum's always saying how reliable she is, though she strikes me as anxious. She might have worried about Oliver's drinking. Perhaps having a stranger felt less pressured. Though he didn't mind me.'

'He knew you wouldn't judge him.' Bella took a photo of the flyer in spite of herself and walked out of the room again. 'Did you find anything in the dining room?'

He shook his head.

She'd thought as much. She made her way back there now. 'Let's check upstairs.'

'Do we have to?'

Bella's hand was already on the banister. She glanced over her shoulder. 'Will you relax if we leave the job half done?'

John looked pained.

She could already visualise him pacing around Vintage Winter again. 'Residual doubts would eat away at you. It'll only take a moment. You know as well as I do that if Oliver had something really secret he'd take it to an upper floor. Downstairs is very open.'

Her father would never have left without checking.

As she mounted the stairs, memories of sitting in his study washed over her. He'd talked to her about his casework: people who might run into trouble, vulnerable individuals, situations that needed defusing. He'd shown her his methods, too. All on condition that she never told a soul. He'd lock the door whenever they left the room. No danger of visitors wandering into that private space.

She creaked her way onto the landing at the top of the steep stairs and found two bedrooms. The first was impersonal, with nothing to trigger alarm, unless you counted the horrendous curtains.

The second was clearly Oliver's. Seeing his horn-rimmed glasses on the bedside table pushed practical thoughts aside. They looked as though he'd just taken them off. The books and rumpled bed linen were so normal. Poor man. How was it possible he wasn't coming back?

It was only as she bent to check under the furniture that something made her pause.

She pulled back, crouching on her haunches. If only she could wish away the object she'd just glimpsed. She'd wanted to comfort John.

Her eyes met his as she looked up.

'What?'

Goosebumps ran over her forearms. 'You'd better have a look.'

Oliver had been sleeping with a hammer under his bed.

SIX

MORE QUESTIONS THAN ANSWERS

Bella straightened up in the almost-dark room. She was rocked by what she'd found, her stomach quivering lightly. Oliver's words about the women and the playing cards had sounded melodramatic but his fear had been real enough. She wondered what had triggered it. It could have been in his head.

'Do you have any idea who the playing cards represented?' she asked John, as they climbed a second flight of stairs, up to attic level. 'Fellow poker players perhaps?'

But he shook his head. 'That lot came and went. There were no long-term participants, I don't think. His niece and great-nephew are the only close connections I know of.'

The niece had to be a candidate then.

They reached a largeish space in the eaves, part workroom, part dressing room, with a writing bureau as well as a built-in wardrobe and mirror.

The bureau was a beauty: satinwood with neoclassical painted decorations. But it was locked. Bella raised an eyebrow at John. 'Tell me you didn't ignore my suggestion.'

'It was only a suggestion?' He took his lock-picking kit from his coat pocket. 'It came across as an order.'

'Three younger sisters does that to you.'

'I'm the eldest in our family,' John said lightly, 'so I think there's more to it than that. Should we really be doing this?'

She thought of the hammer under Oliver's bed and the fact that Oliver had locked the desk in the first place. The contents had to be worth exploring. They needed to know if the danger he'd sensed was real or imagined. 'Yes. But it's a beautiful piece of furniture. Can you do it without leaving a mark?'

He raised an eyebrow and bent over the keyhole. 'I find your question wounding.'

In under a minute, the desk was open.

With the flap pulled down, they were met with the usual multitude of cubbyholes and drawers. She leaned forward, glancing swiftly over the contents. If Oliver had secrets, here's where he'd keep them. At least John and she were both used to handling precious objects. She eased one of the drawers open as John lifted a pile of correspondence from a nook.

They were both absorbed. Bella was on her third drawer when she found a smart card. A key? She held it up for John to see. There were no markings on it – no name, or photo ID. No lanyard attached. 'It's not his university key card. I found that two drawers ago. So what's it for?'

'Good question. He has a garage but there's a standard key for that in the kitchen drawer. I had to use it once when he'd shut Smudge in by accident. Who uses a key card at home, anyway?'

It might be for somewhere else, but it was odd. She could understand an organisation not announcing themselves on it; it was sensible on security grounds. But no marking at all would make it totally impractical. You'd expect a photo of Oliver or *some* identifying feature.

It was John who made the next discovery. She saw him pull a letter out of an unmarked envelope, then rest his chin on his hand as he read. Silently, he set the paper on the bureau's flap and turned it to face her.

It was typewritten.

I KNOW WHAT YOU'VE BEEN UP TO, AND YOU'RE BEING WATCHED. IF YOU DON'T STOP, I SWEAR TO GOD I'LL STOP YOU MYSELF.

So the feeling of threat wasn't just in his head then...

John took a deep breath. 'That might explain the hammer under the bed.'

'Yes.' But it was only a partial answer. The sort that reeled her in. 'We need to know what it refers to. It might be the nighthawking, but I haven't found anything that suggests he made a habit of it.'

'Nor me.'

Bella picked up the threatening note. 'The paper's an odd choice.' It was thick. Glimpsing something beyond the words, she backlit it with her phone torch. 'There's a watermark.' Two intertwined 'A's. 'Could you photograph it while I keep it lit?' He obliged. 'Who sends a threat with an identifier like that? Maybe it's misdirection.'

'Or someone who didn't notice because they were in a hurry. Like we should be.' He tapped his watch. 'I think we've done all we can.'

She hesitated. She wanted an explanation for the smart card, but they seemed to have run out of house. 'All right.'

They put everything back. She let John relock the bureau and at last they started their journey down the stairs. They were on the middle floor when it struck her.

She dashed between the two bedrooms, looking up at the ceiling.

John shook his head. 'The excitement's got to you.'

'No hatches to the attic space.'

'Because the attic's been converted into a room.'

'But not all of it.' There was a strip of attic missing.

She ran to the stairs.

'We shouldn't be going back up again. Time's getting on.' John's tone was urgent, but he was on her tail.

There was no door or hatch in the wall by the bureau. If there was a way in, there was only one possible answer. She opened the wardrobe. It was full of clothes: tweed suits, slacks, shirts, all worn and comfortable, not smart. They smelled of cologne and cigarettes. Bella normally liked it when objects gave something away about their former owner. Here, it reminded her of a life lost. Feeling behind the clothes, she traced her fingers around the back of the wardrobe. To the far left-hand side, she felt hinges.

'Have you found a way through to Narnia?'

'Could be.' She'd need to move the clothes. The rail was heavy, but designed to lift off. She handed John some of the weighty suits and at last she was able to lift the rest clear. They draped the lot over a pair of chairs, and she found a fingerhold to pull the rear panel free.

Behind it was a door. 'And we'll now be needing that smart card.' She gave John a bright smile.

He raised his eyes a fraction and went back to re-pick the bureau's lock. She could tell he was nervous now. The operation wasn't quite as smooth as before. She listened for any sound in the house. Nothing. But they were two floors up...

Bella tapped the edge of the wardrobe subconsciously with her nails.

'So sorry to keep you waiting.'

'Sarcasm doesn't suit you.' She took the card from him and held it to the reader in the door, which glowed green.

'Prop it open,' John said, taking the key. 'I'm going to put this back in case we need to leave in a hurry. It'll take us long enough to get the clothes back in the wardrobe.'

Bella took her boots off and used them as a wedge, then entered the hidden room. It smelled of old wood – intense from being shut up. At first, she was still using her phone torch to see and caught a glimpse of cabinets and glass cases, but no windows. She found a light switch. A moment later, she was glad of the chair to the right of the door.

'John, leave the key card for now,' she said, as she collapsed into it. 'You need to see this.'

SEVEN

A DANGEROUS SECRET

A moment later, John was standing in the small, windowless attic room, lips slightly parted, staring. Bella got up again and approached the display cases and dusty old chests of drawers. It was unbelievable. Gold torcs, probably Iron Age, with exquisitely twisted strands of precious metal, medieval coins in abundance, precious Anglo-Saxon necklaces and pendants inlaid with garnets. Everywhere she looked there were more.

Oliver Barton hadn't been at the ruins of Raven Hall by chance. You wouldn't get what he'd found without a targeted approach spanning decades. And even then it was incredible.

'It's like a museum,' John said at last, his words slow and drawn out.

Bella wondered if her dad had had any inkling of Oliver's secret. How and why had they met? If he'd got a hint, he'd have talked to Oliver about it; tried to convince him to declare what he'd found. It had been his way. Making it official would have been a last resort. But Oliver would have had a heck of a lot of explaining to do.

After putting on her gloves, she opened a drawer and found hardback notebooks. They were full of details about the treasure. Dates, maps and diagrams of where he'd found each piece. He'd trespassed all right. Then studied what he'd found, gone about it with an academic's curiosity and precision, but not to further collective knowledge. He'd kept it all to himself.

John was peering over her shoulder, matching the entries in the book to the treasures in the cases. 'Wait. This one's missing.' He pointed to Oliver's spidery writing: 33. *Medieval gold iconographic finger-ring with a depiction of the resurrection.*

He was right. In a drawer which contained a number of smaller finds, the space next to label 33 was bare. It was the same for exhibit 44. She turned the page. *Medieval flower-shaped gold and diamond brooch.*

'Maybe he sold some of the smaller pieces when times got tough,' John said.

But a creeping sense of unease was sending butterflies through Bella's stomach. 'He could have. To pay off a gambling debt perhaps. But looking at the loving way he's kept this haul and his notes, I can't imagine him doing it unless it was a very last resort. And his collection's organised. Something tells me he'd have rearranged his finds so he didn't keep looking at gaps.' Seeing the blank spaces would have been a constant reminder of having to let something go. He'd had a serious addiction. She was sure he wouldn't have done it lightly.

'What if someone discovered his secret, just like us? They might have been here since he died. Maybe they're gradually helping themselves to the more portable pieces.'

'You're thinking of Nan?'

She nodded. His niece had to be a possibility. 'She might have had a key for emergencies, even if he didn't ask her to feed his cat. Or perhaps she's his executor and she's got one now. Other people might have copies too. Old girl- or boyfriends. Current ones. Your school friend Meg Jones, if he hired her to clean.' Though that idea seemed odder still, given what was under his roof. You wouldn't think he'd want anyone inspecting his house too closely.

She took some more photographs, then backed out of the room. It really was time to leave.

John was reversing too. Bella retrieved her boots and pulled the door to the hidden room shut. 'I don't think we should leave the key card in the desk. Or the threatening note.'

'Why not?'

'Because we'll have to tell the police about this. I don't fancy explaining we broke into the desk. If we want them to come and look, they'll need the key, and this way, we can avoid them damaging the bureau.'

'I love your sense of priorities.'

Bella's mind was on her solution. It wasn't ideal. If someone had been helping themselves to Oliver's finds, they might come back for more. They'd discover the key was missing. Know someone had unearthed the secret. But she couldn't see a way round it. 'I'll set the wardrobe to rights.'

Panicking wouldn't help. She paused to draw breath, then replaced the clothes rail and hangers.

Ten minutes later, they'd hidden the key card between some books on a shelf, tucked the letter under a paperweight and were creeping back down the stairs. She fought the urge to recheck each room. She was certain they'd left everything else as they'd found it. They peered through the front window, then let themselves out when they saw the lane was quiet.

After that, they walked up the road without looking back, but Bella had taken note of the houses to either side of Oliver's. Still in darkness. 'You mentioned he has a garage. Where's that?'

'Round the back. Off Holt Lane. He has a vintage Alfa Romeo Giulietta Spider. Red. You'd love it.' His face clouded. 'He joked about it. Called it his late-life-crisis car.'

'I suppose he could have sold some treasure to afford it.' But she still thought it was unlikely. The attic room spoke of an extreme passion, and of spoils that wouldn't be sacrificed, even for a car that special. 'I wonder if he bought it from Harvey Howard.'

'Maybe. Think it means anything?'

'Probably not.' But it was a link. Her dad had taught her to look out for those.

'So, we're going to the police?' John sounded miserable.

'We have to.' Quite how she'd explain their trespassing was an interesting question, but there was no way round it. There was enough treasure in Oliver's attic to furnish a new wing at the British Museum. 'I'll go. I can talk to Barry Dixon, the detective sergeant who worked on Oliver's death. You get back home. But the police might contact you eventually, I suppose.'

She could see John was agonising. 'I know you're right. But how on earth will you—'

'I'll think of something. I'll tell you what I've said so we can get our stories straight.'

John nodded at last. 'Thank you. Can you promise me we won't get arrested for breaking and entering?'

'Of course.' *Probably.* They'd had a key. It couldn't possibly come to that.

EIGHT

A VISIT TO DS DIXON

An hour after she'd parted from John, Bella was in Thomasina, driving towards Shrewsbury, after grabbing a halloumi & grilled vegetable wrap from Narin's on the high street. Her main mission was a drink with her godfather, a retired cop who'd worked alongside her dad. But she decided to call in at the police station on the way. It was well after seven and she doubted Barry Dixon would be around, but she had the urge to get the meeting out of the way.

Or she thought she had. When a constable appeared at the front desk and called her bluff, her enthusiasm evaporated. She wasn't entirely happy with her plans to sanitise her story.

The constable took her to an interview room, where Barry Dixon had already arrived. He managed to drag himself to a standing position to shake her hand before sinking back down and gesturing for her to sit too. He leaned over the table between them, notebook and pen in hand. She noted his five o'clock shadow, and his collar, one tip tucked under his jumper, one not. She yearned to set it right. He reminded her forcefully of an overgrown schoolboy.

'What can I do for you?'

'It's in relation to Professor Oliver Barton. My colleague was a close friend of his and we were both knocked sideways by his death.' She gripped the table for show. 'I didn't recognise him when I found his body.'

He nodded. 'Not surprised, what with his head being crushed and everything.'

Ten out of ten for sensitivity. 'In the end, we decided to use my colleague's key to go to Oliver's house.'

Dixon frowned. 'You need permission now he's dead.'

Bella bit her lip. 'Sorry, we didn't think of that. Oliver let my colleague nip in and out when he was alive and we wanted to lay the ghost.' She looked down and sniffed. She was glad she'd left her hat on. It helped to cover her face.

Dixon shifted awkwardly in his seat. He hadn't written anything down. 'Happy to forget it, given you're upset.'

'That's kind of you. Anyway, while we were there, we found some things that worried us.'

She told him about the hammer under Oliver's bed, the treasure in the secret room and the threatening letter. She left out breaking into Oliver's desk and implied they'd found the key and the letter lying about.

At last, he started to write, though she sensed it was unwillingly. 'So how did you access this secret room again?'

'A door in the back of the wardrobe.' She wished it didn't sound like a fever dream. 'I wouldn't have thought of it, only we realised there was a bit of attic unaccounted for. The contents are incredible.'

She handed him her phone and showed him the photos. It wasn't working. He barely reacted. She enlarged an image with her finger and thumb, then pushed it under his nose. 'You can see how special his collection is.'

'Possibly.' He sounded even more dejected now.

'The combination of the hammer, the threatening note and the treasure is worrying, under the circumstances.'

'The circumstances?'

Was he being deliberately obtuse? 'The way Oliver died.'

'It was an accident, Ms Winter.' He seemed to catch her look. 'But I've noted all your points. Where was the hammer again?'

For the love of Sweet Agnes... 'Under the bed.'

'He could have left it there after some DIY.'

Seriously?

He closed his eyes for a moment. 'If he was worried for his safety, why go stumbling about in the dark on someone else's land?'

Annoyingly good point. 'I think he had a habit he couldn't kick: a passion for ancient artefacts.' She imagined he'd been deep in his digging. She could understand that. If she was engrossed at a fair, she was the same. A pride of lions could probably walk past and she wouldn't notice. She expected Oliver had meant to watch out, but his focus would have been dragged towards the holes he'd dug. He could have been killed. All she wanted was for Dixon to take the possibility seriously and investigate. 'There were at least a couple of items missing from the professor's hoard, too.' She wished she could come up with a better name for it. Hoard conjured up images of caverns filled with gold, like something from Tolkien, but treasure was worse: the stuff of Enid Blyton. 'We wondered if they'd been stolen.'

'Most likely he removed them himself.' Behind the exhaustion she could see a glimmer of hope in Dixon's eyes. 'How do you know these items are genuinely valuable? Maybe he'd already declared them to the coroner, and they weren't found to be treasure trove. Or perhaps no museum wanted them.'

This was ridiculous. 'If you saw the whole collection, you'd know that's not believable. And besides, if that were the case, why hide them?'

He looked pained but a reply came a moment later. 'They could have been valuable to him, but not to anyone else.'

'I've never heard of anyone going to those lengths for something that's objectively worthless. And they were ancient, according to his notes.'

'Maybe they're old but not rare.' He was glancing at his phone as a message popped up.

'I'd stake my life that they're both.'

His bleary eyes met hers again. 'And you'd know, because?'

'I work in antiques.' He'd taken her details when he'd interviewed her. Expecting him to remember had clearly been over hopeful.

'And ancient artefacts are your area of expertise?'

She was forced to admit that they weren't. 'But there's the threatening note.'

Dixon shrugged. 'People threaten each other all the time.' He sighed and closed his notebook. 'You did the right thing to come. I'll take everything you've told me into consideration. We'll send someone to the house when we can. Of course, we'll need permission or a warrant,' he added, rather pointedly. 'Leave it with us.'

When we can... If Dixon had any conception of the professor's collection he'd be progressing this right now. Bella bit her tongue and strode for the door.

NINE

NOT YOUR AVERAGE GODFATHER

Bella left the police station ready to throw something at a wall. She was incredulous that DS Dixon hadn't realised the magnitude of the situation.

On her journey to Shrewsbury, she assessed the consequences. John had been right. There was a problem. And Dixon's reaction wouldn't set his mind at rest.

Deep inside, a little voice was telling her that if he wouldn't act, she'd have to. Because if you wanted something doing...

She tried to damp the voice down. Looking into Oliver's death could be dangerous. There were vast sums of money at stake, in the form of the hoard. It was quite possible someone had already killed over those riches, and managed to pass it off as an accident. They'd either been lucky or, more worryingly, clever.

But she was her father's daughter. His only child. He'd taught her how to investigate. And her career had built on that. She was used to spotting fakes, liars and cheats. And well versed in charming people. Even her upbringing was relevant: the seamy characters who came and went. Her rebellious younger sisters. She'd got good at reading people. Making judgements. Acting on instinct.

As she neared the Mitre, a spark of temptation built inside her. Warmth at the thought of finding out more. Because solving puzzles – from what fifteen-year-old Thea had been doing until three o'clock in the morning, to tracing the history of an antique – was in her blood. Getting in there, getting her hands dirty and steering a course, kept her own personal pilot light lit.

Besides, she'd found Oliver's body. The spark burned brighter.

But then the craziness of the escapade overwhelmed her again. Dixon should be doing all of this. She had a new business to run. She sighed. She'd share the whole thing with her godfather, see what he thought.

She marched across the swirly carpet of the real-ale pub towards Tony Borley. Captain, his black Labrador, trotted over to meet her and put a warm friendly face to her hip. Stroking him was soothing.

'What's up?' Tony asked. 'The look in your eye could kill a man at ten paces.'

She took her umpteenth deep breath. 'I spoke to DS Barry Dixon on my way here. I found it hard to instil a sense of urgency in him.'

He grunted as he stood up and clapped her on the back in a half hug. 'Not surprised. I was going to ask what you'll have to drink but that answers my question. A stiff gin.'

'I'm driving.' Bella cast her eyes over the bar. 'I don't suppose this place does hot chocolate.'

He raised an eyebrow. 'You're so judgemental.'

'They do, then?'

'Well, no.' He looked defensive. 'But they might have. What about a Coke?'

'Can we meet at the Bee's Knees next time?' It specialised

in sparkling lights and live piano music and didn't smell of must and carpet shampoo. To be fair, the Mitre might smell a lot worse if someone hadn't done the cleaning.

'I'll pretend I didn't hear that.' Tony moved towards the bar.

A moment later they were back at the corner table he'd chosen.

'It's good to see you. Looking swish as ever. But put out. And fresh from a visit to the nick. I take it this isn't just a social call?'

'It's nine tenths social.'

He raised an eyebrow.

'All right. Six tenths. I've been longing to catch up, a hundred per cent. But I wouldn't mind your advice on something.' She took off her wrap, hat and coat.

He sat back in his seat and swigged his Hobsons Twisted Spire. 'Thought as much. It's about the death at Raven Hall, I suppose.'

She put her Coke down. 'How did you know?'

He smiled and Bella could tell he was trying to look mysterious. 'Ways and means.'

She waited, fixing him with her gaze.

'All right. There's a committee I still sit on. They like retirees – we're able to take a step back. I keep a watching brief over some of the current cases. Check everyone's dotted their i's and crossed their t's. That little incident caught my eye. If your dad was still alive, he'd have been all over it. Dixon's boss, Lydia Moss, is having a mare at the moment. Too much pressure, too little time. She let Dixon cover the Raven Hall ruins death, but he's snowed under too. He's doing the legwork on this spate of jewellery robberies in the well-to-do homes of Shropshire.'

Bella made a mental note to watch out for stolen goods at the shop. 'I suppose that explains why he looks so exhausted.' She felt marginally less cross.

Tony shook his grizzled head. 'They're always pressed.

Barry's virtually comatose most of the time. His wife's a vet. She presses him into service sometimes, if he's off duty. He was brought up on a farm.'

Bella remembered the straw.

'Plus, they've got four kids under seven.'

Her sympathy stretched a little further. Memories of her own childcare duties made his situation relatable. Her mother had pressed her into service too.

'I can see why any complications will come as a blow, but he can't just ignore them.'

Tony met her eye and raised an eyebrow.

Okay. Maybe he could...

'So, what's rattled your cage?' He took another drink. 'You've got worries about the death?'

She explained everything, from Oliver's mysterious connection with her dad, to what John had told her about the playing cards and the medieval coin.

'I didn't tell Dixon about the cards. It sounded a bit too Agatha Christie.'

'Very wise.'

Bella finished with what she and John had found in Oliver's house. And how.

Tony grunted. 'Chip off the old block. Your dad always said you'd make a good detective.'

'I thought you'd tell me I'd overstepped the mark.'

Tony gave a low chuckle. 'It's not as though I'm speaking on the record. I trust you, and it would be unrealistic to leave it all to Dixon.'

So much for him discouraging her. 'He promised to send someone to look at Oliver Barton's hoard.'

'In a week or two, if you're lucky. With the agreement of his niece, who inherits the house.' His eyes met hers. 'Yes, she does. So she'll get the treasure. Wonder if she knows about it... That's a nice little motive for murder right there.'

'She's a housekeeper. She works for John's parents.'

'Oh, well, cross her off the list then.'

'Seriously. Do you think someone might have killed him?'

Tony absorbed more of his beer. 'What you found in his house is enough to make me wonder. I can tell you what I know about the case. Shouldn't, obviously, but as it's you.' He took a notebook from his pocket and flipped back a few pages. Bella wondered if the powers that be knew he was pottering around the local pubs with confidential information. 'Mrs Howard, who lives in Raven House, was woken by a loud crash in the garden. She doesn't know what time it was exactly, but she went to bed at midnight and was asleep by half past, so some time after that. She woke her husband, who wasn't keen on leaping out of bed to investigate. Can't say I blame him. He thought it was probably a fox, knocking something over.'

'That ties in with what they told me.'

He nodded. 'Mr Howard went out the following morning at around eight twenty and found their ladder on the grass. The shed lock had been broken but nothing else taken, leaving him and his wife mystified.'

'And at eight thirty I found the body.'

'All noted in the records. You told the Howards. Mrs Howard called the police. Then they each of them went down the drive far enough to glimpse the corpse, but not to identify it.'

'And even though I stood over him, I didn't recognise him. With his face hidden, you'd have to have known him well to work out who he was.'

'The Howards knew him, apparently. Mr Howard and the prof were members of the same local history group, and the prof bought a classic car from Mr Howard.'

'Ah. I'd wondered about that.'

Tony raised an eyebrow. 'Detective's instinct.'

'Dealer's hunch. Why aren't you telling me how dangerous it was to sneak into Oliver's house? Call yourself a godfather!'

Tony smiled, then shrugged. 'Consider it a compliment. I agreed with your dad. Always thought you'd be good at this. Plus, if you don't look into it, who will? I can help in the background, obviously.'

'Getting bored in your retirement?'

'Do you want to know more about the car, or don't you?'

She gave him a weary look. 'Go on then.'

'Bought it a few months back, apparently. Probably not relevant, but you never know.' He flipped the page of his notebook over. 'As for the prof, he'd been drinking at the Blue Boar that night. Enough to be quite merry.'

'Though John says he likes his whisky, so his tolerance was probably high.'

'Fair point.'

'Any idea who he drank with?'

He frowned at his notes. 'No one specific mentioned, just that the proprietors, Jeannie and Peter Jenks, noted his presence. Of course, Dixon wasn't treating it as anything more than an accident. The salient point was that he'd been drinking and there were witnesses. The prof doesn't have a criminal record. Respected academic, though known to like an evening out: wine, women and song. And cards. For money.'

'I'd heard.' It all fitted with the impression Bella had got: a clever, charismatic man with an addictive personality who liked to take risks. By turns a party animal and a keeper of secrets.

'He'd left the Blue Boar by ten fifteen.' Tony raised an eyebrow. 'After that, he went on a bat walk with his greatnephew.'

'Seriously?'

'Apparently, they make a habit of it. But the nephew, Cal, had school the next day, so he was home before eleven. His mum had already called the pair of them to tell them not to stay out too long.'

It sounded on the late side to Bella too. Then again, her

sisters had stayed out far later than that as teens. And not to
look at bats.

'That said,' Tony frowned, 'the prof called him on his
mobile after that, at eleven thirty.'

'Seems like an odd time to ring.'

'Your professor doesn't sound too conventional. The boy
said he often called out of the blue. This time it was because
Cal had asked for help with his history homework. The prof
had a last-minute genius idea he wanted him to include.'

It fitted with the exuberant side of his personality.

'The doc reckons time of death was between ten p.m. and
two a.m. All Barton's belongings were still on him. Wallet,
phone, what have you. And it looks as though his finds were too.
The holes he dug weren't deep. He had the odd coin – relatively
modern. A bit of copper pipe. Nothing interesting apparently.
Of course, if someone killed him, they could have taken the
precious stuff, but it doesn't look like it. He had a notebook in
his pocket. Just like the ones you found in his secret room, by
the sound of it. He was recording his dig as he went and there's
nothing special mentioned. Though something must have
sparked his interest. He'd written a question mark, followed by
an exclamation mark, next to his notes.'

'Maybe he expected something good and was disappointed.'

'Could be.'

Bella visualised the professor at work. 'He can't have been
that drunk, if he was making detailed notes.'

'Hmm. If the record-keeping was habitual, he might have
managed it, even hammered.' Tony's eyes met hers. 'We're on to
the ladder next. It was near a higher bit of remaining wall, so it's
possible Barton used it to look over the top. Or *at* the top, is my
thinking. Because looking over doesn't make sense. He could
have just walked round. The ladder came from the shed. Looks
as though he used something to lever the shed's lock off. His
trowel maybe. Dixon noticed rust on the prof's hands and the

ladder was corroded, so that all ties up. Whatever he was up to
with it, it seems he went back to digging afterwards. Appears to
have had his head down, looking at his work, when the stone
fell. Maybe he'd clambered on that wall beforehand and made it
unstable.'

'Or someone could have pushed the stone onto him.'

'Using the ladder to reach it?'

Bella shook her head. 'That bit of wall wasn't high. If there
was a killer, they'd have had to keep their head down to avoid
being seen.'

Their eyes met. 'Perhaps that's just what they did,' Tony
said. 'It's not certain, but if no one digs, it never will be.'

'Oh, put me on the spot, why don't you? I don't like to be
steered. If there's any steering to do, I'll do it myself.' She
drained her Coke, feeling almost as annoyed with Tony as she
had with Dixon.

He grinned. 'Wouldn't have mentioned it if I didn't think
you were tempted already. Choice is yours, obviously.'

Bella left the pub a short while later, climbing into Thomasina
and slamming the door closed. Tony's words echoed in her
head. *Chip off the old block.* She already knew what she was
going to do. Her dad's image played in her mind. He wouldn't
have left Oliver Barton's death to CID if he thought they were
missing something. He'd have kept his ear to the ground. Used
his local knowledge. Gathered information until something
came clear. He'd minded.

Back at her flat, she put her feet up on her velvet sofa with
the glass of red she'd promised herself many hours earlier.

Oliver Barton, John's friend and a man who'd known her
father, had been threatened. He'd implied he was afraid for his
life. And now he was dead. The only official who might find
justice for him was a permanently sleep-deprived detective-

cum-vet's assistant dealing with a string of jewellery robberies. She got up and put Edith Piaf on her vintage record player. For some reason she found the crackles of vinyl tremendously comforting.

She was a Winter, just like her dad, and she was going to find out more. She hadn't turned her back when she'd unearthed wrongdoing in London, even when it turned colleagues against her.

She wouldn't do it now.

TEN

THE STEPS

Bella found two texts on her phone the following morning. The first, sent around 1 a.m., was from Tony.

If you go for it, you know where I am.

Unusually tactful of him. She was quite sure he'd known what she'd decide before she'd left the pub.

The second was from John.

Tell me the worst. Are we under arrest?

She texted back and they arranged to meet for breakfast at the Steps for a proper debrief. The fact that the café was next-door-but-one to the antiques centre and run by John's brother made it a regular haunt.

Bella had rediscovered the place five days after moving to Hope Eaton, climbing up a narrow flight of steps, a red-brick wall sprigged with pellitory-of-the-wall on one side, gateways to snug hillside cottages on the other. Hope Eaton was full of these narrow steps, leading from the river up towards high town. Bella's reward for reaching the top had been to find the café.

The arched doorway she'd come to, cut into the wall, had looked like the entrance to a secret garden. It had been July and people had sat at the ironwork tables outside. Distant memories had come back of going there with her dad for scones with jam and cream.

She'd been welcomed by an effervescent guy called Leo, loud and warm with extravagant wavy hair. His colleague in the book section was Bernadette, a woman with poppy-blue eyes who moved around as though she was on springs.

Little did Bella know she'd end up employing Leo's brother as her assistant manager. Or that John and Leo were brothers of her neighbour. As she'd said, the Jenkses were everywhere.

Leo was easy-going like John, but a hundred times more extrovert. He and Bernadette had started to treat her as an old friend from the second time she'd visited. The café was one of her favourite places. The atmosphere was good, the prices decent and the coffee superb.

Leo slapped her on the back as she transferred from icy chill to warm fug.

'How are you? And how's my disreputable brother?'

'That's no way to talk about John.'

Leo laughed. 'I already know how he is. He beat you here. I meant Matt.'

'I wouldn't know. He keeps very odd hours.'

He grinned. 'All that gigging.'

Bella had seen him heading out of his flat with a guitar case. A band member, just like her mother's disastrous post-divorce boyfriend number three, father of her youngest two half-sisters. He'd gone off to New Zealand to find himself and presumably got lost, as he never came back.

'Matt's playing tonight, as a matter of fact, in a pub down the valley,' Leo said. 'Fancy joining us?'

'Kind of you to ask, but I'm planning a quiet night in.' She wouldn't get drawn into his antics.

'Fair enough.'

Close to the counter, Leo's teenage daughter, Lucy, sat writing in a book, her short straight hair falling over her face. 'John's over there.' Leo pointed to a table by a window in the far corner of the café. 'What have you done to him? He's all aquiver.'

'Long story. I know you'll listen in anyway, so come and sit down if you want the gossip.'

'Temptress! I might just manage it, although we have Poppy helping today.' He glanced at the waitress who was trying to read a Jilly Cooper and prepare a bacon sandwich at the same time. 'What'll you have? John's already ordered.'

Bella eyed Poppy and decided to plump for one of the simpler options. 'The Eaton sausage sandwich please. And a black coffee.'

He saluted. Bernadette was twinkling at her, approaching from the book section at speed. 'I've got just the thing for you. A 1950 edition of *A Shropshire Lad*. Beautifully illustrated. I put it by as soon as it came in so you could look at it before anyone else.' She took a breath at last.

It was for Bella, not Vintage Winter. Her father had had a copy, but she didn't know where it had ended up.

'Thank you!' She'd been holding out for an edition she'd love. She followed Bernadette, who was virtually skipping to the book counter.

The moment she saw it she knew it was the one. Her heart sang as she touched the pages. 'I'll take it.'

'I knew you would,' Bernadette said happily as she took Bella's money.

As Bella turned to join John, she saw Leo's wife Carys come in, looking harried. She was one of the most beautiful women Bella had ever seen, with long dark hair and clear blue eyes, but her job teaching at the local primary school guaranteed a frown at this time of day.

She grabbed a bacon roll, which Leo must have had on standby, and came to sit with Bella and John.

'Look at you!' She indicated Bella's retro tweed suit. 'I long to have a job where I get to dress up. If I wear anything I mind about, ten to one I'll end up covered in sick or paint or something. What have you two been up to?'

Bella explained. 'Now John wants to know what happened after I left him.'

John leaned forward, his shoulders tense. 'That's overstating it. I'm bracing myself for the news.'

'You'll have to wait. Leo wants to hear too.' You had to love a dramatic pause.

Leo appeared a moment later with her breakfast. The smell of the local sausage and mustard put her in seventh heaven. She filled them in, between mouthfuls.

'Sounds highly suspect,' Leo said. 'But the police aren't taking it seriously?'

'The sergeant I dealt with is trying to catch a jewel thief who's terrorising the great and the good of Shropshire, as well as having hundreds of children and a part-time job as a vet's assistant. As far as he's concerned, Oliver Barton was a naughty old drunk who got into mischief.' She paused to sip her coffee. 'I've somehow let my godfather talk me into seeing if I can find enough evidence to convince the police to look more carefully.'

'I want in,' Leo said.

'You would.' Carys shook her head. 'You look worryingly excited.'

Bella took another mouthful of her breakfast. Sumptuous. She suspected Leo had prepared the sandwich, rather than leaving it to Poppy's tender mercies. Loyal of him.

'Doesn't it set something off in you, though?' Carys asked, turning to Bella. 'I mean, with it being a family tradition. Your dad had the respect of the whole town. People confided in him. If something was off, he always knew it.'

The question tugged at her heart strings. Her dad had regularly aired the idea of her following in his footsteps until it was clear she had other plans. He'd never pushed, but deep inside she felt she'd let him down. 'I use my skills in my own career. I don't feel as though I'm missing out.' Or at least, she hadn't up until now. But the fire that had ignited inside her yesterday evening was burning ever brighter. She'd gone from *wanting* to know what had happened to *needing* to. It was possible the police had missed a murder. Oliver Barton might have been naughty, but he'd been sparky too. Fun. Friendly. Again, she wondered if her dad had been onto him. Had unfinished business he would have concluded had he lived. Maybe she was watching the next part of the story unfold. She took a notebook from her bag. If they were going to make plans, she wanted to ink them in.

'Wait a minute!' Leo snatched the book from her. 'That's new. And very pretty.'

Bella hadn't been able to resist it. The cover and the edges of the pages were marbled in blue.

'It's the kind of notebook people save for a special purpose.' Leo's eyes were on hers. 'You don't go jotting randomly in a beauty like that. You *are* keen!'

He'd got her. 'Oliver was a friend of John's. That matters. And my godfather's right. The time to act is now if we think there's something off. And I do.'

John nodded. 'So do I.'

Carys rolled up her sleeves as Leo went to rescue Poppy from a bacon bap disaster. 'Right, then. If we have to do it, we do it together. I'm not missing out on a distraction from a class full of six-year-olds. Let's pool resources.'

ELEVEN

THE LOW-DOWN FROM THE LOCALS

Bella wrote a timeline in her pristine notebook.

Sunday

9.50 p.m.: *I sneak off to bed early at Raven House*

10.15 p.m.: *Oliver leaves the Blue Boar and meets his nephew Cal for a bat walk*

11.00 p.m. approx: *Cal arrives home*

11.30 p.m.: *Oliver rings Cal with homework advice*

Midnight: *Alexis Howard goes to bed at Raven House*

12.30 a.m.: *Alexis asleep*

Some time later (but before 2 a.m. – end of time-of-death window): *Alexis woken by a crash in the garden.*

She wakes husband Harvey who decides it was probably a fox and encourages her to go back to sleep.

Monday

8.20 a.m.: *Harvey goes into the garden and finds their ladder on the lawn, close to the Raven Hall ruins. Puts ladder away and discovers shed lock is broken. Postman also saw ladder and exchanged words with Harvey.*

8.30 a.m.: *I leave to attend an auction, but spot Oliver Barton slumped against one of the ruins' walls.*

8.40 a.m.: *Alexis Howard calls the police.*

She turned to her collaborators. 'Evidence and questions next.'

John leaned forward. 'The queen cards Oliver referred to after we played poker.'

The Agatha Christie element. 'Remind me what he said again?'

John repeated his words and Bella wrote them down:

Queen of hearts, spades, clubs and diamonds – 'Three passionate women. One who loves too much, one who's full of fear, and one who's striving for immortality. And then the fourth. An enigma, but one who worries me.'

'We need to know who he was thinking of.' John frowned as he took a delicate bite of his bacon sandwich. 'And who might have written that threatening note.'

Bella nodded, lowering her voice. 'And whether his niece knew about the treasure stashed in his attic. Oliver kept her at arm's length, which could have been to keep his secret. But she might have found out. We must look into the history of Raven Hall, too. I wonder what Oliver thought he'd find.'

Leo glanced up and caught Bernadette's eye. She came bustling over and nodded vigorously as he spoke to her, her smile getting wider by the second.

A moment later, she was crouching down amongst the polished mahogany bookcases. She reappeared with a battered old hardback, *Hope Eaton Through Time*. 'This is what you need. There's a whole chapter on Raven Hall. I don't suppose anyone's bothered putting that much detail on the internet.'

Bella handed over more money. She loved watching Leo and Bernadette sell. Artists at work.

She turned to John. 'We should get a list of the people he played poker with. I know you said there weren't any regulars, but we can't leave them out.'

'Mum or Gareth might be able to help.'

Gareth worked at the Blue Boar. He was the chef, as well as being Jeannie Jenks's wingman and John's partner.

'Mum will have views on Nan Gifford too,' John added. 'We should pay her a visit.'

'Sounds like a plan.' Bella scanned her notebook. 'We need more information on the Howards.'

Leo leaned forward. 'We stock Alexis's poetry books if you want to have a look. She comes in sometimes.' He glanced in Bernadette's direction. 'We don't think she's very happy in her marriage. She's always looking at travel books and self-help volumes. Stuff about believing in yourself. She volunteers at the local school – helps the English teacher instil a love of poetry. Lucy tolerates her.' He nodded in his daughter's direction. 'Harvey comes in sometimes too. Buys non-fiction. History and politics. He's rather stiff, just like his dad. I remember him. Very upright and soldierly.' He pulled a haughty expression.

Carys turned to him. 'You look like a camel.'

'So did he.'

'Has Raven House been in their family long?'

Carys shook her head. 'Harvey's dad, the brigadier, bought it. And he didn't believe in making things too easy for his son. Harvey inherited it a few years back, but the family money went to fund a school overseas.'

It sounded as though the brigadier had wanted to test Harvey. If he'd behaved like that in life, it mightn't have been great for Harvey's self-esteem. He could have mixed feelings about his dad.

'Harvey came up trumps in the end,' Carys went on, 'but only after some bumps in the road. His wine business went south, and I gather he'd started to sell his dad's furniture, but Howard's Classic Cars turned his fortunes around. He's clearly made a packet. Their son's in his teens. Off at boarding school, so they can't be hurting.'

'I didn't realise they had children.'

Carys nodded. 'I think Alexis wishes he was at the local school. If I ask about him she always gets emotional.'

'So Harvey drove the choice for him to board, presumably.' It didn't surprise Bella. He'd seemed like the traditional sort.

'Still trying to conform.' Carys shook her head. 'He always seemed to want his dad's approval.

'You know Alexis is giving a poetry recital this week? I go along to do some adulting. Stop my brain turning to mush.'

'Tomorrow night? I wasn't sure if it would go ahead.'

'She hasn't told us otherwise.' Leo pointed to a poster pinned to the Steps' noticeboard. 'Come along?'

'I think I might. Oliver bought his Alfa Romeo from Harvey. Do you know any of his other customers?'

Leo laughed. 'They'll be way out of our social league. Probably come to him from across the county.'

'It was certainly an extravagant purchase of Oliver's. I doubted he'd sell his treasure to fund it, but he might have.'

Carys lowered her voice to a whisper. 'Not from what I

hear. He took out a loan on his seventieth birthday. I shouldn't know but I'm friends with a woman from the bank. We were marvelling at how much some people spend on luxuries. He borrowed fifty-five thousand. Told her all about his plans.'

John looked at Bella. 'That answers that, then.'

She frowned. 'So it looks as though someone else has taken the missing pieces of treasure. Since he died, maybe. We shouldn't forget about Meg Jones. If Oliver decided to hire her, she's another one who might have a key.'

'I suppose we could go and see her.' John spoke with the utmost reluctance. 'We were friends, once upon a time. We still chat if we meet in the street.'

'We definitely should.' Bella added her name to her list before John changed his mind. 'Now we know about the treasure, the idea of him employing her seems even odder. Why take the risk? She was bound to go all over the house. She might easily notice part of the attic was walled off.'

John was glancing at his watch. 'We should go and open up.'

'True. Any last thoughts before we do?'

Leo had been distracted by Poppy, who'd failed to clear a table. He stopped gesticulating and put up an eager hand.

'Background intel on Nan Gifford, since I imagine John's been too upstanding to say. Her husband's in jail. He—'

'Hush!' Carys cocked her head and gave him a disapproving look. 'What her husband's done isn't relevant. She's her own woman.'

Leo shrugged. 'Of course. But she's keeping that household going. And her husband dealt with some ropy types. If he's in debt to anyone, financially or morally, she might need to pay them off.'

Carys tutted. 'Your imagination is overwhelming.'

Bella thought Leo looked rather proud. She was tempted to

probe further but at that moment Carys checked her own watch and leaped up.

'Sweet Agnes, I must go! But I have a contribution too. Meg Jones cleans for the Howards at Raven House.'

Trade was good that morning. Between sales, Bella went to buy a pack of playing cards from the toyshop on Market Street. Later, in a quiet moment, she fixed some A1 paper to her beloved mid-century drawing board in Vintage Winter's office. She liked to imagine the architect who'd used the board previously, leaning over the slanting surface, poring over their designs. She'd been using it to record her plans for the shop. Resting her paper on such a beautiful bit of furniture made every idea feel momentous. She spent a moment appreciating the expanse of unmarked white paper, then stuck the four queens down its right-hand side.

John popped in while she was lost in thought and raised an eyebrow at her work.

'For case notes. Don't tell Leo.'

As he watched, she noted her priorities near the bottom of the page:

Talk to Nan Gifford – find out if she knew about Oliver's treasure.

'If so, she has to be the top suspect, as his beneficiary.'
John looked uncomfortable.

Research Raven Hall – what did Oliver think he might find and who knew he'd be there on Sunday night?
Investigate the watermark used on Oliver's threatening note – to try to identify the sender.

John had brightened up and Bella knew why. The last two points could be done in the peace and quiet of the shop.

Consider the Howards – could they have been involved?

'It doesn't seem likely,' Bella said, glancing at John, 'but he was on their land. We need to work it through, step by step.'

Talk to Jeannie and Gareth – try to identify the four playing-card women from amongst Oliver's contacts (including fellow poker players).

'Of course, the card women might not have anything to do with his death,' John said, and Bella nodded.

'But they must have been a key part of his life. His relationships with them will be revealing.' Her dad had taught her that much. Understanding the victim's personality was crucial for any crime that might have a personal element. She could feel him urging her on.

Later, while she rearranged the stock after a couple of sales, Bella broached the plans that had been forming in her head.

'It's nearly lunchtime. Let's go and knock on Nan Gifford's door. If she works as a housekeeper she might be done by now.'

'What on earth will we say to her?'

She'd been wondering how he'd react to that part of her scheme. 'I've got an idea. Let's talk about it.'

TWELVE

THE SURVIVING RELATIVES

Bella adjusted her expectations of Nan Gifford when the woman opened the door. Her name had somehow conjured up a matronly figure. In reality, she looked younger than Bella and was fine featured, with wavy mid-brown hair. Her face was pinched, with shadows under her eyes, but the woollen dress she wore was neat.

Nan gave a small nod of recognition when she saw John, though her brow furrowed as she spotted Bella beyond. They'd agreed John would do the talking. It had taken Bella five minutes' determined persuasion.

'We're so sorry for your loss,' he said in his gentle voice. 'I was very fond of Oliver.'

A tabby cat had appeared behind Nan, its bell jangling. It snaked its way around her ankles and trousered John, who bent to give it a fuss. 'Hello, Smudge.'

'He's feeling proper lost,' Nan said quietly.

Bella bent to fuss the cat too. His eyes closed as she stroked him under the chin.

'This is Bella, my boss,' John said, as she stood up again. 'She's worked with antiques all her life and I asked her advice about something Oliver gave me. Could we come in and talk to you about it? I wondered if you might like it back.'

Nan's eyes took on a wary look.

Bella had thought John might not like her gambit, but he'd leaped on it as a decent excuse to get them inside. ('It's not as embarrassing as I'd thought.') She'd worried that offering his coin to Nan might hurt, but John said he was uneasy about keeping it anyway.

The approach meant they could ask questions without showing their hand.

Despite Nan's frown, she stepped back in the hallway, almost tripping over a sports holdall slung carelessly on the hall floor and a pair of scruffy trainers chucked to one side. It looked as though Oliver's great-nephew, Cal, must be home for lunch.

Nan took them to a living room with a kitchen-diner at one end and a sofa, coffee table and armchairs at the other. A teenage boy sprawled at a table, side-on to them, his hair hanging down over the laptop he was scrutinising, a glass of Coke at his elbow. A plate with a sandwich sat to one side, as though he'd pushed it away.

Nan introduced them and the boy looked them up and down. His eyes were appraising, like those of Bella's most difficult customers: the ones who knew exactly what they wanted but weren't prepared to pay for it.

Bella caught a flash of anxiety in Nan's eyes as she tore her attention from her son and motioned them to seats on the street side of the room. It meant Cal was outside their circle, but close enough to listen in.

Bella glanced around. The sofa she sat in was comfortable, the house well-loved, but the odd repair needed doing. There was a crack in the window behind them. A patch of damp near the chimney breast. Cal had his computer, though. She must mind about his education.

'What did Oliver give you, John?' Nan perched on the edge of a small armchair.

Straight to the point, and no offer of tea or coffee. She didn't want to extend their visit, clearly. She looked wrung-out, like a pretty cloth that had been washed over and over and been through the mangle a hundred times. Bella wouldn't welcome visitors at a time like that either – Nan had had a terrible week – but she wondered if there was more to it than that.

John took out the medieval coin with the hole in it and Bella looked on, watching Nan and Cal Gifford.

She heard Nan's sharp intake of breath, but Cal's reaction was just as interesting. A split-second flicker of anger, quickly suppressed. And then he was up and out of his seat, with a smile which didn't meet his eyes. He drew a dining chair round so he could join them.

Nan darted him a quick, nervous glance.

'He said he wanted me to have it as a thank you for feeding Smudge,' John said. 'But when I showed it to Bella, she said it was probably hundreds of years old and that it might be valuable. Special anyway.' He took a shaky breath. 'And now that Oliver's dead, I thought maybe you'd like to have it. As a memory of him.'

Bella couldn't have done it better herself.

But Nan shrank back in her armchair, her eyes huge. 'I don't know anything about that sort of thing. He intended it for you. You must keep it.'

Bella was sure Cal would have taken it. He turned towards them, smiling still. But behind the façade, his look was as appraising as ever. His gaze flicked to the coin. 'Have you found out any more about it?'

John shook his head.

'It's not my specialist area,' Bella said. 'It's only a single coin, of course. Not treasure trove. But interesting.' She'd decided in advance to be economical with the truth. She didn't want them to think they suspected Oliver of anything.

Her eyes met Cal's.

For a moment he held her gaze but then nodded. 'It's the kind of thing they like us to bring into school.'

'There are other things you can take.' Nan spoke quickly, putting a hand on the boy's arm.

He twitched, and she withdrew it quickly, blinking.

At that moment, a mobile sounded inside her pocket. She fished it out, glanced at the screen, and caught her breath.

'Excuse me a moment.'

Cal looked after her as she left the room. 'Another one of her mysterious calls. How many mums keep secrets from their kids?'

Lots, Bella imagined.

She was conscious of Nan's footsteps on the cottage stairs, and then the sound of creaks on the landing. At last, there was no sound overhead. Nan must have taken the call as far away as possible.

'She's pretty obvious about it, don't you reckon?' Cal said. 'Makes you wonder, doesn't it?' His look turned from challenging to sly. He was deliberately winding them in, wanting them to speculate. Not pretty behaviour.

Bella smiled innocently. 'Do you tell her everything you and your friends talk about?'

Cal shrugged and she asked him about school. He claimed he loved history, and that his great-uncle had encouraged his interest, but the sly smile was back. Then he asked to look at the coin. His interest in the treasure was real enough.

She watched as he peered at it, then turned it over in his hand.

'Oliver often talked about you,' John said.

Cal raised his chin now, a truculent look. 'Really?'

'He mentioned your bat walks.'

The boy's eyes part closed and he grinned. 'Loved them. Made the guys at school jealous. I thought Oliver was an embarrassment when we moved here. Weirder than the other kids' relations.'

'But you were close by the end?' said Bella.

'Very.' Cal folded his arms. He was still holding the coin.

'When did you move here?'

'When my dad got banged up.'

Well, that was nice and straightforward.

'We used to live at the far end of the valley. My dad was poaching. Shot another guy. It was an accident. He never meant to kill him, but they made it out to be some kind of feud. Gave him life. It was just after my grandparents died. Oliver said Mum should come and live here so he could help out.' He scoffed. 'Reckon she's too prickly to want help. And he never knew all the things she gets up to.' He held the coin between his finger and thumb. 'Why are you so interested?'

But at that second his mother swept back into the room, her eyes darting from her son to Bella and John.

'Give the coin back, Cal.'

He shrugged and chucked it to John, who was clearly meant to drop it, but didn't.

Bella smiled at Cal's twitch of annoyance. *Serves you right. You don't know who you're dealing with.*

'We were just talking about Oliver and Cal's bat walks,' she said to Nan. She wanted the conversation back on the dead man and his habits.

The woman gave a sharp nod. 'They went out on one the night Oliver died, though Cal was back here by five to eleven.'

'Oliver and my dad were friends,' Bella said. 'I saw a photograph of them together, walking in the hills. They looked happy.'

Nan raised an eyebrow. 'Your dad's dead too?'

She nodded. 'Twelve years back.'

'I'm sorry. Who was he?'

'Douglas. Douglas Winter.'

Nan shifted in her seat at the name. 'I didn't know him. Not personally. If you'll excuse me, I must get on now.'

'Of course.' John stood up.

'Look after that coin,' Cal said, with an edge to his voice, as they walked towards the door.

In the porch, Nan hesitated. 'I'm sorry about Cal. He's out of sorts at the moment.' She lowered her voice. 'He'll miss his uncle.' Her eyes were pleading.

'We understand,' John said.

A nicely ambiguous answer. Bella felt she understood Cal too.

As they emerged from the house, she caught movement. The edge of someone's overcoat, just visible behind the thick trunk of an oak tree across the road. She walked on, as though she hadn't seen.

'I pity poor Nan. Cal strikes me as a prize toad.'

Bella had had her work cut out with her younger sisters, but she'd rather three of them than one Cal, any day. She thought of the way he'd bad-mouthed his mother, and thrown the coin at John, hoping to humiliate him. Of course, he might be jealous. Maybe his great-uncle had never given him a present. And they didn't know much about Nan yet.

'He's had a tough time,' John said, mildly.

'Granted.' A difficult upbringing didn't cover it. Losing his grandparents, being separated from his dad. Prejudice directed against him and his mum after his father's conviction. Switching areas. Having to find new friends. There were umpteen reasons he might be troublesome, but letting him behave like a beast wouldn't help.

Bella risked a glance over her shoulder. The edge of the overcoat was no longer showing behind the tree, but a man had appeared beyond it. He was facing away, his head down, covered by a hat. But at that moment he glanced over his shoulder, started at the sight of her and quickened his pace.

Bella turned quickly to John. 'Do you know that man?'

But as she pointed, the tails of his overcoat disappeared around the house on the corner.

'I know this sounds far-fetched, but I think he was watching us as we left Nan Gifford's house.'

John shuddered. 'Not a good thought. Was he young and musclebound?'

Bella smiled. 'No. Senior and slender. And anxious not to be seen. In fact, anxious full stop.'

'I like him better already.'

'Let's see where he goes.'

They doubled back to catch him up, but when they rounded the house on the corner there was no sign of him.

Bella looked at John. 'Not keen to chat, I'd say.'

'Interesting. If you see him again, I'll try and identify him.' He put his gloved hands in his pockets as they retraced their steps. It was bitter. 'What did you think when I showed Nan and Cal the coin?'

'That they knew about the treasure.'

John nodded. 'Or Nan at least.'

'I'd say both of them. Cal looked angry the moment he saw it. Why would he, unless he knew? We only explained how old and special it was after that. And Nan was desperate to distance herself. She didn't want to show any interest in the coin, or for Cal to take it into school. Though I doubt that was really his plan.'

As they turned onto Hollybush Lane, back towards Uppergate and the shop, Bella added: 'It felt odd when Nan told us what time Cal got home on Sunday night. As though she was trying to give him an alibi. Or provide one for herself, maybe.'

He nodded.

'Did anything strike you?'

He looked uncomfortable.

'Spit it out.'

'Cal's got a rather nice new computer.'

'How do you know it's new?'

'I popped into Nan's cottage with Oliver on Friday evening to move a bit of heavy furniture. Cal was working on an ancient-looking machine and complaining about it.'

'Did you notice the make of the new one?' Bella had only seen it side on.

He frowned as they paused to cross the road towards St Giles's Lane and the close. 'A MacBook Air.'

Bella took out her phone and googled. Just over a thousand pounds. *Right.* 'Well, I know I couldn't afford it.'

'Nor me,' John said.

'You think she's already sold some of Oliver's trinkets to buy it?'

John looked unhappy. 'I don't know.'

'And why all the secrecy when Nan took the call?'

'And who was the man hanging round outside?'

It all felt significant, but it was as though they'd wandered deeper into a forest, their route getting darker. 'The take-home point is that Nan and Cal both stood to benefit from Oliver's death, and it looks like Nan has a secret income. Plenty of food for thought.'

'What next?'

'Actual food. Quick and lots.' They'd used up their lunch hour. They'd have to snatch sustenance between customers. 'Then research into the Raven Hall ruins when there's a quiet moment. And I want to know the origin of the watermarked paper.'

THIRTEEN

SIENNA HEARST'S REVENGE

After John had eaten his lunch and Bella had demolished hers, they cast their eyes over the shelves which lined the walls of Vintage Winter's office. They contained stock not yet displayed, most of it needing some kind of attention before it was put out. The larger items were stored in the former coach house at the Blue Boar. Offering John a job had put Jeannie very much on Bella's side.

After they'd identified which goods should take priority, Bella indicated the drawing board and its piece of A1 paper. 'We should update this before we plough on with the day job.'

John took up a marker pen and looked at her.

'Go ahead. I was planning to put the names of Oliver Barton's contacts down the left-hand side. If any of the women seem to match a card, we can pair them up, though I don't think we should restrict our suspects to females.'

John leaned over the board and wrote the names they had so far in his neat italics. After that, they threw out ideas and comments until the key players were annotated with notes.

Nan Gifford (niece), housekeeper, Blue Boar – Top motive.
Inherits Oliver's estate but too soon for her to have benefited
from that legitimately. Son has expensive new computer.
Sensitive on the subject of John's coin, and cagey about her
phone calls. Cal implied she has secrets. A lot to cope with,
husband in prison, parents dead. Seems concerned for Cal. She
and her son alibi each other but that doesn't feel solid.

Cal Gifford (great-nephew), student, Hope Eaton High School
– also has motive – worldly-wise, asks questions, looked angry
when he saw the coin/heard Oliver had given it to John.
Antagonistic towards Nan.

_Meg Jones (mentioned on a flyer at Oliver's place), cleaner
(already works at Raven House)_ – touting for business.

_Harvey Howard (knew Oliver through the local history group),
runs Howard's Classic Cars_ – owns the land on which Oliver
was found, sold him an Alfa Romeo, found the ladder he
pinched the morning after his death.

_Alexis Howard (knew Oliver through husband Harvey), criti-
cally acclaimed poet_ – woken by the crash the ladder made.

At that moment the shop bell jangled. John handed her the
marker. 'I'll go.'

Across the bottom of the paper, Bella wrote the key
questions:

_Who knew about the treasure before Oliver's death? (Nan and
Cal Gifford likely.)_

_Of them, who removed some and what have they done with it?
(Is Cal's expensive laptop significant?)_

Who wrote the threatening letter? And what did it refer to?

She wasn't certain it was Oliver's nighthawking. There was passion in that note. She could imagine someone he'd stolen from feeling passionately angry, but about their own loss, not about Oliver's ongoing activities. Maybe the note was about something else. Cheating at cards? Sleeping with married women? Double-crossing someone at work? The possibilities were endless.

She scrolled back to the photos she'd taken at Oliver's house and found the typewritten note:

I KNOW WHAT YOU'VE BEEN UP TO, AND YOU'RE BEING WATCHED. IF YOU DON'T STOP, I SWEAR TO GOD I'LL STOP YOU MYSELF.

She left the office for the shop's front room, where John was taking money for a Sweet Agnes candle and the next cheapest item in the shop, a Wade Whimsies tortoise. Bella gave the customer her best smile and hoped they'd come back with some extravagant friends.

As they left, Sienna Hearst, the new owner of the Hearst House Museum, swept through the door. She looked like just the sort of person she was, with her sharp eyes, sharp bone structure and expensively dyed blonde hair. Bella almost expected her to have fangs when she opened her mouth.

Sienna nodded to John and ignored Bella. Bella knew she'd wanted John to stay and run the museum for her, and she could see why. John was a gem. Sienna had lost him fair and square by being foul.

Sienna cast her gaze over Vintage Winter's contents. Quickly. As though nothing required more than a moment's attention. Bella felt her blood heat instantly.

'I'm rejigging the museum, John,' she said, picking up a

Sweet Agnes candle and dropping it back into its jar again. 'Throwing out some of the old rubbish. I can't think why you didn't convince my aunt to have a clear-out sooner.'

John didn't say anything, which was probably wise. Bella found it hard to talk to Sienna without being rude.

Sienna paused a moment. 'The travel candlesticks are already gone.'

Bella watched as John's hand tightened on the back of the chair he was standing next to. She fought the urge to tell Sienna just what she thought of her. John had shown her the items when she'd visited. They were officer's campaign candlesticks dating back to 1800, neat and clever, the pair fitting into a bun-shaped brass container. She knew how fond he was of them. She couldn't help wondering if Sienna had found out and come in especially to taunt him. Selling them made no sense.

'I didn't bother bringing them here,' she said, turning to Bella. 'They're not in keeping with your stock.' She returned her attention to John. 'I've got shot of the medicine chest too. It wasn't to my taste, but it turned a profit.'

She *was* doing it on purpose. She must be. The small chest had belonged to a Royal Navy surgeon with a connection to the Jenks family. Bella felt waves of hate running through her. Who would be so vindictive?

Sienna laughed lightly. 'I actually thought I might find some replacement pieces in here, but I was wrong. It's not quite... Well, never mind.'

She gave a wave of a hand, all poisonous elegance, and strode out of the door, letting a gust of cold air reach into the shop, like a clammy hand.

Bella looked after her. 'I'm going to find those pieces, John. I'm going to find them, and buy them, and you can take them home.' She didn't know how she'd do it, but she had contacts and she was steaming with pent-up fury.

'You don't have to do that. It doesn't matter.' He didn't look at her.

But it did. Wretched Sienna Hearst had made John sad. And Bella had caused the rift by employing him. Even though it was entirely Sienna's fault.

FOURTEEN

TWO LEADS IN ONE AFTERNOON

Bella was glad of the customer who arrived moments after Sienna Hearst left. It gave her the chance to calm down and channel benevolence. It had to be good to flex those muscles. The woman was a regular and Bella was able to ask about her children, her aunt's hip operation, and show her the new stock that might be of interest. They were both so nice to each other that Bella's equilibrium had almost returned by the time the woman left, a wrapped purchase swinging in the bag on her arm.

When John had finished cleaning some china, they settled down at the refectory table with their laptops and the book of Hope Eaton history. The sky outside had darkened, low cloud hugging the town. Inside, the shop was cosy, the radiators warm, the gleam of the 1930s chrome desk lamp illuminating the table. Once the rain started, they weren't much disturbed by customers. It was all very well for the time being; Bella wanted to get on with her research. All the same, if she wanted to keep Vintage Winter warm and cosy, she couldn't afford too many afternoons as quiet as this.

John was trying to find an organisation that used two

entwined 'A's as its logo, matching the watermarked paper. He'd set about it with admirable focus, his brow furrowing. Now he was biting his bottom lip. A second later he pushed his glasses further up his nose.

Bella was looking at an old aerial photograph of the Raven Hall site and reading about the family who'd once owned the place. Once she'd got the gist, she flicked regular glances in John's direction. *At last!* He'd shifted in his seat. She took the opportunity to interrupt him.

'It's odd. I can't find any reason for Oliver to have targeted the ruins. According to Bernadette's book, the family who once owned the hall, the Millingtons, lost it in a game of cards. Shades of Oliver.'

John nodded.

'They hadn't a penny by the time they left, and the man who won it never bothered with the place. He already had bases in Scotland, Wales and England, so, you know, he just hadn't the time to pop over.'

'Poor man. How exhausting.'

'Quite. Bit by bit, the hall fell apart. So sad, and such a waste. I'm sure there were people locally who could have made use of it. And the Millingtons had nowhere to go.' She imagined the family's despair at the father of the household, who'd staked the hall in the game. They would have been powerless to stop him. 'Ultimately, a descendant built the new house on the site. It sounds as though they stripped the hall of anything saleable at that point.'

John took his glasses off and polished them. 'So the likelihood of finding buried valuables seems pretty much zero.'

'Yes. Yet we know what a serious collector Oliver was. I can't believe he'd hare off to the ruins on a fishing expedition.'

'He must have known something the history books don't. Anything else?'

Bella nodded. 'The hall ruins are a scheduled monument. I

found them on Historic England's website. There's not much detail though. The listing says the record's been generated from something called an "old county number", whatever that is. It hasn't been reviewed under their Monuments Protection Programme, so it's a dead end as far as further information goes.'

They went back to their respective research. Bella book-marked several pages. Once again, she was waiting for John.

'Anything yet?' she said at last.

'Oh yes. Found the answer hours ago. I'm on Facebook now.'

'Oh har-de-har. The idea of you on Facebook!' It wasn't John's thing. 'I've found local news reports about the vandalised lights at the ruins. Oliver would have known they were out.' She took a deep breath. 'And so would his killer, if he was killed.'

'What do you think of the Howards? We haven't unpicked their possible motives yet. Could they have attacked him if they were in it together?'

'I wondered about that. Or Alexis could have sneaked out earlier to kill Oliver. Perhaps the ladder came down sooner than she said, and she lied about the timing and shook Harvey awake to muddy the waters. But why would either of them want him dead? I could maybe see it if Oliver had discovered something amazing.' She frowned. 'They could have seen a priceless trea-sure, gleaming in the moonlight, and wanted it for themselves.'

'Wouldn't they have simply called the police and stopped him taking it? It's not as though Oliver was armed.'

'If they called the police, any treasure would have to be given up. Even if Oliver had dug with permission, he and the Howards would have been legally bound to declare treasure trove to the coroner. They might have ended up with a reward or even the treasure itself, if no museum wanted it. But there would be no guarantees. And the Historic England listing is restrictive. No one's allowed to dig there. The Howards aren't entitled to give permission.'

John frowned. 'So they could have killed Oliver to *secretly* take possession of the treasure.'

'That's right. Except Oliver was recording his dig and he hadn't found any.'

'Didn't you say he'd written a question mark followed by an exclamation mark in his notebook though?'

'Yes, according to Tony. But not because of a spectacular find, I don't think. He was working methodically, like the academic he was. My sister's the same. And when he was killed, he had his head down. He was busy digging again. If he'd found something prior to that, he'd have updated his records. And if he'd discovered anything in that last hole, the killer would have had to move the stone and his body to get at it.'

Bella was convinced Oliver had drawn a blank, so what had triggered the excitable punctuation? 'Something must have surprised him. I wonder if it made him fetch a ladder from the shed. Tony suggested he might have been trying to look on top of one of the walls, because using it to look over them isn't logical. And he's right. You could just walk round.'

John nodded. 'That makes sense. But the upshot for the Howards is, we don't think there was any treasure to kill for?'

'That's right.' Bella recalled her breakfast at Raven House. 'I think Alexis was telling the truth about the disturbance in the night anyway. Her body language was natural. Nan and Cal Gifford seem like stronger suspects.'

John's gaze reverted to his laptop. 'Fair enough.'

Bella had just attended to an isolated customer, who'd clearly come in to get out of the rain, when she heard John whistle.

'I've got it! Or at least, the logo matches exactly.' He frowned. 'It's the Alexandra Arms near Much Wenlock. A three-star hotel. Maybe the sender of the letter wasn't even local. They could have been staying there.'

That would be inconvenient. But a moment later, Bella's spirits surged again. 'They have to be local. How could they keep an eye on Oliver, otherwise? And how would they know what he was up to in the first place? Maybe the letter was sent by someone who works there but lives here.'

'We can but hope.'

'I'll start dropping the hotel into conversation around town. See if anyone twitches.'

John was about to reply when they were distracted by the jangling shop bell again.

It was his brother Matt, grinning, his unruly dark hair dripping. His stubble made Bella wonder if he'd spent most of the day in bed after doing who knew what the night before.

'Happy news,' he said. 'I've just seen Sienna Hearst step on some chewing gum. She'll be hobbling all the way back to her four-by-four.'

John gave a flicker of a smile. 'We had her in earlier.'

'Just an antisocial call?' Matt shook his head. 'I still can't believe she's related to old Mrs Hearst.'

'Even close relations can be very different from each other.' Bella was thinking of her and her sisters, but John and Matt were the most immediate example. Chalk and cheese.

Matt laughed and patted John on the shoulder. 'Each of us perfect in our own way.'

And modest with it...

'I've just come from the Steps.'

A late-afternoon breakfast, perhaps.

'Leo told me what you're up to. All about Oliver Barton.' He was looking at John now. 'You know how sorry I was to hear what happened.' He shrugged. 'I thought you might like to know that I heard someone talking about treasure at Raven Hall.'

'What? Where was this? When?' Bella had stepped forward automatically.

'A couple of weeks back at the Black Swan, down the valley. We were halfway through our set, and I passed someone on the way to the gents who mentioned it.'

'You didn't recognise them?'

He shook his head. 'But I'm playing there again tonight.' His blue eyes met Bella's. 'You can come along and ask some questions if you like. John's coming, aren't you, John? And Leo and Carys.'

He strode out again.

'Change your mind?' John said, with a small smile.

She'd been wondering if she should make for the Blue Boar. Talk to Jeannie and Gareth. But this was more urgent. They might discover why Oliver had decided to dig at the ruins. And crucially, who knew he'd be there.

'Yes. I think it's time to deploy Thomasina. Plenty of room for you all. It's what she was made for.'

John grinned. 'Leo will love that. Carys says he's obsessed with your taxi.'

FIFTEEN

HOWARD'S CLASSIC CARS

Between customers, Bella plotted her approach for that evening, but as soon as she got home she turned her mind to Sienna Hearst. She made Bella so angry she could hardly think. She took a deep breath and began to work out who might have bought the candlesticks and the medicine chest. She'd already nipped into the other outlets at the antiques centre, just to be sure, but of course, Sienna hadn't made it that easy. There were a couple more specialist shops in the Kite Valley, but Shrewsbury seemed the most likely place. She started to ring round, leaving messages, asking if Sienna Hearst had been in to sell items from the museum. It wasn't the best way to go about it. The shop owners would know she was keen. They might charge over the odds, but this mattered. And if she waited until she could scour the length and breadth of the town, she might miss them. She only hoped someone would call back.

By seven o'clock, Bella was driving John, Carys and Leo down a dark country lane. Matt was travelling with the band. Bella had Thomasina's reassuring headlamps on full beam as occasional creatures scuttled into the grass verge. The rain had stopped, and a crescent moon was visible between the clouds.

'What's new with the case?' Leo asked, craning forward over the front seats.

Bella and John filled him in.

'This route takes us through Upper Bewley, where Harvey Howard's salesroom is,' Bella said. 'If Oliver *was* killed, I doubt they're involved, but I'd still like to see it.'

'You're just in love with the classic cars.' Leo laughed.

'I'm being thorough. Don't listen to him, Thomasina. I'd never look at another vehicle.' Bella patted the car's steering wheel.

They found Harvey's showroom beyond the village, isolated except for a small cottage next door. It was closed, of course. The noticeboard said it didn't open at all on Tuesdays and Wednesdays, but Bella pulled up in the forecourt anyway and they got out.

'I assume you don't mind featuring on Harvey Howard's CCTV,' John said.

'I'm sure he'll understand. He knows about my passion for vintage.' She walked over to the dimly lit showroom. There were some beauties. An old Lancia Fulvia Coupé Monte-Carlo, a seventies Triumph Spitfire and a fifties Riley. Just for a second, she felt a quiver of disloyalty over that one and took a photograph or two.

'It is quite cold out here, you know, Bella,' Carys said. 'Leo's shaking like a jelly.'

'Like a jelly?' Her husband shook his head. 'I'd always imagined you saw me as a tough guy.'

Carys laughed and patted his shoulder. 'Bless. I hate tough guys.'

'I'll be right there,' Bella said. 'Shelter in Thomasina.' She was just taking one last picture of a 1920s Bugatti, when the sound of screeching tyres made them all look round.

A young man was getting out of a James-Bond style Jaguar, well away from the CCTV cameras. He pushed his hair out of his eyes, his anxious face morphing from a frown into a smile. As he bounded over to them, Bella saw a young woman extricate herself from the passenger seat, eyes down, her long blonde hair gleaming in the moonlight.

'Hello, hello!' The young man spoke as though they were long-lost relatives he'd been pining for and held out a hand. 'I'm Tyler. Tyler Smith. I'm so sorry I wasn't here when you arrived. I'm afraid we're closed, but I live just next door. I'm usually out like a jack-in-the-box when people show up.'

He glanced at Bella's taxi. 'You're after something with a little more...' He hesitated, his eyes on Bella's, and changed tack. *Very wise.* 'You're interested in expanding your collection? Taxis are perennially popular, of course. I'm sure we have just the thing for you. Would you like me to open up the showroom?'

'Is it warm in there?' said Leo.

'We were just having a look from outside,' Bella said firmly. 'We can come back for a proper browse when you're open. Do you sell many?'

The young man nodded as though his life depended on it. 'A lot. People travel to reach us. Are you local? How did you hear about us?'

'I stayed with Mr Howard and his wife recently. We talked about it then.'

Bella saw the young man's eyes flick over his shoulder towards the Jaguar. 'Ah.'

'An old friend of John's bought his Alfa Romeo from you. It was on my mind because he died last Sunday in an accident on Mr Howard's land.'

The young man dragged his worried gaze back from the Jaguar. 'I saw the news. The old professor who got crushed by a falling stone?'

Bella nodded.

'I remember him. Mr Howard came over to help him

choose.' Bella watched him flush in the moonlight. 'Poor old s — Poor man. He was excited when he came here. Full of plans. Kept talking about the open road. He was a romantic, I reckon. Wanted to whisk a girlfriend off her feet with that car.'

'He talked about someone?'

'Well,' the young man frowned, 'nothing specific. I think he was building up the mystery a bit. Mr Howard was asking about her, telling the professor he was a dark horse. But he just tapped the side of his nose.'

That sounded familiar. Bella thanked Tyler for his time and let him get back to his evening.

As she reversed round and exited the forecourt, she saw his blonde companion buffing the Jaguar they'd been out in.

'Was that, or was that not, worth the shivering?' Bella said.

'All right. You win. It was.' Leo patted her on the shoulder. 'So, Oliver was being secretive about his lover.'

And enjoying Harvey's curiosity, by the sound of it. He'd had a sense of the dramatic. Some people had said the same about her.

'If he was seeing a married woman,' Leo went on, 'a jealous husband could have come after him.'

'Would it fit with the threatening note?' Carys asked.

'"I know what you've been up to, and you're being watched. If you don't stop, I swear to God I'll stop you myself."' John recited it from memory.

'Not if the note was from the husband or partner,' Bella said. 'They're saying this is your last chance, as though they've been watching him for a while. That doesn't sound right. A partner wouldn't bide their time.'

John grunted his agreement. 'And how would this person know where Oliver would be?'

'Good point.' Bella bounced as they went over a bump in the road. 'If Oliver was killed, maybe his attacker had been following him. They could have discovered his secret hobby that way, listened in on his conversations even.'

'You think he'd talk publicly about it?' Leo put in.

'It might depend on the company he was keeping. Matt overheard someone discussing treasure at the Black Swan. Maybe we'll find out more tonight.'

'What's the plan, then?' Carys asked.

Bella focused on the dark road. She'd thought it through already. 'If there was gossip about the treasure at the pub, maybe Oliver heard it there. His name's been all over the news. It might be easiest to start by chatting about him. We can see if the staff saw him and what they say about it. I've thought of a cover story. I'll kick things off.'

'Excellent.' Carys sighed. 'This comes as welcome relief. After an afternoon corralling thirty children into gluing pasta onto sugar paper, my patience is at an end.'

SIXTEEN

DODGY DEALINGS AT THE BLACK SWAN

Tony Borley would have felt at home in the Black Swan. It wasn't quite spit and sawdust but it was... rough and ready. Dark and crowded, smelling of spilled beer, dodgy aftershave and stale fried food. Tony's tastes were deeply mysterious to Bella.

He would have been less keen on the guy at the bar, a big man with a dark beard and a ruddy face. He was complaining about his pint to a beleaguered barmaid – demanding she top it up now it had settled.

Bella suspected he'd had a good slug, and was trying it on.

'Useless,' the man was saying, leaning forward, crowding the barmaid. 'That's what you are.' He turned to an older woman behind the bar. 'Why don't you get some proper staff round here, Sandra?'

Tony would have relished wading in to give him what for. Bella opened her mouth to do the job when the older woman rolled up the sleeves of her bulky jumper. 'Say that one more time, Bob Berrow, and you're out of here. Go and sit down and stop making a nuisance of yourself.'

The man grumbled as he shuffled off to a table near the fire.

Matt and his friends were setting up on a stage to their right as the woman in charge leaned forward to take their order.

'Here for the band?' She raised an eyebrow.

It wasn't the most welcoming look Bella had ever seen. She didn't imagine they got many strangers coming in. She'd worn her least conspicuous outfit – a figure-hugging black dress with her faux astrakhan coat on top – but anyone not in jeans, leathers or a jumper would jar. That included her and Leo, who'd teamed his dark trousers with dress shoes, a white shirt and a huge checked scarf. John and Carys had done a better job.

'That's right.' Bella smiled. 'A Coke please, and whatever they're all having.' She indicated the others. 'Can I get you one?'

'Don't mind if I do. Thanks.' Sandra unbent slightly as she poured herself a half of lager. Leo, Carys and John ordered pints of Twisted Spire.

'I haven't been here before,' Bella said to the woman. 'I live up the valley in Hope Eaton, but a friend of my dad's used to come in. Oliver Barton. You probably heard that he died last Sunday.'

Sandra unstiffened further, her face falling. 'Terrible thing that was. Yes, he used to come in quite often.' She gave a sigh that ended on a half laugh. 'He stuck out like a sore thumb in here. Always in that rumpled brown suit of his, and a twinkle in his eye.'

'Did he have any regular drinking partners? Only we're trying to collect names to contact about the funeral.'

The woman's gaze shifted uneasily along the bar, then over to the corner table where the big man with the dark beard was slouched in his chair. 'One or two. Though I don't know as they're the sorts to go to funerals.'

'The man who was making trouble about his pint? They were friends? Or played cards together?'

Sandra raised her eyebrows. 'I never saw the professor play cards.'

Interesting. From what John said, poker playing was part of who Oliver was. If he hadn't played at the Black Swan, he must have come for another purpose.

'I'm not sure I'd call Bob Berrow and the professor friends,' the woman went on, 'but the professor talked to him and his mates. I wouldn't bother with Bob though. He's not worth it.'

As Bella picked up her Coke and turned towards the room again, she found John waiting quietly next to her. Carys and Leo had taken their drinks and gone to say hello to Matt.

'Talking to this Bob Berrow is the least appealing prospect I've had all day,' John said.

'Worse than dealing with Sienna? At least this is in a good cause. But let's speak to Matt first. I want to know if it was Berrow who mentioned treasure.'

They struggled through the throng. After Bella asked her question, Matt stopped tuning his guitar and cast a subtle glance in Berrow's direction. 'No. It wasn't him. It was a smaller guy with straw-coloured hair, sticking out from under a beanie. But I've seen that bloke before. He got into a fight after a gig once.'

'Perfect,' John said, under his breath.

'Once more unto the breach.' Bella gave him a shove in the right direction as Carys laughed.

'I'd hoped for more sympathy,' John muttered as they skirted tables in the crowded pub to reach their destination.

'Excuse us,' Bella said, inserting herself between Bob Berrow and the fire. 'We're here for the band, but we were friends of Oliver Barton, the professor who used to drink here. We're taking the names of anyone who might want to attend his funeral and the woman at the bar said you knew each other.'

Berrow looked at her meditatively and picked at his teeth. It was a moment before he spoke. 'Oliver who? I didn't know the guy. Sandra doesn't know what she's talking about. None of them do.' His voice rose. 'They're all useless.'

He was already nine tenths of the way down his pint.

'He was in his seventies. Wore a rumpled brown suit. Jolly. Lectured in archaeology.'

Berrow shrugged. 'No idea who you're talking about. What are you after? You're pretty pushy for someone passing on news about a funeral. Get lost and leave me in peace.'

Charming. Bella didn't think she could push it any further, but she hated letting him have the last word.

They went to join Carys and Leo, who were managing to dance in the tiniest space imaginable between two tables. Lacking room for manoeuvre, Leo was making energetic vertical arm movements.

'You're such an idiot,' she heard Carys say, but her smile was fond.

Behind them, Bella's gaze met Matt's and he grinned, a twinkle in his eye. An unexpected warm spark lit somewhere deep inside her. *Seriously?* Maybe she was her mother's daughter after all. But she wasn't going to repeat her mother's mistakes. The musician she'd gone out with had been one in a long line of disasters after Bella's father. Bella raised an eyebrow at Matt and turned to update Leo and Carys, taking off her coat at last and finding a shelf to cram it onto. 'Berrow's lying, so he must have something to hide.'

As she joined in the dancing, she cast her eyes over the clientele, looking for someone with blond hair and a beanie. Or anyone looking furtive. Leo kept distracting her, egging her on with outrageous moves. John was refusing to participate, which made her and Carys all the more extravagant.

'Stop it!' he groaned. 'You're all deeply embarrassing.'

When the barmaid who'd had the misfortune to serve Bob Berrow approached them, Bella almost elbowed her in the stomach.

'Sorry. Didn't see you there.' She pushed herself back

against a table so the woman could get past to collect some empties. But instead, the barmaid paused next to her.

'Can I have a word?'

Bella felt the others' eyes on her as she followed the woman to a far corner of the pub, behind some coat hooks. They were out of sight of most of the room now.

'I was standing behind you when you talked to Bob Berrow.'

'I should have known he wasn't worth the effort after the way he treated you.'

'He's always like that – and worse. He was banned for a while, but he's related to my boss Sandra's husband, so,' she shrugged, 'it's complicated. He's not a bit like the professor.' She gave a sad smile. 'I liked him. He was kind. Friendly. Cheeky but polite. That's why I was surprised him and Bob always ended up talking to each other.'

Bella frowned. 'You heard him deny it?'

She nodded. 'That's why I came to talk to you. If he doesn't want people to know then there's something off about it. If you're after information, I'm happy to help. I don't owe him anything.'

Bella would want to pay him back too. 'Was it just the two of them who used to talk? Or should I be looking for anyone else?'

'There's a group of them. They don't all come at once but they're in and out. I don't know the others' names. They're cagey.'

'Maybe I can find them another way. Do you know what drew them together?'

The barmaid gave a wry smile. 'I found out after a bit. I listened in. If Bob complains about me, knowing his secrets might shut him up. He's a nighthawker. One of those people who creeps onto other people's property after dark and digs, hoping to find something valuable. Don't imagine he's much good at it, though. Too drunk most of the time.'

Bella couldn't see him and Oliver collaborating, but she could imagine Oliver wanting news of any finds.

The barmaid's eyes were sad. 'Do you think that's what the professor was involved in? The papers didn't mention it, but he was found at the ruins. He seemed too nice to do something like that.'

Bella was loth to disillusion her. 'I suppose people surprise you sometimes. I liked him too. Have you heard anyone mention Raven Hall? We were wondering what made him go there.'

The barmaid's eyes were anxious now. 'There was a stranger in at the same time as the professor. This Saturday last. A guy with light hair, with a black woollen hat.'

The man Matt had seen.

'He went and hung around with Oliver, Bob and their group, but he wasn't here long. Just the one drink. When he left, they were buzzing. I knew something was up. And when I went to clear a table, I heard someone mention treasure and the ruins.' She frowned. 'There was a woman here that night too. With the professor, I mean. She's been in once or twice. Long, dark wavy hair. Greying a bit. Younger than him by twenty years or so I'd say. They didn't arrive together, but she hung around near his group, watching.

'When the professor saw her, he looked startled. But he kissed her on both cheeks, and they had a drink. She looked fond of him. If you find her, she'd probably like to attend his funeral.' She sighed and shook her head. 'If he was a nighthawker, it was probably that night that he decided to go to the ruins. I've peeked over the wall there. You can see the danger notices. It's tragic.'

By the time Bella rejoined the others, she'd taken the barmaid's number, in case she had further questions, and John had bought her another drink. Leo and Carys were still dancing. It was too loud to fill them in. She'd wait for the return journey.

At last, the band played its final encore and they managed to drag Leo and Carys away.

They were installed in Thomasina when Matt came out, laughing, a woman with long auburn hair on his arm.

He waved them off. 'Thanks for coming.'

'I assume Ada's a thing of the past then,' said Carys, looking over her shoulder at the pair. She was in the front this time, next to Bella.

'Ada?' Leo was looking too. Bella could see him in the rear-view mirror. 'She must have been short-lived. I hadn't realised I'd missed one.'

A heartbreaker, evidently.

'To be fair, none of the women he dates seem to be after anything permanent, any more than he is,' Carys replied. 'Still, it's time he moved on.'

Odd. It sounded as though he was moving on all the time. Leo interrupted her thoughts.

'So what did the barmaid say?' He leaned forward, his voice booming.

She turned out of the Black Swan car park, her mind not on the woman's words, but what they meant. 'Sit back in your seat like a good boy and I'll tell you.'

SEVENTEEN

A CLANDESTINE STROLL IN THE DARK

Everyone was silent for a good minute after Bella had told them what the barmaid said.

'You've had longest to think about it,' John said at last. 'What do you reckon?'

Bella stared at the dark open road in front of her. 'It's interesting that Oliver found nothing at the ruins, despite the talk of treasure. If his death was murder, maybe the killer started the rumour.'

'To lure him to Raven Hall, you mean?' John asked.

'Yes. Otherwise, why didn't the guy with the black beanie just go and dig for it himself?'

'But how could they be sure Oliver would be the one to turn up, not the others?'

Bella had wondered that too. 'They couldn't. But if it was someone who knew Oliver well, they'd know how keen he'd be. And he lived in Hope Eaton, nice and handy. They might figure he'd make it a priority – that he'd go that very night or the one after. They could have waited for him on Saturday, and again on Sunday, at which point their gambit paid off. If someone else had turned up, they could simply have cancelled their plans.'

'They took a chance, and it paid off?' said Carys, taking a packet of mints from her pocket and popping one into her mouth.

'Maybe.'

'Why would Oliver delay until the Sunday?' John asked.

'There could be any number of reasons.' Bella dipped Thomasina's headlights at the sight of a lone oncoming car. 'Maybe he tried on Saturday but got interrupted. Or perhaps he thought it was too risky, digging on his own doorstep, but changed his mind as temptation gnawed away at him.'

'Do you think we need to be looking for this blond man with the black hat?' Leo asked.

'I suspect someone paid him to go into the pub and plant the story. If that guy was planning a murder personally, I doubt he'd let anyone see his face. Especially not Oliver.'

John's eyes glimmered in the rear-view mirror. He shook his head. 'I find it hard to believe, but I suppose Nan Gifford's still most likely in terms of motive. Assuming she could shift the stone that landed on poor old Oliver.'

'I imagine she could. It wasn't high up, and the warning notices about falling masonry must mean it's unstable. Oliver's hoard is all hers now. That's a lot to gain if she can sell it on secretly. And we know she's got some mysterious extra income – maybe she's already started.'

'It's a horrible thought.' Bella could hear the frown in John's voice. 'I'd never have imagined she could be that ruthless. And Cal says she came to Hope Eaton because Oliver invited her. He wanted to support her after her parents died and her husband was sent to prison. Would she really kill him, despite all that?'

'To be fair, we don't know what their relationship was like. They didn't sound close. It was you who fed Oliver's cats.'

'But she'd have been risking her freedom when Cal has no one else to turn to,' Carys put in.

That was more persuasive. Nan seemed anxious for her son. 'She'd have to be truly desperate. I agree, she wouldn't have killed just so she could buy Cal a new laptop.' Bella was adding to a mental to-do list. 'We need to find out more. Did she have an urgent need for large amounts of money? Perhaps some of her husband's old enemies have debts that need paying, like you said, Leo.'

She saw him bounce in his seat. 'You see, Carys? I knew it was worth mentioning. We need to find the woman with the long dark hair, too. The one who met Oliver at the Black Swan. I'd say she's a person of interest.'

'You read far too much crime fiction,' Carys said. 'I must ask Bernadette to broaden your horizons.'

'Don't. She doesn't need any encouragement.'

When they arrived back in Hope Eaton, Bella dropped John at his and Gareth's tiny cottage on Uppergate, then took Leo and Carys back to their place on Holt Lane. Lucy was at a sleepover, so their house was in darkness. The lane led up to St Giles's Holt, with no through road. Bella did what felt like an inch-by-inch manoeuvre to turn back the way she'd come. Thomasina's turning circle was good, but she was built for London streets.

As she approached the main road, she saw a lone figure scurrying along in the shadows opposite. Head down, body pressed to the side of the pavement, in amongst the shrubs.

There was something familiar about the neat outline. As Bella drew nearer, and saw it from behind, she was sure. It was Nan Gifford, Oliver's niece. She glanced at her watch. Past midnight. Where was she off to at this time? She was moving rather awkwardly. Carrying something under her arm. Bulky but not heavy.

On impulse, Bella pulled up on the main road to watch. Nan was crossing over, disappearing down Old Percy's Lane. Where her uncle's house was.

If Nan was the thief, that needed to come out. Her godfather's words came to her: *If your dad was still alive, he'd have been all over it.*

She could hardly call the police. They'd tell her Nan was her uncle's heir; she had every right to go to his house. And every right to his belongings too. Even if she was jumping the gun a little, Bella couldn't imagine them taking action.

She continued to think as she parked and pulled on her bucket hat. She couldn't come up with many reasons for Nan to go to Oliver's place in the dead of night. Stealing bits of treasure fitted the bill. Nan couldn't admit to knowing about it. Not declaring it was illegal, just as acquiring it in the first place had been.

Bella bet Barry Dixon hadn't progressed the investigation. He'd only had a day. Tony had said he might easily take a couple of weeks. If she wanted answers, she'd have to find them herself.

She got out of Thomasina and locked up, turning up her collar against the cold. Within a minute, she'd reached Old Percy's Lane. All was quiet. Nan must already be inside Oliver's house. The row of cottages was on her left; to her right, a worn red-brick wall with trees just beyond, masking St Giles's Close and the church. There was a set of steps that allowed pedestrians to move from the lane to the close and Bella took them. She could watch Oliver's house from there, beyond the trees, without being seen. Behind her, St Giles's was dark against the night sky.

Bella kept very still, grateful for her black coat and hat, not visible, she hoped, to anyone up late. She watched Old Percy's Lane from behind the reassuringly thick trunk of an oak, but the dim glow of the street lamps showed the way was deserted. Time ticked on. Bella glanced at her watch, thinking of opening Vintage Winter the following morning. Springing out of bed was a struggle at the best of times. Whatever Nan Gifford was up to, she wished she'd get on with—

It was at that moment that Oliver's front door opened. Frustratingly slowly. Nan was being cautious, but this was ridiculous. Bella would have marched out with confidence; it would be far less suspicious.

At last, Nan appeared, looking left and right. She waited a moment longer, then pulled something awkwardly over the threshold.

A shopping trolley. The collapsible sort. The bulky thing she'd been carrying under her arm.

Was she moving larger amounts of the treasure now, for fear of losing it? Perhaps Bella had wronged Barry Dixon. Maybe he'd dragged himself out of his torpor and called Nan to request a visit. She might be reacting to that.

Bella heard the bump as the trolley landed on the narrow pavement. No clanking. Nan must have the precious pieces well wrapped if that's what she was moving. She looked anxiously up and down the row of cottages, but it was past one o'clock now and no one stirred.

Bella had expected her to walk back towards her house, but in fact she was heading towards St Giles's Close. Not using the steps like Bella had, but the lane. They interconnected eventually. Where on earth could she be going?

Bella stayed well back until Nan had skirted the church. After that, she followed, keeping close to St Giles's walls, creeping in the shadows.

Beyond the building, she could see Nan struggling to get the trolley over the edging stones that marked the church's border. Then over the close she went, and made for St Giles's Steps.

It would be a job getting her precious load down there, but Bella could see the logic if she wanted to travel in secret. It was a lonely route. But why was she headed that way? Perhaps she was meeting someone. They could take the treasure and be over the river and away in no time.

Cautiously, Bella followed. The steps descended at an angle, to make them less steep, and the lamps lighting the way were few and far between. She'd given Nan a head start. Although she couldn't see her, she could hear the trolley, a regular thunk as it landed on each new step. It wasn't loud. Bella guessed Nan must be attempting to take the weight off the contents as she lowered it each time. She was young and probably strong.

Bella trod softly, judging how far ahead Nan was by the sounds she could hear. Eventually, it went quiet, and she knew Nan must have reached Boatman's Walk, which led down to the river.

She was in time to see Nan turn north, away from St Luke's Bridge, the main river crossing.

Curiouser and curiouser.

Bella followed at a distance as Nan descended onto Kite Walk, just beyond Bella's own home, and continued along the river out of town.

It was an eerie, isolated route, with the dark mound of Kite Hill and the stone circle to their left, and the wide inky-black river to their right. The thought of Nan making the journey with what might be hundreds of thousands of pounds' worth of treasure was alarming. If anyone knew, she was vulnerable. And Bella, following just behind, was ripe to be caught up in the trouble.

Leo's thoughts echoed in her head. Nan's husband was in jail. For murder, as she now knew – although Cal had claimed the death was an accident. The quarrel that had got his dad there sounded personal, but that didn't rule out a financial element. Maybe a surviving relative was ready to collect. Carys had scoffed at Leo for being judgemental, but here, alone in the dark, Bella's imagination ran wild. A serious debt, demanded with threats of violence, would explain Nan's desperation.

Bella was grateful for the trees that lined the riverside walk: leafless willows and rowans, blackthorns and hawthorns. They meant she had something to dive behind.

Nan Gifford bumped along the rough path ahead of her. Bella couldn't imagine what rendezvous point she might be making for. Though perhaps a four-by-four could get over the next bridge, the North Crossing, if they used a farm track on the other side.

It was that direction Nan took, heaving the trolley behind her up onto the bridge. The river was wide there, and she paused in the middle of the crossing.

At first, Bella thought she'd stopped to rest. Then, as Nan looked around her, she wondered if that was the meeting point, though it was more exposed than waiting on the bank.

Bella scanned the immediate area. There was no one to be seen. It was the dead of night now and they were well out of town. Farmland stretched to one side of the river, the deserted hill to the other. Cloud hid the moon.

Bella could just see Nan open her trolley and delve inside. She pulled something out. The cloud shifted and Bella could see better.

Not treasure.

Something small, flat and rectangular. Dark.

Taking one more look around her, Nan dropped the object over the North Crossing's parapet. As it fell, the dark shape shifted, expanded, revealed a paler inside.

Pages. A book.

Nan reached into her trolley for another. Then an armful of them. And another one.

They all went into the river. Individual books landed on the surface and were carried away by the current. The ones thrown in a bundle dipped below the water.

The books looked just like the one she'd found in Oliver Barton's secret room. The records of what he'd found, and where. They'd all sink eventually. The writing would be obliterated.

Bella was rooted to the spot. Nan was ensuring no written record of her uncle's thieving remained. Maybe Dixon had been in touch after all. Was she destroying notes which would reveal she'd stolen part of Oliver's hoard? She could rearrange the treasure to hide any gaps. Or perhaps she was simply getting shot of the books before selling the valuables. Bolstering her finances to ensure a secure future for her and Cal.

It took her a moment to realise that Nan had almost finished her work, after which she'd no doubt return the way she'd come.

She needed to make herself scarce. She spun round, silently cursing as her coat snagged on a hawthorn. The moment she'd pulled free, she shot back up the river path, her breath short as she darted glances over her shoulder.

Once again, she could hear Nan as she moved. The sound of her trolley, much lighter now, jouncing off pebbles.

The sense of being pursued took over and Bella started to run. She tripped on a root and only saved herself by flinging out a hand and grasping a branch. At last, she was back on Kite Walk, with its old-fashioned street lamps. She didn't stop until she was standing in the doorway of Southwell Hall.

She shrank into the shadows, undecided. Nan might remove more treasure from her uncle's house next. If she didn't follow, no one would ever know – not now his inventory was gone. She sighed, and set out again, the moment Nan had disappeared up the steps.

Half an hour later, she finally returned home, exhausted. Nan had carried her folding trolley straight back to her house. Whatever she had planned for the treasure, she must be saving it for another night.

Just outside the door to her flat, Bella could hear laughter from Matt's place. She looked forward to shutting it out.

As she let herself into her cosy, secure home, the latest revelations washed over her. She'd have to call Barry Dixon in the morning. And fetch Thomasina too. In the meantime, she needed to work out what this evening's business meant.

EIGHTEEN

DOING BATTLE WITH BARRY DIXON

The following day, having risen far too early and rescued Thomasina, Bella sat at the table in the kitchen area of her living room. The winter sun streamed in as she sipped her coffee for strength.

She'd already texted her godfather to let him know what she'd seen the night before.

I'm going to call Dixon. I have to report it.

He'd replied with:

Good plan, but I wouldn't get excited. You know what he'll say.

She finished her toast and marmalade, then tried the police station. Tony was right. She did know. He'd ask how she knew the books Nan had chucked into the river were records of her uncle's finds. Then tell her they had it in hand. He'd barely believed in the treasure. Even if Nan had gone to the river in response to the threat of a police visit, she doubted he'd leap into action.

Her call was transferred and Dixon's voice came on the line.

'You're not ringing to hurry me along, are you, Ms Winter?' The sergeant sounded defensive. As though she was his mum, asking if he'd done his homework.

'No. But have you contacted Nan Gifford?'

'We've been overtaken by events.' He sounded doleful.

'I beg your pardon?'

'Mrs Gifford's just been in.' He sighed. 'She's told us all about her uncle's finds and the secret room. It's all in hand.'

Bella felt the ground shifting. Not what she'd expected.

'Everything will be gone through,' Dixon added. 'Recorded, run past the proper authorities.'

From his tone, she imagined he was visualising mountains of paperwork.

'So you never called her?'

'It was next on our list, but it makes no odds now, does it? Mrs Gifford has done the right thing. Told us about her uncle's habit. It's over, bar the paperwork. Unlike the Kite Valley jewel thief. They burgled the chief constable's mother-in-law last night, one of my twins is teething and for some reason there was a pig in our garden when I got up after two hours' sleep.'

'Yes, all very distressing.' Bella's mind wasn't on his woes. She was rattling through the implications. Nan hadn't ditched Oliver's records because of a threatened police visit. Nor had she been offloading them prior to selling the hoard.

Instead, she'd voluntarily confessed her uncle's thieving after putting the notes beyond reach. To disguise the fact that she'd taken some of the treasure, Bella assumed. But she hadn't wanted the whole lot. Now she thought about it, it made sense. She could imagine Nan doing battle with her conscience. And of course, she'd have realised someone else had discovered Oliver's hoard too, the moment she tried to find the key to the hidden room. That could have urged her on. She might have suspected her son and wanted to act before he got into worse trouble. Or maybe she'd worried it was a dodgy contact of Oliver's who might be dangerous. Either way, her first instinct had been to cover her tracks then come clean, not remove more valuables.

'You do remember I mentioned there were at least a couple of artefacts missing from the professor's collection?'

'*Yes. And I remember telling you he probably removed them himself. They were in the attic of the house he owned in a secure room. Is that all?*'

She didn't want him to ring off yet. She needed to work out what to do. She asked a ridiculous question about procedure to play for time, then ignored his answer as her thoughts rushed on.

Nan's actions changed things. John had found it hard to imagine her killing for money. They'd agreed she'd have to be utterly desperate. A huge debt to an old contact of her husband's, perhaps. Someone who was a danger to her *and* her son. Bella was convinced Carys was right. She'd never risk jail and the knock-on effects on Cal otherwise. But in fact, it seemed she'd only stolen a few small items. They might still be worth a great deal if Nan found the right buyer, but crucially she appeared to be using the income to support her son and fund the odd luxury. Risking her freedom for that seemed unthinkable.

So if she wasn't the killer, should Bella be ramming home the fact that she was probably a small-time thief? Thoughts vied in her head: the irreplaceable missing artefacts set against Nan using the income for a computer to benefit Cal. And all that against the backdrop of the terrible time Nan had had. Should she really face jail for giving in to temptation?

'*So, if there's nothing else?*' Dixon sounded desperate to hang up.

What would her dad have done? Not pulled out all the stops to get Nan prosecuted when she was the sole carer of a son who was already partway off the rails. He'd have talked to her. Told her he knew what she'd done and not to repeat it. Probed to see if the goods could be recovered. Passed on information about the larger players who'd bought the treasure.

But most of those options were closed to Bella, as a private citizen.

She screwed up her eyes. 'Nothing else.'

She hung up feeling utterly thwarted. Nan looked like a dead end and Bella couldn't even use the police to make sure the missing treasure was recovered.

She threw a magazine that had been on the table across the room to relieve her feelings. It sailed through to the seating area and landed on her mid-century armchair from behind, to be met with a furious yowl.

Bella jumped out of her skin and bolted to where the sound had come from. How had Matt's cat got in *again*? He must have sneaked around her ankles when she'd dashed inside after tailing Nan.

'Come along, Cuthbert. You can't be in here. You can see it's dangerous and Matt will wonder where you've got to.' She hoisted him up, feeling the warm weight of him. He put his head against her chest, kneaded her with his paws and started to purr. For a moment she gave in and cuddled him, but then hardened her heart. 'It's no use trying to get round me.'

She popped him into the hall, next to Matt's cat flap. He couldn't be that hard done by. He was gloriously glossy.

She went back to her flat and picked an assortment of tabby hairs off the chair.

Once she'd finished, she took a deep breath and called Tony.

'*Thought you'd ring.*'

'I need to talk to someone who's awake.' She heard him laugh. 'But more importantly, someone I can be honest with.'

'*Terrible, this requirement to tell the police the truth.*'

She explained that she'd told Dixon nothing in the end, then justified herself.

'*You are your father's daughter. Though I hope you don't come to regret not speaking up.*'

'You think I will?'

'*There's always more to a situation than meets the eye.*' She imagined him shaking his head. '*But I can see why you did what you did.*'

'I doubt me telling him would have made a difference anyway. The books are long gone. It's not as though Dixon would have dragged the river.'

'*Sounds right. Your information would just have been back-ground knowledge for our boy Barry. It might have become relevant, somewhere down the line. Other than that, it's case closed as far as he's concerned. The professor died in an accident. The police already knew he had a quirky hobby. Now, thanks to Nan, they know the extent of it. It'll make the headlines, that's for sure, but beyond that? It'll just be a heck of a lot of paperwork.*'

'The missing treasure might trip Nan up, though, if she's our thief. I suspect she'll have rearranged things so it's not obvious. That'll make Dixon wonder. I'd already told him there were gaps but he's sure it was Oliver who created them.'

'*He won't be tempted to make a fuss. Not if there's as much left as you say there is. But I'll keep an ear to the ground. Find out the way the team's minds are working.*'

'Thanks.' She couldn't quite let go of her regret at the loss of the missing pieces.

She turned her mind back to the fallout from the latest development. 'It's quite something, Nan coming forward about the hoard. She must have had a hellish time after her husband

was arrested. I imagine she was all too glad to move away from
their village. She won't welcome the press and the gossip.'

'*Probably felt she had no choice. Declaring it quickly proves
it was her uncle's doing, not hers.*'

Bella thought of Nan's reaction when she'd seen John's coin.
She'd been desperate to distance herself. And if she'd kept the
odd piece to sell, 'coming clean' ought to stop the police looking
in her direction.

'*Where does this leave you with the prof's death?*'

'I don't buy Nan as the killer any more.' She explained her
reasoning. 'But she's a strong candidate for thief. She's keeping
secrets and there's Cal's new laptop.' She explained what she
and John had seen on their visit to Nan's place. 'And she knew
about the treasure and how to access the room. She could have
taken the two missing pieces. Maybe more.' Bella visualised the
woman. 'I wouldn't have said she was the sort, but she's been
through a terrible time and she's worried for Cal. I can imagine
the prospect of buying him a standout laptop to help with his
schooling would have been tempting. And ditching the notebooks is damning. Of course, she could have jettisoned Oliver's
inventory to protect Cal, if he took the missing bits. That I
could definitely imagine. But it's Nan who's in the money.'

'*He could have bought himself the laptop.*'

'Without her asking questions? And besides, I can't imagine
him choosing that luxury. A new phone, yes, but not a
MacBook.'

'*Fair enough. So, if Nan's our thief, what about Cal as the
killer?*'

Bella pictured him. *Ugh.* 'Motive-wise, I'm pretty sure he
knew about the treasure too, but it wouldn't be as easy for him
to remove it. Nan's the heir. She's got the keys and besides, I'd
imagine she watches Cal pretty closely.' Bella would, if he was
her responsibility. She thanked Sweet Agnes that that wasn't
the case. 'Still, he could have killed in the hope that he could

pinch the odd item. Or simply because he thought his lifestyle would improve. They'll come in for a nice house, or the profit from selling it. He'd have to be ruthless.'

'*Think he is?*'

'He struck me as angry. The other kids at school might give him a hard time if they know what his dad did. It could add up to feeling dispossessed. Kicking back at the world, his uncle included. I could imagine him following Oliver and acting in the heat of the moment. I can't really see him starting the rumour at the Black Swan though, and it does look as though the whispers were fake. Oliver had been nighthawking for years with a shattering level of success. If there was something to find, he'd have found it.'

'*So it's back to the drawing board?*'

Bella thought of the board in Vintage Winter's office. 'We've got other leads.'

'*Right. Well don't lose track of Nan and Cal. Keep an open mind. She's got secrets, like you say, and he could have a clever friend who egged him on. Keep me posted.*'

Bella was thoughtful as she carried her coffee cup to the dishwasher, but as she stowed the crockery she shifted gear. She had updates to give, and there was work to do.

She went to put on her green crystal earrings, which John had called self-advertising. That was exactly why Bella liked them. She felt a renewed burst of energy as she exited the flat.

NINETEEN

OLIVER'S SECRET COMPANION

The weather was cold and crisp and the customers at Vintage Winter more plentiful, helped by a coach load of day-trippers. They came and rummaged in the corners and dashed into the back room, oohing and ahhing over curiosities which had filled Bella with competitive excitement at the sales where she'd vied for them.

They snapped up the carved wooden bear with the glass eyes and the sycamore and penwork snuff box with its house-finch design. In an hour and a half Bella had sold more than she had in the previous two days put together. And the day-trippers weren't local, so no one bought a Sweet Agnes candle. It was refreshing.

In quieter moments, Bella told John what she'd seen the night before, and what she'd said to Barry Dixon. She didn't ask if he approved of her holding back, and he didn't comment. No raised eyebrow though, so she imagined he agreed with her.

'Poor Nan,' John said. 'I wonder if she'll get a reward for reporting the treasure.'

It could have been a motive, at a stretch, but it didn't wash. 'I think it's unlikely. People who dig with permission sometimes do. They're usually shared with the landowner.' In Nan's case, the authorities would probably never work out what came from where without Oliver's notebooks. It was a crying shame.

'What time did you get to bed?' He peered at her intently from behind his glasses.

'Threeish?'

'How are you still standing?'

'Coffee. And chocolate.'

'For breakfast?' He shuddered. 'I won't tell Gareth.'

'I can mend my ways with one of his heartening lunches at the Blue Boar. It's time to quiz your mum. Oliver was at the inn, the night he died. I want to find out what he did and who he spoke to.'

Bella's first memories of the old coaching inn dated back to her childhood. Her father had taken her there for ploughman's lunches in summer, and huge pies in winter. She remembered lying on the floor afterwards, having overdone it.

The bars were full of rich, dark furniture, glowing lamps, gleaming glasses and shining brasses on the beer taps. Its oldest parts dated back to the 1400s, and its courtyard was timber-framed. It was the type of place that was genuine enough to appeal to her godfather, but clean enough to meet with Bella's approval. It had changed over time, of course. By the seventeenth century, the inn was a stopping point for stagecoaches. Bella imagined the stamping of hooves and the shouts of the drivers each time she crossed its courtyard. She liked the idea of travelling by stagecoach. It would have been uncomfortable but exciting too. A journey would have been an undertaking – have meant something. Those days were long gone, but the clamouring hubbub remained when the inn was busy.

It had been run by John's parents, Jeannie and Peter Jenks, for as long as Bella could remember. She could still visualise the pair of them behind the bar in her childhood. Jeannie front and centre, holding forth to a group, with the occasional comment to someone across the bar. Her voice carried. And Peter in the shadows, talking quietly to a chosen customer or attempting to read his newspaper. Introverted Peter dealt with the business side of the pub. Jeannie insisted that his parents had picked her as a match for their son, knowing she'd be the perfect host for the Blue Boar when they got too old. She often said (loudly and with a great deal of drama) that it was her cross to bear.

Jeannie was sixty-eight now, but she seemed almost unchanged. She still wore her chunky beads with shirt dresses over slacks. Her unruly hair was still thick and wrapped in a scarf, and she still had smudges of paint here and there, betraying her hobby.

As they approached, she was looking critically at a painting as one of the bartenders, Bill, held it up against a patch of honey-coloured wall. Bella could see it was one of Jeannie's works. Abstract. Or at least, that's how it appeared. Jeannie moved to view it from different angles. Bill wore a look of hesitant hope which faded as she shook her head sharply. 'A little further to the left.'

Bella wondered how long they'd been at it as Jeannie looked round and saw them.

'Oh, John!' She waved at Bill to put the painting down again and he did so, leaning it against the wainscot and rubbing his arm.

'We didn't mean to interrupt.' John walked forward.

'Well, no, but you're here now and the painting's not important.' Bill closed his eyes and appeared to silently count to ten as Jeannie swept out from behind the bar. She kissed her son on both cheeks.

'And Bella!'

Bella submitted to a hug too. It seemed she counted as extended family now she worked with John. She'd been vetted, and besides, Jeannie had known her father. But she treated the entire town a bit like schoolchildren for whom she was responsible, a worried look in her eye as though they couldn't really be expected to cope on their own. Bella saw her as a ruffled mother hen with a vast number of chicks. She hadn't shared the image with John.

'I'm glad you're here,' she said, steering them towards the bar and pointing at some high stools as she returned to the business side. 'Bill will get your drinks.'

Bill was at her side at the sound of his name. He must have a lot more patience than Bella did. After John had asked for a sparkling water and Bella a St Clement's, Jeannie leaned over the bar. 'Leo's told me what's going on. Something odd about Oliver Barton's death?' Her voice had lowered. She shook her head. 'I used to have to tell him off sometimes, when he'd drunk too much. He would do it. But I was fond of him. His Monday-night history classes were popular, and they made him more responsible. It was so good for him to have some structure in his life.'

'But he worked at the university, didn't he?' Bella said.

She waved aside the idea. 'Academics are very loose with their timekeeping, and he only gave the odd lecture these days. He could be frustrating at times, but the idea of someone deliberately killing him... It's unthinkable.'

'We don't know for sure,' John said.

'No, but it's not the kind of thing we can overlook. Though what was your godfather thinking, Bella, when he encouraged you to investigate? That's obviously a job for the police.' Bella cursed Leo for going into so much detail. 'The thought of you putting yourself in danger... I want to hear no more about it.'

Bella and John's eyes met briefly.

'I completely agree.' Bella knew how to look guileless.

Jeannie peered at her narrowly. 'But Leo said you were forming some sort of team.'

'You know how overexcited he gets,' John said.

Jeannie shook her head. 'It's just as well he's got Carys to keep him grounded.'

Bella made a mental note to tell him to stop blabbing.

'I've already been thinking who it might be, of course.' Jeannie ran her eyes over the clientele. 'But they're good people. Apart from the obvious ones – and I don't think they even knew Oliver.'

'We need to go carefully with the speculation, Mum.' John's voice was as calm and measured as usual. 'It's as you said. It could be dangerous.'

'Of course I know that! You're as preposterous as Leo sometimes.'

Peter had been approaching as she spoke, emerging from wherever he'd hidden himself to greet his son. At the sound of Jeannie's raised voice, he tiptoed away again with a look of sympathy and a wave of his hand.

'It's only natural to talk about what's happened, John,' Bella said casually, sipping her St Clement's.

'Of course it is! Thank you, Bella.'

Bella ignored John's eyeroll. 'I presume people have been discussing it in here?'

'Extensively,' Jeannie said. 'It's good for people to share their feelings. But if you're going to tell me your worries, then food comes first. You two can't run a shop on empty stomachs.' She pushed a menu under their noses.

Bella asked for the game pie with buttered potatoes and broccoli and John chose the sausage casserole.

Once their order was in, Jeannie frowned at them. 'So, tell me, what have you heard?'

They explained how Bella had found the body, and about the metal-detecting equipment not mentioned in the newspaper.

Jeannie's eyebrows shot up. The news of Oliver's hoard

hadn't spread yet, clearly. 'The local history group had a talk in the function room about nighthawking a couple of months ago.'

And Oliver and Harvey Howard were both members. Bella needed to think what that might mean.

'Gareth said Oliver was in here on Sunday evening,' John said, 'but he was stuck in the kitchen so he couldn't see what went on.'

'That's right.' Jeannie shook her head. 'Oliver had had too much to drink as usual, but he wasn't out of control. I'd have refused to serve him if he had been. It got a bit quieter after he left.' She sighed again. 'That was usually the case, of course, but there was something on television that people wanted to catch. An Agatha Christie dramatisation, I think. Though why slouching in front of the box should be preferable to meeting friends here at the inn, I'm not sure.'

'Did you ever hear him mention the Alexandra Arms? The one just outside Much Wenlock?'

'What an odd question,' Jeannie said. 'Why do you ask?'

'I spotted a threatening letter on their paper last time I visited his house,' John said. Bella was glad to be saved a more complex explanation.

Jeannie blinked. 'It was anonymous? I don't like the sound of that.' She frowned. 'But the Alexandra Arms... Someone did mention that place recently, though it wasn't Oliver. It'll come to me.'

'It must feel odd, having seen him the night he died.' Bella knew she could slip in more questions if she was careful. 'I hope he enjoyed his last evening. I keep wondering about it. Did he get his cards out? You must know the people he played with, I suppose?'

Jeannie shrugged. 'He didn't play on Sunday. And apart from John, the people who joined him weren't regulars. Maybe I put them off. I never let them play for money; it only leads to trouble, but I heard tell of some private sessions...' She shook her head.

Bill was passing, a white cloth over his shoulder, contrasting his black shirt. 'He wasn't a ruthless player when people laid bets.'

Jeannie put her hands on her hips. 'And how would you know that?'

He blushed and she gave a deep sigh and walked towards the kitchen.

Bill looked after her nervously.

'So you played with Oliver?' Bella said.

He nodded. 'A group of us would meet at his house. He was a generous host. The drinks flowed. And he'd listen if you'd had a tough week. That sort of thing. One time, I'm convinced he deliberately played badly to let another guy win. Normally, he'd just play fair and square, but this bloke, Joe, he was drinking too much, and he couldn't hold it. He wanted to carry on betting, even though he kept losing. Oliver told him no at first, but in the end he gave in, and they played, just the two of them. It was clear we shouldn't join in. He let him win all his money back. That was the kind of guy he was.'

He sounded like a fascinating mix. Bella wished she'd been able to get to know him personally. She had a feeling they'd have got on. They'd have argued like crazy over certain things but she'd have enjoyed trying to bend him to her will. A thief, with several addictions, but with a generous spirit. Interested in other people and their problems. Yet happy to steal from his fellow citizens. The artefacts he'd dug up belonged to everyone. It was quite a blind spot. Of course, Bella understood the pull. The excitement of finding something fantastic, in the truest sense of the word. But to keep it all to himself? She could imagine fantasising about it, but not for more than a second. Could she have talked him round, if he'd lived?

Jeannie reappeared.

'This whole thing is so sad,' Bella said. 'I wonder who knows more about the professor's last evening, if the poker lot weren't about. It might help the police if they noticed anything odd.'

'That's a thought,' Jeannie replied. 'He was chatting with Julia Sandford.' She glanced at John.

'Carys's old university tutor?'

'Of course. How many Julia Sandfords do you think there are in Hope Eaton?'

John didn't rise; everyone knew what to expect from Jeannie, especially her sons. Locals described her as robust but good-hearted.

'Carys still sees her. I've seen them chat at the Steps. Julia's there with a coffee and a load of paperwork every Friday. She's a historian. She and Oliver must have been in the same department at the university: History and Archaeology.'

Jeannie gave them a thoughtful look. 'They sat outside on Sunday. I did wonder about it, because it was bitterly cold. Julia went off at around eight, then Oliver came inside and propped up the bar.'

'Did you mention her to the police?'

Jeannie's eyes widened. 'Of course not. They didn't ask. All they wanted to know was what time he left and how much he'd had to drink.'

'What does Julia look like?' Bella asked John, after Jeannie had left them to speak to another customer.

He gave her a significant look. 'Long, dark wavy hair. Greying in places.'

A match for the woman the barmaid saw at the Black Swan on Saturday night.

TWENTY

A STRANGER IDENTIFIED

Bella was poised to work on Jeannie again when she reappeared.

'We spoke to Nan Gifford yesterday. John wanted to offer his sympathy.' Her and John's eyes met for a moment. 'Her son Cal was there too.'

Bella still wanted to know what Jeannie thought of them. Nan's motive no longer put her top of Bella's list, but the more they knew about Oliver's relationships, the more they'd know about him.

Jeannie shook her head, wisps of hair waving about from under her scarf. 'Oliver got Nan to come to Hope Eaton so that he could care for the pair of them. Not that he was really adult enough for the job, of course. His heart was in the right place, but he was desperately impractical.'

Bella added 'frustrating' to her mental picture of Oliver.

'I told Nan to take some time off when the news broke,' she added. 'It's her first day back today. She's been very quiet this morning.'

Bella wasn't surprised. She'd have been fresh from her visit to the police, and recovering from a broken night.

'I tried to talk to her about the death,' Jeannie went on, 'but she's not a chatter, which is a mistake. Bottling things up is never the answer. She's around and about, so have a care. I don't want her upset by idle gossip. She's a treasure.'

An ironic choice of word. Bella hoped she really was, and that she hadn't been wrong to hold out on Barry Dixon.

'Have you noticed anything unusual about her behaviour?' she said. 'Not today, I mean, but over the last few weeks? John was a bit worried about her, weren't you, John?'

He managed to hide his surprise in a split second. 'A little.'

Jeannie stood up straighter. 'Now you mention it, yes. She's been looking tired for the last two or three months. Pale, with bags under her eyes. I recommended cocoa before bed, but if people won't listen, what can you do?

'Of course,' she went on, 'it can't be easy, looking after Cal on her own. It's as though butter wouldn't melt, when I see him.' She shook her head. 'But he doesn't fool me, of course. I overheard him at the grocers recently, saying he'd prefer to share a cell with his dad than be here with his mum. And boasting about how good he is with an air rifle. Pure bravado, of course. It's a horrible age. But he said it in front of Adele Lewis, who we all know is the biggest gossip in the valley. I wouldn't be surprised if it got back to Nan.' She sighed. 'She loves him so much, too.'

At that moment, Gareth, John's partner and head chef at the inn, came into the bar, clutching a cognac glass filled with deep amber liquid. His eyes lit up when he saw them, but a moment later his gaze was on the drink and a frown etched his brow. He attempted to retreat again.

Jeannie whisked round, sweeping a notepad off the bar with her elbow. 'Marvellous. Don't go away.' She grabbed the glass from Gareth and pushed it under Bella's nose. 'Try this.'

Gareth's eyebrows drew down further. 'It's not ready yet.'

'Nonsense,' Jeannie said. 'Go on, have a sip!'

Bella took the glass and sniffed. Ginger. And pineapple, perhaps? With other ingredients she couldn't identify. She put it to her lips. Warming, fiery, sweet and tart all at the same time.

Jeannie watched Bella's face with a smile. 'Gareth's patent winter warmer. New this season. Non-alcoholic, though there's a version with quite a kick to it for later in the day.'

'Magnificent.' Bella raised the glass to Gareth. 'Truly.'

He was shooting mutinous looks at Jeannie. 'The recipe's not right.'

'Oh, piffle!' the landlady said loudly. She turned to Gareth. 'I know you're a perfectionist, but you have now achieved perfection. Let it be.'

Gareth headed back to the kitchens, muttering.

'I'll just have a quick word,' John said, nipping behind the bar to follow him.

Bella excused herself too. She needed to visit the facilities before her food turned up.

Even the loos at the Blue Boar appealed to her, with their large mahogany-framed mirrors. She checked no one was watching, then posed for a second, sucking in her cheeks.

As she exited the room, she was fantasising about a vintage jacket she'd seen online the day before. Far too expensive, but absolutely exquisite... The sight ahead of her made her stop short.

There was Nan Gifford. Nothing wrong with that. She worked there after all. But she was creeping along, very much as she had been the night before, and she was making for the Blue Room, the inn's snug.

Bella watched as she entered, still visible thanks to the room's internal windows, then crossed the hall cautiously for a better look. Her scalp tingled. Nan was talking to the elderly man who'd watched Bella and John leave her house the day before. This seemed to be a surreptitious meeting. They spoke in low voices, their heads close together, Nan in front of him, as though she was deliberately blocking the view of anyone who might walk past.

Bella turned swiftly and recrossed the hall to the main bar. What was Nan's connection with the man? And why had he been watching Bella and John?

Back at the bar, John had reappeared, and her food had arrived. The rich smell of the gamey gravy wafted out of her pie as she cut into it.

'This is superb.'

'And that's not all,' John said, carefully cutting up a bit of sausage. 'Mum's remembered the connection with the Alexandra Arms. You'll be interested in the answer.'

Jeannie nodded. 'Meg Jones. John was at school with her. Her cousin works there. I overheard her recommending it to someone who wanted to stay locally. Frankly rude, when we have such nice rooms here. That's why it registered, only it took me a moment to remember.'

Meg Jones, who cleaned for the Howards at Raven House and whose flyer Oliver had had on his pinboard. 'Interesting.'

'Could be coincidence,' John said.

She pulled a face, but was distracted from replying by Jeannie, who'd moved down the bar. She was serving the man who'd been in the Blue Room.

Bella nudged John. 'Don't look now. That's the guy who was watching us when we left Nan Gifford's house.'

She guessed the man might be in his late sixties. He was immaculately turned out in a beautifully cut suit, but its line was spoiled by his hunched shoulders. He leaned on the bar, his hand to his forehead, his mouth moving quickly. She could tell he was agitated but couldn't hear his words. A moment later he glanced in their direction and caught Bella's eye.

She smiled and gave him a little wave. After all, they'd almost met. He stood and gave a tiny bow, then turned away and disappeared with his drink.

You seldom saw that sort of dated etiquette. Bella was interested. He'd clearly wanted to run and hide as soon as she'd caught his eye, yet manners had trumped the desire, if only for a second.

Jeannie turned back to face her and John, a questioning frown developing as she saw Bella's expression.

'Who was that man you just served?' Bella asked. 'He looked upset.'

'Frank Fellows. He used to teach history at the local high school.'

History? Was that a coincidence? 'He seems almost from another age.'

Jeannie nodded thoughtfully. 'I've often thought the same thing. He holds doors open, even if I'm miles away, so that I end up dashing. He was a very good teacher, apparently. Passionate about his subject.'

'What was worrying him?'

'He was asking about the history group Oliver belonged to. He's a member too.'

Another one.

'He wanted to know if any of the others have been in,' Jeannie went on. 'And what they've said about Oliver's death. He must be worried as well. I doubt he'd ask otherwise.' She frowned at them. 'Meg Jones joined the group recently too, so that's a coincidence.'

Or is it? Bella wondered.

'Meg? When?' John's brow was as creased as his mum's.

'Around five months ago, I should say. I was surprised. Music's her first love, not history. She's always on the periphery. Doesn't mix with the committee members like Harvey or Frank, though I saw her exchange the odd word with Oliver. The society's quite large now.' She smiled. 'I always encourage the townsfolk to broaden their horizons. Frank's been quite active. He organised a trip to see the Staffordshire Hoard in Birmingham last year.' Shaking her head, she sighed. 'Perhaps Oliver saw the treasure and got the idea to go digging himself. He always was one to get into mischief.'

But of course, Bella knew he'd have started way before that. It was interesting that Frank had a passion for ancient artefacts too.

Back at Vintage Winter, with the door shut against the cold and coffee on to brew, Bella and John revisited Bella's drawing board. Bella reviewed the existing list of what Leo had called 'persons of interest' and added Julia Sandford of Acton Thorpe University and Frank Fellows, retired teacher and member of the Hope Eaton History Group.

After that, they updated the key questions. The list now ran:

Who knew about the treasure before Oliver's death? (Nan and Cal Gifford likely.)

Of them, who removed some and what have they done with it? (Is Cal's expensive laptop significant?)

Who wrote the threatening letter? And what did it refer to? (Meg Jones's cousin works at the Alexandra Arms, the hotel whose headed paper was used. Meg recently joined the local history group too – another link with Oliver. Coincidence?)

Why did Oliver and Julia Sandford meet outside in the cold at the Blue Boar the night Oliver died?

Who was the woman Oliver referred to when he shopped at Howard's Classic Cars? Was she a current lover when he died?

Who was the woman who tracked Oliver down at the Black Swan? Could this be the same woman referred to at the salesroom? Could it have been Julia Sandford?

Were Oliver and Julia lovers?

Why was Frank Fellows watching us leave Nan Gifford's house? What's his business with Nan? Why is he so anxious to talk to members of the history group? How deep is his interest in ancient artefacts?

Is it relevant that the history group hosted a talk about nighthawking a couple of months ago?

Was the rumour about treasure at Raven Hall spread with the sole intention of getting Oliver to the site?

'This is making my head spin,' John said.

Bella stared at the playing cards, then looked at her notebook.

Queen of hearts, spades, clubs and diamonds – 'Three passionate women. One who loves too much, one who's full of fear, and one who's striving for immortality. And then the fourth. An enigma, but one who worries me.'

To Bella, all of the women so far were enigmas. She needed to know why Julia Sandford had tracked Oliver to the Black Swan, if it had been her. The barmaid thought she'd been fond of Oliver, but that he'd been startled to see her. Could she be the woman who'd loved too much? And on paper, Alexis might be after immortality, through her poetry. In her mind's eye, Bella could see her mother saying, 'Immortality, darling. We all want it.' *Honestly...*

But there wasn't much of a connection between her and Oliver. She probably wasn't even a card...

'The cards are all very well,' John said, 'But what about the slightly more pressing question of who killed Oliver, assuming someone did?'

'Nan seemed to have the best motive, until she reported the treasure. We couldn't see her killing unless she had a desperate need for large sums of money. I'd say she's unlikely now. Cal's troubled and has a mean streak, I reckon, but any benefits for him would be indirect: a nicer house to live in, more money for Nan. He could have banked on stealing *some* treasure, but he'd have had a lot of organising to do: planting the rumour about the ruins, if that was part of the plot, sneaking his uncle's keys from his mum, removing the treasure without access to a car, meeting with a fence. He could have done it, but I'm not convinced.

'Julia Sandford's interesting though. She's highest in my mind right now. What was she up to, chatting with Oliver in the garden of the Blue Boar, the night he died? It was freezing. I'm prepared to bet she met him at the Black Swan too. If so, she was trailing after him, and on the spot when the rumour started. You said she's at the Steps each Friday, doing her marking?'

He nodded. 'I've seen her there. She comes after work.'

'Then we'll catch her tomorrow. I'm going to ask Leo to contact us the moment she shows her face.'

John grimaced. 'I'll do it, if we have to go and quiz her.'

'We do. If she doesn't appear we can make other arrangements.' Bella found a mugshot of Julia on the Acton Thorpe website and texted it to the barmaid at the Black Swan. She ought to be able to tell them if it was Julia who'd met Oliver on Saturday night. 'As for Meg Jones, she could be Oliver's enigma. She's popping up all over the place.'

'*Slight* exaggeration.'

Bella smiled. 'Your attitude wouldn't have anything to do

with the fact that she's an old school friend and you feel
awkward about talking to her?'

'Her connection with Oliver's nebulous.'

'That's precisely why we need more information. She's not
up there like Julia Sandford, but she and Frank are both oddi-
ties. We can't ignore them.'

John sighed, and Bella's mind turned to Alexis's poetry
recital that evening. People were bound to talk about Oliver's
death. It might reveal something. She thought of what Tony had
said about Oliver's climbing.

*The ladder was near a higher bit of remaining wall, so it's
possible Barton used it to look over the top. Or at the top, is my
thinking. Because looking over doesn't make sense. He could
have just walked round.*

Was there any chance she could get a look at the top of that
bit of wall? She didn't know exactly where the ladder had been,
but she'd seen Harvey pick it up. It must have been between
Oliver's body and the house. Neither Harvey nor the postman
had seen his corpse. Bella could make a rough guess.

She explained her plans to John. 'But we'll have some time
between work and the poetry recital.'

'I was thinking I might use that for supper.'

'You're so conventional.' Bella enjoyed meals immensely,
but she could eat at speed when required. 'Joking apart,
supper's encouraged, but beforehand, we must talk to Meg
Jones.'

TWENTY-ONE

THE MYSTERY OF MEG JONES

An hour before they shut up shop, the barmaid at the Black Swan texted Bella back. It *had* been Julia who'd accosted Oliver at the pub the night before he died.

Bella showed John. 'So they were definitely together two nights running. That has to mean something. The knowledge will give us the upper hand when we meet.'

It was dark and the wind was getting up by the time Bella and John left Vintage Winter. They walked up St Giles's Lane and turned onto the high street, where people were leaving other shops, locking up, shivering in thick winter coats. All around them street lamps illuminated the half-timbered buildings, including the grand moot hall in the centre of the wide thoroughfare.

They passed a delicatessen Bella had been admiring, but the prices were far too high. They were still serving, and Bella peered inside to see Nan Gifford standing at the brightly lit counter. She was gesturing at one of the cheeses under the glass and the man serving – good-looking, Bella noted, with dark eyes and glossy dark hair – was moving the cheese slice across to increase the size of the portion she wanted to buy. After that, she bought some overpriced salami, then pointed to some bottles behind the counter. The man nodded and smiled, reaching to the shelf. She was buying a liqueur. It would be a lot cheaper at the local supermarket. And now she was adding some artisan biscuits to her collection.

'Nan's spending big,' Bella said. 'I don't want to insult your mother's rates of pay, but how can she possibly afford that lot, unless she's using proceeds from some of the treasure?' She wondered again how much Nan had taken and if she'd been right not to tell Dixon about the dumped notebooks. 'The stuff in there's lovely but the mark-up is crazy. I'd already judged the clientele as being weekenders who work in the city. Am I being unfair?'

John looked in the same direction. 'No,' he said quietly. 'I'd guess the spending has to be connected.'

'Even if Nan's innocent of murder, I'd like to understand her part in all of this.' She thought of Tony's warning not to discount anyone. 'I might nip in after her. Get myself something small.' She could just about stretch to it in return for information.

'It'll make us even later for Meg Jones.'

Nan was leaving the shop.

'I'll be fast. Promise.'

The guy behind the counter gave her a smile.

'Welcome. I've seen you about. Haven't you opened the new outlet at the Antiques Centre?'

'That's right. I've been wanting to come in here for a while. I thought I'd treat myself.'

He grinned. 'What would you like?'

The smile was a disaster. Bella went from being determined to choose the cheapest thing in the shop to buying a small – but horribly expensive – bottle of apple liqueur and a tiny packet of upmarket biscuits. She didn't want him to think she was cheap.

'I saw Nan Gifford in here just before me,' Bella said. 'I could see she was splurging and I suddenly thought, why not?'

'Ah, I didn't know her name.' The man behind the counter put her purchases into a posh paper carrier bag. 'But she's become a regular over the last couple of months. It's nice to have a few proper, local customers.'

The length of time was unexpected. Bella nodded as she picked up her spoils. 'Thanks. See you around.'

'I hope so.'

Bella found she did too. She hadn't dated anyone since she broke up with Simon, her ex in London. They hadn't seen eye to eye over the scandal. He'd thought she could have dealt with the fraud more tactfully. When the fraudster ended up in court, some of the private, high-value dealers she'd worked with had distanced themselves from her. She assumed their practices were questionable too, and they were running scared.

Simon thought Bella should have protected her career. That she'd been selfish to put her foot down, not thinking of their future. Remembering his reaction still left her livid. There could be no half-measures for someone so despicable. That went for Simon and the fraudster.

To cap it all, the fraudster had got off. She blanked it from her mind. No use crying over spilled milk.

Outside, John looked at her bag.

'A present for you and a sweetener for Meg Jones.' If she was giving away her purchases, they didn't count as self-indulgent. 'The liqueur looks good, but it might not be up to Gareth's standards. You can always sneak helpings when he's at work. The take-home point is that Nan Gifford's a regular. Has been for a couple of months. So she must have had access to extra funds before her uncle died.'

'You think he could have been giving her bits of treasure to sell, then she helped herself after his death?'

Bella tried to make that fit, but couldn't. 'If she was struggling, I think he'd have given her money from his pay packet. He wasn't hard-up. Think of the wine and the truffle butter in his house. But I can't see him subbing her to buy deli food and a MacBook Air. And certainly not giving her precious treasure to exchange for luxury goods.'

'You think she could have got access to Oliver's secret room sooner, then? Sneaked in and started thieving back then?'

'It's possible.'

John pulled a face. 'But hard to imagine.'

'Think about it, though. We can't begin to appreciate what she's been through. How she might have yearned to treat Cal to something special. And she didn't seem that upset at Oliver's death. Anxious about his coin and worried for Cal, but not heartbroken for herself. If she didn't like him, and abhorred his thieving, she might have thought, to heck with it. At least once. Perhaps she found the hidden room somehow and grabbed a piece or two on the spur of the moment. She'd have been in a state of shock at the sight of all that treasure. She could have chosen something buried deep in one of the drawers and shifted things around in the hope Oliver wouldn't notice. Then not have taken anything more until he died. I'd guess the gaps we saw must have been left since his death. The thief would have covered their tracks otherwise.'

John shrugged helplessly.

'Your mum says she's been looking tired for the last two months. Maybe she's eaten up inside.'

'Very interesting, I'll give you that.' He glanced at his watch. 'But Meg will be cooking supper by now.'

He hadn't been keen on the visit from the start.

'Perfect. She'll have every reason to answer our questions quickly. We can't leave it until tomorrow. She'll probably be working and so will we.'

'Couldn't we catch her on Sweet Agnes's Eve?'

On Saturday evening, pretty much everyone in Hope Eaton

would gather at the Blue Boar, then descend into the valley and process over a narrow bridge to Agnes's Haven, the small island in the centre of the River Kite, where Agnes was said to have done much of her mystic stuff. It was coming up fast, but not fast enough.

'Tony said it's crucial to act quickly if it was murder.'

John sighed again. 'All right, what do we want to know?'

'How well Meg knew Oliver. Did he approach her to clean for him, and if so, what drove his choice? Was it Meg who wrote the threatening note? And does she know anything useful about the Howards?'

'Harvey and Alexis don't seem likely murderers in terms of motive, and not great for opportunity.'

'True, but Oliver was on their land. How did Meg come to clean for them? Is there a reason she's connected to them *and* Oliver or is it coincidence?'

John shuddered. 'Well, it should be *very* easy to slip all of that into conversation. Please tell me you have a plan.'

'Of course. Once you've done the introductions I'll lead. You can chip in.'

Meg lived on Kite Street, on the other side of the river. It was at least a twenty-minute walk. Plenty of time to work out her approach.

Meg Jones lived in a terrace with a red front door and a narrow, arched front window. John had been right. They could see her lit up at the back of the house, standing over a stove.

He knocked at the door.

Meg frowned as she opened up and pushed her thick blonde hair out of her eyes. Then her expression cleared. 'John? It is you!' She looked pleased, her cheeks suddenly rosy. 'Haven't seen you since I brought my sister's kids to the museum.'

She clapped him on the arm in a friendly gesture. John responded in kind, while looking desperately uncomfortable.

'Sorry to bother you at supper time.'

'Go on with you, it's all right. Do you want to come in?' She glanced over John's shoulder at Bella, one questioning eyebrow raised.

'This is my new boss.' John introduced them. 'Bella runs Vintage Winter in the Antiques Centre.'

Meg's smile broadened. 'I've seen it. Been meaning to come in for a nose. I'll have to do that.' She shook her head. 'Isn't the woman who took over from old Mrs Hearst at the museum awful? I can see why you left.'

'It's so sad that Sienna's in charge now.' Bella was glad of the common ground as they moved inside. 'But it's lucky for me, because I get to work with John. I asked if he could introduce us, but it's true, it's an inconvenient time.'

'Don't be daft. Just let me turn off the gas.'

Bella instantly warmed to her easy friendliness.

She ushered them down a narrow hall with coat hooks and a shoe rack, into the brightly lit kitchen area beyond the living room. Bella noted a pair of man's shoes as well as some she assumed were Meg's. John had said she was a widow. Maybe she had a new bloke in her life. She hoped so, and that they were happy. A moment later Meg told them to take a seat and was offering coffee.

'It's fine thanks. We mustn't hold you up.' Bella looked up from her chair. 'Though we brought some biscuits in case you fancy them later. It's so nice of you to invite us in. I wanted to ask you about Oliver Barton.'

Meg had been heading back towards them, having abandoned her attempts to make them a drink. Her smile faltered, though she covered it in a flash.

'I knew you knew him,' Meg said to John. 'I think I saw you

together in the Blue Boar once.' Her voice was rather flat; the cheery bounce had gone out of it.

There was a pause. Meg's face was expressionless as she turned to Bella. 'Why would you want to talk to me about him?'

'John used to feed Oliver's cat when he was away. We ended up going in together once and we saw your flyer on his cork board. He'd put a question mark next to your name so we guessed he must have considered approaching you. I wondered if he had in the end, and if so, how much you knew about his life. Only I've discovered he knew my late father. I only met Oliver once – we never got to talk about their connection – and now it feels like a double loss. It's clutching at straws, I know, but I thought if you'd ended up chatting while you cleaned, he might have mentioned my dad. All I've got is a photograph of the pair of them.'

'Was your father a gambler?'

Bella frowned. 'No.'

Meg shook her head quickly. 'Sorry, I just wondered. That's the one thing I know about Oliver Barton. He never asked me to work at his house. I'd lost a couple of cleaning slots, so I needed to canvass for extra business. I dished out loads of leaflets, and a few came good.'

The explanation made sense. But Meg hadn't met Bella's eyes as she'd spoken. She suspected she was lying – or leaving stuff out. But why? She'd seemed so open and straightforward up until then.

'You didn't send him a letter?' Bella asked, to a wince from John, who clearly thought she was getting herself into dangerous waters.

The woman faced her directly now, her brow furrowed. 'No. What makes you think that?'

Bella was pretty sure she hadn't sent the threatening note, despite the watermark. She didn't look suspicious or uneasy, just puzzled. 'Doesn't matter. It was just that we found a note from someone in his house. The sheet with the signature was missing and John wanted to reply.'

Bella hoped Meg didn't know Nan Gifford. If word got back, they'd have some explaining to do.

'Well, it wasn't me. I only knew him by sight.'

'Didn't you both attend the local history group though?'

Her cheeks tinged pink. 'There are a lot of us. But yes, I remember seeing him there. We exchanged the odd word, as you do. He was noticeable. Larger-than-life. It was a shock to hear what had happened to him. I turned up to clean at Raven House as usual, the day his body was discovered. Alexis and Harvey hadn't thought to warn me. They were too shaken.'

'I found him,' Bella said. 'The Howards put me up the night before. Alexis is a friend of my mother's and they rescued me from a boiler disaster. You could probably tell I'd been there if the police let you carry on.' Bella was wondering if anything had struck her as out of place that morning. She didn't think the Howards were guilty, but it was worth checking.

Meg gave a brief smile that was no longer meeting her eyes. 'There was only your bedding and you'd stripped that.'

'I'm sorry you've been having a tough time,' John said. 'What are they like, the Howards? I hope they're understanding. I barely know them.'

Meg put her head on one side. 'Harvey's a bit of a snob – us and them. Constantly reminding everyone of his wealth and status. But it's a good job. Their old cleaner put me onto it when she retired. Three mornings a week, and I like Alexis.' She turned to Bella. 'You didn't lose a glove when you visited, did you? Only I found one just outside the perimeter wall on Monday. Brown with a faux fur trim.' She seemed relieved to be talking about something practical.

'No, it's not mine.'

Meg sighed. 'I left it on the wall. Hopefully someone will find it.'

They said their goodbyes and left Meg to get on with her cooking.

'What do you think?' John asked.

'She was seriously tense the moment I mentioned Oliver.'

He nodded. 'I've always liked Meg, but I think she was holding back.'

'And that she didn't like him much, which is odd, if she barely knew him.'

He gave her a sidelong glance. 'She has to stay on the list?'

'Yes.' Bella pulled on her gloves, pushing between the fingers until they were properly in place. 'She's not as strong a contender as Julia Sandford, but I'm sure there's more to find out.'

John gave her a speculative look as they walked back up Kite Street towards the river. 'I must say, you lie with worrying ease.'

'Thank you. I wanted to be on the stage when I was a pre-teen.'

'I can so see that.'

TWENTY-TWO

ALEXIS'S POETRY RECITAL

At the poetry recital, it was clear that the news of Oliver's treasure had got out. The room was full of it.

'To think the old devil had all that under his roof,' a man with white hair and a beard said as Bella entered the room.

'It fits though,' the red-haired woman next to him replied. 'He liked to do things for kicks. That crazy car Harvey sold him, the drinking and the gambling. And now this! But what a turn-up for the books. I wonder if Nan knew. It's hard to believe no one did.'

Another guest joined them. 'My son's at school with Cal. He heard him boasting about his uncle's "treasures", then clamming up. It all makes sense now. And if he knew, I'm sure Nan must have.' She gave a fake-sounding sigh. 'I don't want to be mean, but given her husband's history it's not so hard to believe she knew and kept it quiet.'

Bella shot her looks of dislike and hoped she could feel them. Whatever the truth about Nan, tarring her with the same brush as her husband was deeply unfair.

The man looked disapproving and sniffy. 'I'm sure we shouldn't judge her for her unfortunate marriage.'

His patronising tone meant he got Bella's glares next.

The red-haired woman raised an eyebrow. 'She did choose him.'

The bearded man inclined his head. 'True, true... So young Cal knew about the treasure, then. I wonder if Oliver was giving Nan odds and ends to sell.'

It hadn't taken him long to overcome his principles and join in the tittle-tattle.

Bella still didn't believe Oliver had given Nan anything from the hoard. She must find out the truth, though whether that would save Nan from this hateful gossip or create more was a moot point.

The conversation added to her hunch that Cal was an unlikely murderer. He wasn't mature enough. If he'd master-minded a plot to kill for the treasure, she doubted he'd gossip about said treasure with his friends.

When she'd finished eavesdropping, she and John joined Carys and Leo and filled them in on the latest developments.

Five minutes later, Leo was fidgeting in the chair next-door-but-one to Bella's. She, John and Carys were ignoring him on the grounds that he shouldn't be encouraged.

'He doesn't normally come to these events,' Carys said, 'but what with Oliver's death, he was too curious not to.'

Alexis appeared on a dais in front of the assembled audience and someone lowered the lights in the Howards' grand sitting room so that one spotlight remained on her. Other than that, it was just the faint glow from pairs of wall lights with classic shades. A moment later, Harvey joined his wife, standing at her side. He put one hand on her arm.

It might have been to encourage her, but to Bella, it looked more as though he was highlighting their marriage. Not that he was being proprietorial – she was his – but more to show that he was hers. She'd chosen him and that mattered. Meg had implied he was arrogant. He was certainly conscious of his position as the owner of land with a lot of history, but Bella sensed he was leaning on it for support. Beneath his exterior, there was a vulnerability.

'Welcome everyone,' Alexis said. Her voice was slightly croaky, as though she was fighting a cold. 'Thank you for coming. We debated about carrying on this evening, after the tragedy in our grounds. It feels wrong, but several of you encouraged me. And you're right. I'll feel awful whenever I do it. But I'd like to dedicate this evening to the memory of Professor Oliver Barton.' She took a breath. 'We have a collection by the door for a students' fund Oliver set up at Acton Thorpe University. We'd love it if any of you felt able to contribute.'

Harvey moved to the lectern now. 'I'd like to echo what Alexis has said. It still feels unreal and horrific that Oliver met his death here on Sunday night. We spent many happy evenings together at the local history society.' He cleared his throat and moved back to let Alexis take centre stage again.

She began to read haltingly from her latest collection. Bella let the words wash over her, creating images of the wild Shropshire hills and the villages tucked between them. The sound of birds of prey on the wing and church bells tolling. The power of the River Kite and the feeling of strength given off by the stone circle that stood above it.

When Alexis finished, there was a resounding round of applause and Bella resolved to buy one of her books. She felt as though she'd spent the last forty-five minutes in a dream.

Leo, on the other hand, was making straight for the drinks table. 'Not my kind of thing,' he hissed, as she, Carys, John and Lucy caught him up.

'She comes to talk to us at school,' Lucy said, as she poured herself an orange juice. 'She gets tearful sometimes, when she reads her work.'

Bella remembered Leo's thoughts on her marriage and

wondered if she felt trapped. Her poems evoked a freedom she might not feel.

Leo was exploring the house a little more thoroughly than might seem polite, peeking into the TV room at the back, beyond the huge reception room they were in. 'Fancy,' he said, grinning, then shut the door again.

'Stop playing the fool,' Carys muttered. 'You can see what I have to put up with,' she added to Bella. 'I work with kids and then I married one.'

Leo looked injured and she laughed.

Lucy had wandered over to a bookshelf and was pulling out a volume. Carys went to stop her but Alexis intervened.

'Please. It's fine to look. Borrow it if you like. That one's one of my son's favourites.' It was called *The Young Person's Guide to Archaeology*. 'Barney's grown up around the ruins, of course. He's been fascinated by them since he was a child. We're lucky to live somewhere so special.' But then her gaze fell on Harvey, and she looked away.

Lucy was already absorbed, her lips parted as she looked at black-and-white aerial photos.

Bella glanced beyond her and realised Frank Fellows was there. She recalled the notes on her drawing board. The former history teacher who'd watched her and John emerge from Nan Gifford's house. He'd met Nan at the Blue Boar too, and he'd been agitated, asking Jeannie about members of the local history group. He might share Oliver's passion for ancient artefacts; he'd organised a trip to the Staffordshire Hoard.

He looked tense now, his eyes on Alexis. Bella thought he might approach her, but true to form, he was too polite to butt in on her conversation. His patience meant he lost out and an attractive blond man, around Alexis's age, came and ushered her away.

'Excuse me,' Bella said to Frank Fellows, 'I think we almost met outside Nan Gifford's house. I saw you as my colleague and I left.'

His pupils dilated and he edged back with a quick shake of his head. 'I'm sorry, but I think you're mistaking me for someone else.'

'But you do know Nan.'

He'd moved back further. 'Doesn't she work at the Blue Boar? I believe I've seen her there. Please forgive me, I must go and catch one of my neighbours. Enjoy your evening.'

He was so keen to leave her that he knocked into a man's glass as he turned, slopping his white wine.

'Goodness me, I do apologise.' Bella could see the genuine consternation in Frank's eyes.

She thought of Jeannie, saying Frank held the door open for too long. He was old-school, clearly, a stickler for manners. But Bella was quite fond of them herself, so long as they were meant genuinely, and applied to men as well as women.

That appeared to be the case with Frank Fellows. He seemed rather special on the face of it. But what had he and Nan got to hide?

She was almost instantly distracted by the sight of Alexis and the blond man. He was leaning in close. Whatever he'd said, it had made her smile, though she was shaking her head, pulling back.

Carys appeared at Bella's elbow. 'D'you think he's making a play for her? I've seen him at her recitals before. I hear he's a fellow poet and a superfan. They met on her American lecture tour.'

'Interesting.' Bella remembered the spark in Alexis's eyes when she'd talked about the tour. She turned to look for Harvey and realised he was standing just behind her. Thankfully, he was deep in conversation, not hanging on her and Carys's words. She tuned in to what he was saying.

'If you want to get him into the cadets, I can recommend

that. My father got me involved, of course. It was the making of me. I'll have a word with...'

Her attention slid away. This time, it was the man from the delicatessen who distracted her.

'We meet again.' He raised his glass to hers. 'I can't stay but I thought I'd say hello. I'll come and find you at Vintage Winter.'

'Please do,' Bella said, before he went on his way.

'You've met before?' John was at Bella's elbow.

'At the deli.'

'I didn't notice it was him serving. Rupert Edgar. He owns the place. I went to school with him.'

'You went to school with everyone. Why, what is it?' She could tell he had private thoughts on Mr Edgar.

'Nothing. He wasn't in my year anyway. He was Matt's contemporary.' He went to refill his glass, leaving Bella to wonder what was on his mind.

Harvey Howard was talking to a woman about Oliver Barton's death now. He was largely drowned out by Leo, who was chatting with Carys. Bella shifted a little, to hear Harvey better.

'... tragic. And a terrible shock, of course. Historic England are sending someone to check the stones are secure – they're fenced off until then. Turns out they were planning to come and assess the site soon anyway. It doesn't have a full listing yet.'

That was interesting. Was there any way Oliver could have known Historic England was about to investigate the old ruins? Had he wanted to avoid the officials getting there first? It might have made him dig immediately. But if someone had spread false rumours about treasure, it was too elaborate to assume they'd relied on Historic England's visit to hurry Oliver along.

Bella decided she ought to talk to the Howards to express her sympathy again, and ask how they were. It felt wrong not to mention it. She made for Alexis now, hovering just behind her and another woman, waiting for a gap in their conversation. She could have insinuated herself into their exchange if she'd wanted, but she chose not to. The more she knew about Oliver Barton's connections the better, and eavesdropping worked well.

The topic was gardens. Alexis looked pale, but very well-dressed in her expensively cut suit, Prada shoes, gold scarf ring and peacock silk square. She had everything money could buy but Bella agreed with Leo and Bernadette: she didn't seem happy. Her understated earrings and glittering gold brooch rounded off her outfit nicely. Diamond or a good imitation? Bella was tempted to switch sides to get a better look, but stopped herself. She mustn't keep valuing everything on sight.

'... looking so beautiful, even in winter,' the guest was saying to Alexis. 'I love the ironwork trellis with the climber. It's a nice way to mark the boundary between your garden and the ruins.'

'Greg, our gardener, came up with that. The climber's Clematis cirrhosa. It's slow growing. It'll be lovely when it's taller. It flowers all winter and the bees adore it.' She sighed.

'I envy you Greg,' her companion said. 'He's done wonders. It feels as though he's only just started with you.'

Alexis's look had been far away. The fellow poet Carys had mentioned was in her line of sight. Perhaps that was where her thoughts lay.

But now, she frowned. 'Actually, it's been a while. He must have joined us six months or so after I came back from my US tour. The last gardener left while I was away. He got terribly unreliable so it was no good keeping him on. Greg's been rescuing us from the wilderness ever since. It's rather nice; he's going out with our cleaner now. Joe, her husband, died a year ago. It's good to think of her having some company.' She put her hands to her face. 'I'm sorry. I normally love thinking about the garden, but at the moment ...'

The woman she was talking to put a hand on her sleeve.

'I'm so sorry; I should have thought. I was fond of Oliver Barton. Such a character. Though the news of his treasure hoard is quite extraordinary—'

Behind them, Bella saw Frank Fellows talking to Harvey Howard. She abandoned her attempt to speak to Alexis in favour of edging round to eavesdrop again. In the background she could see Leo and Lucy, discussing the book she'd been reading. Both looked animated.

'No,' Harvey was saying. 'I was in bed. Asleep, as a matter of fact. I had no idea what had happened until the next day.' He looked pale. 'It was horrific.'

Frank's back was ramrod straight, and he was twisting his hands. Bella wondered if he knew something. She missed his next words but caught Harvey's reply. 'I don't know, but I could imagine it. He was lively, wasn't he? A giddy old goat.' He shook his head. 'I caught him with lipstick on his collar once. I asked him about it of course, but he just smiled and tapped the side of his nose.'

'Shush, Harvey.' Alexis moved closer and took his arm. 'It can't be right to spread rumours like that now he's dead.'

TWENTY-THREE

A SECRET VISIT

Bella glanced at the ruins as their group walked down the driveway of Raven House. A combination of the cordons and the crowds leaving the reading prevented her from looking more closely. It was frustrating. She wanted to check the top of the wall after Tony had suggested it might be significant. It was hard to imagine what might be there, and if it was something portable the killer could have taken it. All the same, it was a lingering question. She wouldn't be happy until she'd investigated.

She looked over her shoulder as they walked on, down into the valley, across St Luke's Bridge and into town. Leo had suggested a nightcap at the Blue Boar, though Carys and Lucy were headed for home.

They waved them off and went inside to be greeted by the inn's welcoming warmth. They got the chance to try the alcoholic version of Gareth's winter warmer. He was a happier man, now he'd tweaked the recipe to his satisfaction.

· · ·

Bella arrived back at Southwell Hall with a warm glow in her chest. She was just anticipating her soft duvet when she noticed the corner of an envelope, peeking out from the slot in her flat's mailbox in the foyer. The thought of something to deal with at this hour was unappealing. The letter must have been hand-delivered. She'd already collected that morning's post on her way in from work. She opened the mailbox and pulled it out.

Her name was written on the front in block capitals.

Inside was a typewritten note.

WHERE DOES NAN GIFFORD GO AT NIGHT? COME AND WATCH THIS EVENING.

All vestiges of warmth from Gareth's excellent cocktail seeped from her body. She glanced over her shoulder, onto Kite Walk and the river beyond, almost black in the darkness. Who had sent this? How did they know she was investigating? Or where she lived?

Had someone been asking about her? Or perhaps she'd been followed. Not a good thought.

It took her a while longer to consider the contents. Had someone got it in for Nan? Or was the writer genuinely concerned? Could they have seen her head to Oliver's house the night before, just like she had? The note implied the outings were ongoing. Perhaps she'd been removing the treasure by degrees, until she told the police. Or maybe the writer was onto something else. Nan couldn't be picking up artefacts if she was heading out tonight. Even if Dixon's team hadn't removed the hoard yet, why report it and then steal from it? It would be senselessly risky.

There was always the possibility that the note writer was luring Bella out... Kite Walk was full of shadows.

She glanced at her watch. She might be a night owl, but even she was short of sleep after the previous escapade. Not as sharp as she might be if she ran into trouble. But the idea of going to bed now was a non-starter. She had to know.

She re-locked her letter box, exited the building and turned to cut up Boatman's Walk. St Giles's Steps was a quicker route to high town, but they were too lonely, this time of night. If someone was waiting for her there, they'd be disappointed.

In fifteen minutes, she was on the corner of Nan's road, Mary's Walk, and already wishing she'd changed into warmer clothes. Frost glinted on the pavement. She decided to wait at the corner with Hollybush Lane. It was thick with foliage, which gave her some cover, though the prickles were a disadvantage.

For twenty minutes, all was quiet. The only change was the level of numbness in Bella's feet. *Come on!* But then she saw movement. The front door of Nan's house opened. Nan pulled it closed after her, with the least possible noise. But if it was for Cal's benefit, Bella could see the effort had been wasted. The curtain twitched in an upstairs window and a pale face peered out, illuminated by the street lamp.

Nan had her trolley again, but this time it was deployed, not folded. Bella assumed she was transporting something from her house, just as she had from Oliver's. She wondered again about Nan taking a small portion of his treasure to sell. She might have it with her now.

As she scurried along the lane towards the corner where Bella stood, the curtain in her cottage dropped back and Bella made her move, hurrying until she reached a stile marking the start of the footpath up Gallows Hill. She pushed herself back and to one side, in amongst the leaves of a viburnum.

A couple of minutes later, Nan still hadn't passed. She'd probably turned the other way, towards Uppergate. Bella risked a look. Sure enough she could see her, dashing along. Bella followed, keeping to the shadows as best she could. She considered removing her distinctive bucket hat, but at least it disguised her hair.

Following Nan onto Uppergate was difficult. There was no cover at all. The snug homes and grander townhouses fronted straight onto the street. On the other side of the road were half-timbered buildings with quaint shops in their ground floors, rather like Vintage Winter. But as Bella watched, wondering how to play it, Nan disappeared onto Holt Lane, diagonally opposite. The road where Leo, Carys and Lucy lived. She loved it there – it was lined with Georgian cottages with pretty front gardens and mature trees on the other side of the lane.

Bella risked crossing Uppergate so she could peer down the road. It was as well she'd looked when she did. Nan was turning off into Back Lane before the road petered out. The houses were larger there. Bella had done lots of exploring since she'd moved. It ranked as highly satisfactory free entertainment.

If Nan was transporting treasure, who was she taking it to? It felt bold, after she'd reported the hoard to the police, but in reality, Bella guessed she had no reason to worry. It wasn't as though she'd been back to her uncle's house and Barry Dixon wouldn't be watching. He was probably in bed, dreaming of jewels.

She hurried after Nan, glancing over her shoulder as she went. She was still worried the letter writer might be following her, but all seemed quiet. Everywhere, frost glinted in lamp- and moonlight. The only thing Bella could hear was the wheels of Nan's trolley, just audible in the hush.

Back Lane curved round, winding back on itself. Like Leo and Carys's road, it had mature trees. Bella did her best to keep behind them as she walked. After the first bend in the road, Nan Gifford stopped outside a navy front door.

The person inside opened up and for a moment, Bella could see nothing. They were in shadow. Then at last they stepped forward, into the lamplight.

It was Frank Fellows.

Bella was thinking so hard about what she'd seen that Matt's voice made her jump as she entered their shared hallway.

For the love of Sweet Agnes... She was on the home straight to a fruit tea and bed. The last thing she wanted was social interaction with a Jenks at this time of night. Especially this one, who was less known, and therefore unpredictable.

'Been out on the tiles?'

'No. I was just getting some air. Have you?'

'Also no. I've been working.'

'Working?' At this hour? The pubs would have long since closed and Hope Eaton wasn't known for twenty-four-hour industry. Unless you were a vet like Dixon's wife, or a farmer with a sick animal.

'Yes, you know. You do stuff and people give you money in return.' He smiled. 'Could I trouble you for my cat?'

'I haven't got—'

At that moment, she heard a yowl.

'I don't believe it.' Bella dug for her keys, opened the door, scooped up Cuthbert and thrust him into Matt's arms.

Matt took him, grinning. 'Much obliged. Night.'

Bella closed the door behind her.

TWENTY-FOUR

THE DEADEST OF DEAD ENDS

The following morning, Bella drank cup after cup of coffee. John was opening the shop. She was due to see a woman who had some items to sell. The visit was not a success. The pieces included an ancient silk christening dress that had been pre-loved not only by its previous owners but by a whole family of moths. It could have been beautiful once. Possibly. She was also not in the least tempted by the most unpleasant-looking Toby jug she'd ever seen. Nor yet the salt and pepper pots in the shapes of leering faces, which would give her nightmares when she finally got enough sleep to dream again.

She recommended eBay for 'items with such specialist appeal' and dashed back towards Vintage Winter, frustrated at the wasted journey.

The weather was marginally milder, the frost replaced by a chilling rain. Dark-edged clouds pressed down over the moot hall as she dashed up the high street. She had her umbrella angled in front of her and only identified Alexis Howard by her Prada shoes.

'Thank you for the reading yesterday,' she said, after their umbrellas had snagged and they'd exchanged polite apologies. 'It must have been hard to go ahead after Sunday.'

Alexis nodded. 'A friend of mine pointed out everyone would quiz us about the death whenever we held the first recital. He thought it was best to get it over with.' Bella wondered if she was talking about the blond man. 'We've had people coming to peer over our wall. Can you imagine?'

Bella thought of her desire to explore the site. 'Terrible. How are you bearing up? It must be difficult, having known Oliver.'

'It made it more shocking.' She hesitated. 'And the press came and parked themselves outside on Monday. They asked lots of questions.'

'And now they're excited over Oliver's treasure,' Bella said. She'd seen it on several newspaper hoardings.

Alexis nodded. 'Poor Nan. It must be hard after all she's been through. Oliver should have thought of that.' She sighed. 'Anyway, thanks for coming last night. Getting the recital out of the way helped. I got my first decent night's sleep afterwards. Please give my love to your mother.'

They said their goodbyes and Bella made for St Giles's Close, entering the shop in time to see John taking money for some candles. The day for burning them was tomorrow. She was looking forward to it being over and knowing clients were in her shop for the right reasons. It was just as well the flyers were due imminently. She'd been too busy to organise them sooner but now was the time to get the word out in person.

Once the customer left, she told John what she'd seen the night before.

'That's disturbing.' He took off his glasses and polished them. 'You've got no idea what was in the trolley or who wrote the note?'

'None. The trolley contents looked quite bulky, but I didn't hear any clanking. I wondered about some of the treasure, carefully cushioned to protect it. Frank Fellows is mixed up in this somehow. He's been jumpy as a cat every time I've seen him. He's very old-school in his manners, but he struck me as genuine. I rather liked him, but he clearly has a passion for the past. He was a member of the same history group as Oliver, as well as teaching the subject. And there was that trip he organised to the Staffordshire Hoard. Perhaps he's a secret collector, just like Oliver, only he prefers buying artefacts to digging them up. His house is quite posh. He could probably afford it.'

John bit his lip. 'It sounds possible. But does it lead us closer to Oliver's killer?'

Bella sighed. 'Probably not. Unless Frank killed him, knowing the treasure would pass to Nan, who'd be willing to sell him some. But that's too convoluted.'

'Agreed.'

'No, talking to Julia Sandford is the next step as far as finding Oliver's killer goes. She's got plenty of questions to answer.' She was due at the Steps that afternoon, if she kept to her usual pattern. It would be easier to chat there. The meeting would seem casual. 'Did you ask Leo to tell us when she shows up?'

John raised an eyebrow. 'Of course.'

They went to look at the drawing board in the office again, with the four queens stuck down the right-hand side.

Three passionate women. One who loves too much, one who's full of fear, and one who's striving for immortality. And then the fourth. An enigma, but one who worries me.

'So you've got Julia down as the one who loved too much?'

'Who Oliver was involved with when he bought his car from Harvey Howard? Tentatively. The barmaid at the Black Swan said she looked fond of him, and that she'd popped up a few times. And I also think their relationship might have been complicated. If he was startled when she turned up, perhaps he was pulling away, but she was hooked. And we know she was with him at the Blue Boar the night he died. Sitting outside, so probably discussing something private. What's the betting she knew he planned to visit the ruins?

'Meg still feels like the enigma. I'm sure she hasn't told us the whole truth, and I sense she didn't like Oliver, despite claiming to have barely known him.' Bella smoothed her hair behind her ears. 'And on paper, Alexis still fits for the woman who's striving for immortality, but I'm not convinced it's her. Perhaps we're missing someone.'

'And who's full of fear?'

'Nan, because she knew Oliver was sailing close to the wind?'

John nodded. 'Could be. So, next steps?'

'We need to talk to Julia, and to Meg again too. If Julia doesn't come to the Steps today, we'll go in search of her.'

John closed his eyes for a moment. 'That's going to be even more difficult than visiting Meg.'

'I want to talk to Frank Fellows again too.' But she'd thought of a natural way to achieve that.

They went through to the shop and John got to work dusting the alcove displays. Outside, Bella saw Sienna Hearst walk by. If she was going to the Steps, Bella hoped Leo served her cold tea. It reminded her that none of the antiques shops in Shrewsbury had got back to her about John's favourite items. She whizzed off some emails to chase. Calling again would have been better but she knew John would feel uncomfortable if he heard her.

It was mid-morning when Rupert Edgar from the delicatessen dropped in, looking sleek and expensive in a long dark coat and tailored trousers. He certainly knew how to dress. John seemed to dematerialise. She could hear him in the back room.

'It's a charming shop,' Rupert said, glancing at the refectory table and a painted blanket chest. Mid-twentieth century. Bella loved that period.

'The chest's the most expensive item we have at the moment. I'm in love with it myself.'

'More expensive than the table?'

'Ah, that's not for sale.' An old family friend, Val Barber, had given it to Bella when she'd moved out of her mother's house. Bella had been hugely fond of Val and loved it more than any other piece she owned. She hadn't considered its value at the time, though Val had said she could always sell it to raise some cash. But Bella wanted it here – in her very first shop – for good luck.

'Why on earth isn't it for sale?' Rupert said. 'People would come from miles around to buy something like that.'

'We have history.' She patted the table.

He put his head on one side. 'I'm intrigued. I wonder, do you fancy coming out for dinner next week? You could tell me about it. Are you free on Friday? Seven o'clock? I'm away for a few days before then.'

'You're missing Sweet Agnes?' Bella put on a tone of mock horror.

'Let's just say I've done it before.' He smiled and gave her one of the deli cards. 'Give me a call. Let me know where you'd like to meet.' His dark eyes lingered on hers for a moment. 'See you next week.'

Bella couldn't help noticing that John reappeared the second Rupert left the shop.

She put her hands on her hips. 'What is it that you don't like about him?'

'What? Nothing. He's fine.'

'You'd tell me if he was an axe-wielding maniac, wouldn't you?'

'Definitely.'

Bella stalked across the room feeling faintly irritated and set about rearranging the window display. With the greatest reluctance she put the bronze-painted lizard in pride of place, resting it on a square of black velvet to show it off to best advantage.

'It's in a good cause,' John said, as she added other animal-themed items around it: a wooden owl book stand, and a nineteenth-century visiting card case, decorated with cranes and cherry blossom.

Just before lunch, the flyers turned up.

Bella stood over John as he opened the box carefully with a penknife.

'They look great!'

The designer had given them a theatrical look. She wanted people to feel a sense of occasion as they walked through her door. Life was short; every experience should count.

She and John reread the flyer. It was heavy on beautiful photos, included their contact details and a footnote saying: 'We buy and sell.' Three sentences summed up Bella's offer:

'A hundred collectibles, a hundred stories, a hundred pieces of history. Buy an item that's touched lives, on a journey to the next port. From pocket-money purchases to standout splash-out pieces and everything in between.'

'But mainly, we sell candles,' she said, giving him a sidelong glance.

'We've done all right this week.'

'It's a start. Now we've got the leaflets, I want to use them. I'm going to start delivering in Back Lane this lunchtime.'

John raised an eyebrow. 'Why Back Lane?'

'It's where Frank Fellows lives, and he's on my list of people to talk to. I was already planning to knock on doors and hand the leaflets over. When Frank opens his, I'm going to be terribly surprised it's him, because just last night, as I walked home after a nightcap at a friend's, I saw Nan Gifford enter his house. Yet he claimed he didn't know her.'

John shook his head. 'Was it really your sisters who played

up when they were young? Your level of guile makes me wonder.'

'I learned from them. I was angelic.'

John looked at her owlishly.

Lunchtime arrived at last and the rain had cleared up. It felt too obvious to visit Frank's house first, but Bella wanted a targeted approach. They could fill in the gaps later. So they began with his next-door neighbour. The result was positive. The woman who answered seemed interested and hadn't yet visited Vintage Winter.

'Here goes,' Bella said, as she rapped the lion's-head knocker on Frank's door. They stood there for a couple of minutes but there was no reply. 'Bother. I'll leave a leaflet anyway.'

The woman she'd already spoken to reappeared with her coat on. 'Not in? I was going to try him again. I've not seen him this morning, which is unusual. Only I noticed there's a crack in his side window. I wondered if someone had tried to break in. I'll catch him later.'

A possible break-in after what Bella had seen last night? And no reply from Frank... On impulse she swung his keyhole cover to one side and bent to peer through.

'Do we have to do this?' John said.

'Yes.' Inside, the key was still in the lock. It didn't prove Frank was in the house. He had a Yale too. He could have gone out, relying on that for security, but instinct told her it was unlikely.

She explained the situation to John. 'Maybe we should check the side window.'

He looked uncomfortable. 'I'm not wildly keen on tres-passing.'

Bella was already on her way. It had the desired effect; she could hear him just behind.

The side window was a traditional sash, two panes over two, and the crack ran across the bottom left-hand pane. If someone had wanted to break in, they'd have had to smash a lot harder than that, and knock out the sash bars too. It didn't look like a determined effort. She glanced over her shoulder. There was no one on the street behind her. Good.

She walked further round the house towards the back and glanced through another window. John marched past her abruptly, to the window furthest from the road.

'You're keen suddenly.'

'Keen for this to be over as soon as possible.'

He peered hesitantly at first, but then pressed his face against the glass, cupping his hand to shut out reflections.

As Bella approached, she heard a noise deep in his throat.

'What is it?'

He stepped away from the window. 'Don't look.'

Bella looked.

There on the floor of a cosy sitting room was the body of Frank Fellows, a cup smashed at his side, his arms splayed awkwardly, a rug rucked under his feet.

TWENTY-FIVE

A JOB FOR BARRY DIXON

After they'd called the police, Bella took the flyers and walked to the end of the road nearest to Frank Fellows's house. She had a terrible sinking sensation in her chest: an aching pity. Shock made her feel as though she'd been slapped, and underlying that was a gnawing sense of guilt.

John followed her, dashing to keep up. 'What are you doing?'

She swallowed down her feelings. 'If the police go door-to-door they'll think we weren't really here to leaflet – unless we cover our tracks.'

'Isn't it a bit unfeeling to be doing this when we know what's happened?'

'It's not that I don't care. I'm processing my emotions while I work. Dad taught me to be clear-sighted when disaster strikes. If you'd rather explain the truth to Barry Dixon, then I'll stop.'

John sighed. 'You win.'

'I think Dixon's more likely to take us seriously if he thinks we've stumbled across this, than if he imagines we came looking for clues.' She glanced at him. 'Frank Fellows is more likely to get justice this way.'

John rubbed his chin. 'You have a point. So you reckon the death is suspicious?'

Thinking time not required. 'Don't you? Frank Fellows has popped up everywhere we look. He's got a secret connection with Oliver's niece. She visited him with luggage after midnight. He was in the Blue Boar, desperate to find members of the local history society. And pummelling Harvey Howard for information at the recital. The more Harvey couldn't answer, the more anxious he got. Now there's a new crack in his window and he's dead.'

John frowned. 'I see all that, but his rug *was* rucked up under his feet. He could have tripped and knocked his head.' He must have read her expression. 'But if we take a leap, and assume he didn't, then what's our theory? That Nan Gifford sold him some of the treasure? Then someone came and stole it from him and killed him in the process?'

'Possibly. And if so, it means I've messed up, big time.'

John frowned.

'I decided not to make a big deal about the missing treasure and Nan dumping the notebooks because I felt for her. But if she was selling some of the hoard to Frank Fellows then this whole thing is much bigger than I'd realised. I could have made the police question Nan. She might never have taken the treasure to Frank if I'd done that.'

'We don't know that she did.'

'Don't try to make me feel better.' She marched on.

'No. Right.'

Bella pushed another leaflet through a letter box.

'What will you do?' John's tone was nervous.

'I'm going to have to tell Dixon what I saw and live with it.' The sinking feeling intensified. She hated guilt. It was unproductive and offered no escape. She kept replaying her reasons for not speaking up, an endless stream of self-justification. And after all that it would be the worst of both worlds: telling on

Nan *and* failing to protect the killer's next victim. She thought of her dad and hoped she could turn things around. If he could see her now, he might revise his opinion of her supposed talents.

They'd reached Frank's next-door-neighbour's house – the one who'd already chatted to Bella and taken a leaflet. Not a moment too soon. Patrol cars appeared, and an ambulance too. They went to explain what had happened and five minutes later, Barry Dixon arrived, almost falling out of his car.

Bella watched as a uniformed officer gestured in her and John's direction and Dixon looked up, shoved his hair out of his face, wincing, and walked towards them.

'Ms Winter?' He closed his eyes for a moment, before his gaze turned to John. 'And this is?'

'John Jenks. My colleague. We were leafleting the road during our lunch break – trying to get the word out about my shop, Vintage Winter. We talked to Mr Fellows' neighbour and she was concerned for him. She said she'd normally have seen him by now and she'd noticed a crack in his window.'

Dixon's baby-face brow furrowed into many creases. 'You knew Mr Fellows?'

'We'd talked briefly. It's a long story.'

Dixon closed his eyes as though daylight was more than he could bear. He took a deep breath. 'Right, right. Let's go and sit in the car. Then you can tell me the whole thing from the beginning.'

Bella and John sat in the back, Dixon in the front. Bella put her hand on the seat and felt something crunch underneath. Looking down, she recognised a broken bit of rusk. A sign of the four kids under seven. It brought back memories, being one of four herself. She jiggled sideways to avoid getting crumbs embedded in her coat.

Dixon turned to a new page in his notepad. 'So, you first met Mr Fellows when?'

Bella explained everything, from how they'd seen Frank

watch them leave Nan Gifford's house, to the time she'd seen him at the Blue Boar, up at the bar, looking anxious, and in the Blue Room, talking secretly to Nan. She wound up with what she'd seen at the poetry recital.

All the time, the bigger bit of news she'd have to confess weighed heavily in her mind. When to slip it in? *Not yet.* 'I thought it was odd that he lied about not knowing Nan. That brings me to the last time I saw him alive,'

Dixon stopped scribbling and craned round to look at her. 'And that was when?'

'Late last night. I'd been to the poetry recital, and then to the Blue Boar for a few drinks. Maybe it was all the nibbles, but I couldn't sleep so I went for a walk to clear my head. I ended up on this street and saw Mr Fellows open the door to Nan. It must have been around half past midnight. She had a shopping trolley with her.'

Dixon's frown deepened. 'Right.' There was a long pause. She sensed he was aching to accept that at face value and move on, but at last he sighed. 'And you're back in the same road today. It's a big coincidence.'

'It would be,' Bella said, 'if it was one, but it's not. I noticed how large the houses were last night. It seemed like a good place to start leafleting.'

'Because they're more likely to afford your wares?'

'Not solely. I stock lots of reasonably priced items. It's because they might have nice antiques or vintage belongings they no longer value. I'm always looking for new stock. So Back Lane was a logical place to start. People in smaller houses are more disciplined – they don't hang on to stuff.'

Dixon's frown was back, but after a moment he shook his head and let it go. Life was full and short, she guessed.

'Did you see Nan Gifford leave again, last night?'

Bella shook her head. 'I didn't hang around. I was back home again by one or so.'

'Can anyone vouch for you?'

'I bumped into my neighbour, Matt Jenks, in the hallway. He saw me go into my flat.'

Dixon's shoulders relaxed as he wrote that down. Something that fitted neatly into place. But then he paused. 'Wait, Jenks?' He looked at John as though they'd played some kind of joke on him.

'John's brother. The Jenkses are a local family. John and Matt's parents run the Blue Boar.' She sighed. Her father wouldn't have needed that explaining. If only there was someone local who really understood the townsfolk.

Dixon was scribbling furiously. He took down John's details next, asked about his movements and learned that Gareth could vouch for him. 'Though it's looking like an accident from first impressions,' he said. 'As though he slipped on the rug and knocked his head on the stone shelf.'

Bella flinched inwardly. The moment was coming where she'd have to tell him the truth. Before that, she could point out the obvious. 'But there's the cracked window. Mr Fellows' neighbour said that was new.'

'He could have broken it earlier in the evening.' Dixon rubbed his forehead. 'Whichever way you look at it, it doesn't make you think foul play. No one could have climbed in.'

Absolutely true. But it was a great, howling coincidence, like her being on Back Lane twice in fourteen hours. She bet it wasn't chance, any more than her two visits were.

'Anyway,' Dixon said gloomily, 'it'll be hours before we know anything concrete. Every detail will be checked.' He put a hand over his eyes for a moment. 'It'll have to be.'

'Will the house be searched?'

Dixon glanced at her questioningly.

'I wondered about the trolley Nan Gifford brought with her and what it might have contained. I'm afraid I have information that could be relevant.'

'Right.' A look of weary acceptance spread across Dixon's face. 'I suppose you'd better explain.'

Bella gave a precise account of Nan dumping the notebooks in the river the night before she'd reported her uncle's hoard. 'I'm now wondering if Nan kept back more than just the two missing items, and sold a collection of them to Frank Fellows. I can't think of another reason she'd destroy Oliver's notebooks. They'd have detailed every one of his finds. If you'd found them, you'd know what was missing and start asking questions.'

She felt better once she'd made her speech. At least she'd warned him about the missing treasure previously.

'What on earth were you doing, following Mrs Gifford so late at night?'

'I saw her by chance, after dropping off some friends in high town. Given what I knew about the treasure, I followed her when she left the professor's house with a heavy-looking trolley.' She fixed him with her gaze, her eyes wide. 'I saw it as my civic duty.'

She thought she heard John snort.

Dixon frowned, then looked as though he couldn't be bothered to pursue it. Decision made, his expression cleared, and he closed his notebook. 'I can see why you didn't tell me. How can you know the books contained records of the professor's digs? They could have been anything. And anyway, I'd never have been able to recover them. I think you can stop worrying now.'

Unlikely. 'Can you at least ask Nan about the books? Don't you think it's a little odd to remove them from her uncle's house in the dead of night and dump them in the river? And slightly strange that she took a trolley to visit Frank Fellows after midnight? Did your team find the gaps left by the missing pieces John and I noticed? Because if not, items have been moved to disguise them.'

She hadn't wanted to put Nan under pressure, but this was

too big a secret to keep. Anything sold to Frank could be the reason he was killed.

Dixon coloured slightly. 'We've got a team going to look at the hoard today.'

'So you'll be able to check. And ask questions.'

His shoulders sagged. 'Happy days. Thanks for your time.'

When they got back to the shop, Bella called Tony to explain what had happened.

'Do you think you might hear more about the investigation?'

'*Don't you worry*,' Tony's gravelly voice rumbled down the line. '*I'll put out feelers.*'

'Fancy a trip out this way?' *Please say yes.* The Blue Boar was a thousand times nicer than the Mitre, but more than that, it was familiar and friendly. That felt all-important right now. Tears pricked her eyes, but she managed to keep her voice steady. 'We could meet at the inn?'

'*You've talked me into it. Shall we say eight?*'

They said goodbye and Bella went back to the drawing board and made a note against Frank Fellows's name. It was so final. The floodgates opened. Her tears dropped onto the paper. *Please don't let John come in.* She found a handkerchief and dabbed desperately at a patch of running ink.

Frank and Oliver's faces flashed up in her head. So vivid. Oliver mentioning her dad. Admiring her stock. Frank's look of concern as he'd knocked that man's glass of wine. The kindness in his eyes. And Jeannie's words. *He was a very good teacher, apparently. Passionate about his subject.*

Two people wiped out.

She could appreciate the beauty and rarity of Oliver's treasure but people dying over it was horrific. Had Frank been unable to resist ancient artefacts, just like the professor? This had to stop. She stood there, fervently wishing that Dixon would treat Frank's death as murder. If he wouldn't, she'd have to find evidence to force his hand.

Who would have killed the pair? Despite Nan's presence at Frank's house the previous night, she still doubted it was her. As before, she could only see her crossing that terrible line if she'd needed vast sums of money for something crucial. The very fact that she'd reported the treasure and used the funds she had for a MacBook Air showed that wasn't the case. She wouldn't splash out on an expensive computer if old contacts of her husband were demanding money with menaces. Cal's physical safety would come first.

Bella went to splash her face at the sink. She hoped to goodness Nan didn't end up in jail because of what she'd told Dixon. Pinching the odd bit of treasure might have felt worthwhile and harmless in Nan's eyes – a victimless crime – but it could still cause her terrible trouble.

But for the murder, she was back to Julia Sandford. If she'd known what Oliver was up to, the night he died, she might know he'd been at it for years. Seen his hoard even. She could have followed Nan, just like Bella. Seen her visit Frank. Guessed she'd handed over some of Oliver's finds and killed Frank to get them. Maybe she wasn't a woman who'd loved too much after all, but one who'd clung to Oliver because of the treasure he'd amassed. She might need money for some reason, or just have wanted the artefacts. She was a historian after all.

She'd have to be utterly ruthless in that scenario. Bella shivered. If she'd followed Nan, she might have seen Bella outside Frank's house too.

She couldn't be the letter writer, though. She wouldn't have wanted anyone guessing Frank might have some treasure.

Bella could hear more than one customer in the shop. She needed to get out there and help. She took a deep breath, checked her face in the mirror, and went to make friends with a woman who was looking at the painted blanket chest Rupert Edgar had admired. She said she'd got Bella's flyer that lunchtime.

Despite everything, a faint spark lit up inside her. This was going to work.

The woman from Back Lane left without buying the chest.

'It's so tantalising,' Bella said to John, as they prepared to lock up for the day. 'She was teetering on the brink. She loved it, and so she should. It's a beauty.' She had a feeling the woman would be back, but she didn't say it aloud. It would be tempting fate and she couldn't afford it.

At that moment, John's mobile rang.

'Ah. Good. Thanks.' His tone didn't match his words.

'What is it?'

He pulled the phone from his ear for a moment. 'Julia Sandford's at the Steps as forecast, doing her marking.'

'Excellent. We'll "just happen to drop in".' Bella had turned the woman into a bogey monster and couldn't quell the thrill of fear that went through her as she got her coat.

John went back to his conversation, looking resigned. 'You heard that?' A moment later, he rang off. 'Leo says to come through the bookshop door and hover in the office. Carys will meet us there. She came by after school; she can oil the wheels.'

. . .

Bella and John entered the café via the bookshop door as instructed. Like the entrance to the eatery's garden, it opened onto St Giles's Steps. The smell of toasted teacakes and hot chocolate floated through from the café area. There was still an hour until closing and customers with rosy cheeks were peeling off layers. Carys was waiting to intercept Bella and John as planned, as Bernadette sold a second-hand Agatha Christie.

'Did you see the adaptation on Sunday?' Bella heard her say to the buyer. 'It was so dark, wasn't it?' Her voice was full of glee. 'I'm not surprised it was on late.'

Carys was in her standard uniform of calf-length swishy skirt, brown boots and drapey cardigan.

'Thanks for helping us out,' Bella said.

'It's the highlight of my day. I love my job, obviously, but one of the little dears put jellybeans down my back earlier, and none of them can spell dinosaur, despite a week-long project.' She gave a fixed smile. 'I want *your* life of vintage clothes, beautiful goods and detective excitement instead. And to that end, Julia Sandford's sitting in the far corner. I spoke to her about Oliver. It seemed only natural. And get this, she's just told me she hasn't seen him in weeks.'

The lie had to mean something. The nervous excitement in Bella's stomach intensified. She could imagine getting addicted to it.

'How are we going to get her chatting?' John was biting his lip.

'I'll introduce you,' Carys said.

'And I've got an idea for the next bit.' Bella had just come up with it. Timing was everything.

'Sorry to disturb your marking,' Bella said, once Carys had done her bit and left, with a promise to pass on their orders to Leo. 'We'll be quick.'

Julia leaned back in her chair. 'Oh, don't worry. I've already got a lot of it done. I'm just about ready to tear my hair out.' She closed her laptop. 'Not that it's bad work. Just the end of a busy week. And I've read it all before.' Her long wavy hair fell forward over her face, hiding her expression, but Bella had already noticed the dark shadows under her eyes. Something had been keeping her awake. Grief or guilt? Either way, she wasn't conforming to the inhuman monster Bella had conjured up.

Leo appeared at that moment with a hot chocolate for Bella, and a tea for John. He looked at them keenly, but Carys tucked an arm through his and steered him away.

'So, what can I do for you?' Julia poured herself another cup of tea, her silver rings glinting in the overhead light.

'John was a good friend of Oliver Barton's,' Bella said, watching Julia as she spoke. She flinched slightly at his name; Bella was sure she was hurting. 'I'm so sorry for your loss. We know you worked together. Only, John wanted to collate a few memories for a memorial. You seemed like a good person to ask.'

She could tell by John's expression that he wasn't entirely happy with her story. It was true that if Julia asked enough questions of enough people she might smell a rat, but it seemed unlikely. It wasn't as though Bella had specified a particular memorial or promised her words would be read in church.

'It's been years since we met regularly.'

It sounded as though they'd had a personal relationship well before Oliver bought his Alfa Romeo, then. 'But you have fond memories from back then?'

Julia looked sad and happy all at once. 'One or two,' she admitted. 'He was wildly charismatic. Fun, intelligent. Adventurous. Full of a zest for life. We used to go out, once upon a time.'

'Once upon a time' sounded like a while back. 'Ah, gosh, I'm sorry. That must make this very painful. But you didn't socialise recently?' It was another chance for her to come clean.

Julia shook her head and sighed. 'I'm seeing someone else.'

She looked at Bella, her eyes watery. 'I heard it was you who found Oliver's body.'

Bella nodded, recalling the scene at the ruins without wanting to. 'He had a metal detector and a trowel with him. And he was surrounded by holes.' She shook her head. 'I was surprised. Did he ever get involved in that sort of caper when you were going out?'

'It's all such a long time ago. Fifteen years have passed. He's probably changed.'

She'd avoided answering the question. Bella couldn't prove his hobby dated back that far, but the contents of his secret room meant he must have been at it for years.

She ran her finger round the rim of her hot chocolate and said casually, 'I wonder if anyone knows why he went to Raven Hall. He didn't tell you what he was planning, I suppose?'

Julia's hair was down over her eyes again. 'No. As I said, we hadn't spoken recently.'

Bella's gaze met John's and she let the look linger, so Julia couldn't miss it.

'What is it?' the academic asked.

'Sorry.' John spoke quietly. 'It's just that my mother said she saw you and Oliver at the Blue Boar, the night Oliver died.'

Julia went pale.

'It struck her because you took your drinks outside, and it was so cold.' Bella let the silence hang.

'I— Yes, it's true. I was with him then, but only for about ten minutes, so I wasn't really counting it as a proper meet-up. We'd bumped into each other on the high street by chance and we sat outside so I could smoke. He was heading indoors when we parted.'

'Actually,' Bella said, 'someone mentioned they saw you with Oliver in the Black Swan the night before too. The two meetings made us think you'd want to contribute to the memorial.'

Julia's grip tightened on her mug. 'No. They've got that wrong. It wasn't me. I'll have a think and put some memories together for you.'

Bella gave her a business card with her email address, her mind on what they'd heard. It was another layer to add on top of their knowledge of Julia. If she had a new man but her relationship with Oliver had rekindled, she could have been seeing him in secret. And she'd been keen on him years back too. Maybe she'd never got over him. If Oliver had wanted to end the relationship again, that could have played into events leading up to Sunday night. She could have invented the rumour to get him to the ruins. She'd been in the Black Swan the night it went round. Perhaps she'd given in to pent-up feelings that had built over many years. If Frank knew her, thanks to their shared interest in history, maybe he'd suspected she was guilty. Bella could imagine her killing him from fear rather than greed. She'd still have taken the treasure though, to avoid the police linking Frank's death to Oliver's hoard.

As they left the Steps, Carys took them to one side. 'I heard what Julia said about meeting Oliver at the Blue Boar. There's just one thing – she doesn't smoke.'

TWENTY-SEVEN

UNPICKING IT ALL AT THE BLUE BOAR

That evening, Tony Borley commandeered the Blue Room at the Blue Boar. Captain lay comfortably at his feet, next to the roaring fire. The snug was at the front of the pub, and Tony had somehow got the other clientele to disappear. It could have been by sitting too close to them or asking odd questions. He had many techniques. The way was now clear to catch up in private. John, Carys and Leo had joined them. Lucy was somewhere behind the scenes in Jeannie's private quarters, reading a book about molluscs.

Jeannie came in to see what was going on. 'What did you do to my customers?' she said, taking them all in with a glance, an accusing look in her eye.

Bella had been worried she'd notice. 'Have they left the pub?' That would make it worse. She felt responsible for Tony.

'No...' Jeannie was still frowning. 'They've gone to the back bar instead.'

Tony chuckled. 'I checked that room first, but here seemed better. I didn't want to disturb the old guy in the corner.'

'Oh!' A look of fury crossed Jeannie's face like a dark cloud.

'That'll be Harry Godfrey. He wasn't napping again, was he? He spends hours doing that. I'm thinking of getting him a dog basket.' She looked at them more sharply. 'Are you plotting something?'

'How can you say that, Mother dear?' Leo got up and put an arm around her shoulders, steering her towards the door.

'If you are, then I'm staying.' Jeannie folded her arms. 'And I'm getting Gareth too. He's finished cooking and you need the finest minds. But I won't have you taking the place of the police. I've already made that clear. It's too dangerous.'

She disappeared through the door.

'Your mother?' Tony said to John and Leo.

'That's right.'

Tony's grin broadened. 'Delighted to make her acquaintance.' Then he turned to Bella. 'Glad you've gathered a team around you. Always good to have plenty of ears to the ground.'

Jeannie dashed back into the room, followed by a reluctant-looking Gareth, still in his double-breasted chef's jacket. As they sat down, Bella performed the introductions. Jeannie and Gareth had brought their own drinks and Tony had a half of bitter. The rest of them were clutching glasses filled with Gareth's hot winter punch. Leo said it would be a much-needed stiffener after the upset of the day.

'So what have you heard, Tony?' Bella asked, bending to stroke Captain's head, loving the comforting feel of his fur. The dog turned and gave her a sleepy look.

'Frank Fellows's death looks like an accident, just as Barry Dixon told you.' He held up a hand before she could interrupt. 'The doc estimates he died between three and five in the morning. The TV was still on when the police arrived and there was a pad and pen by Mr Fellows' side. He'd been making notes on a history show.' Tony peered at his notebook. 'It aired on a specialist channel between three thirty and four thirty. His notes suggest he watched the first twenty minutes before he died.

'The floor's wooden with a rug over it, which was rucked up. The theory is he got up for some reason, stumbled and hit his temple on the mantelshelf.'

'Well, that immediately raises questions,' Bella said. 'Why leave his seat just twenty minutes into the programme?'

Tony shrugged annoyingly. 'It could have been anything, from going to the loo to fetching a reference book.'

It was a fair cop.

'Why was he up so late?' John looked horrified at the idea.

Jeannie shook her head. 'He was an insomniac. I caught him nodding off once. I've been concerned for him recently. He seemed anxious. He wouldn't confide so I suggested long walks and sticking to a routine, but I'm not sure he took any notice.'

'The link between him, Nan and Oliver Barton has to mean something,' Leo said, sitting forward on the leather button-back Chesterfield.

'What link? What do you all know that I don't?' Jeannie eyed them fiercely, so Bella filled her in, leaving out any hint of Nan's possible thieving, let alone violence. She had a strong feeling Jeannie would object.

'And you discovered all this by accident?'

'You know how it is in a small town.'

Jeannie frowned. 'Hmm. But I'd say Leo's right. The link *does* have to mean something.'

'You're not going to gang up on me, are you?' Tony said. 'Ask Bella. She knows. Coincidences do happen.'

'Dad used to say they were more common than you'd imagine.' Bella met Tony's eye. 'But you don't think this is just chance, do you? What about the cracked window?'

His eyes gleamed as he sipped his beer. 'Ah yes, the window. Another coincidence. Or is it? What do you make of it, Bella?'

'I wondered if the killer – if there is one – cracked it to give themselves an excuse to knock on Frank's door. They could have said they wanted to warn him. Perhaps they saw the back room was lit, but the front of the house was in darkness, so they risked giving the side window a tap. Maybe they knew Frank was an insomniac and likely to be up and about.'

From Tony's smile, Bella could tell he'd had the same thought. 'And if there's a killer, why would they do that, rather than simply going the whole hog with the window, climbing in and attacking the poor guy immediately?'

'It would have been noisier if they'd removed enough glass and wood to climb in,' Leo said eagerly.

'He's speaking from experience.' Carys sipped her winter warmer.

Leo grinned. 'I'll never forget my keys again. Especially not when you and Lucy are at your mum's. The houses along Frank's road have windows just like ours.'

Tony nodded. 'You can shift the old-fashioned sort with a knife. Less messy.'

Carys raised her eyes to heaven.

'But leaving that aside,' Tony continued, 'you're right. It would be way noisier. By talking their way in, any killer had more chance of making the death look like an accident. But there might be another reason.'

Bella almost didn't reply. He'd only say she was a 'chip off the old block' and she didn't want to encourage him. At last, she sighed. 'Because the killer—'

'If there is one.'

'*If there is one*, wanted to talk to Frank first. He or she needed to be invited in and treated as a friend.'

Tony nodded. 'That seems like a possibility to me.'

'If Nan Gifford sold Frank some treasure, maybe the killer guessed he might have hidden it and wanted to get it out of him before he bashed his head against the mantelpiece.'

Her godfather shrugged. 'Not so sure about that. They could probably have found it without too much searching unless it was one tiny piece.'

Jeannie turned on the rest of them. 'What do you mean, if Nan sold him some treasure?'

Bella took a deep breath and explained their more worrying thoughts about her employee.

'Nan Gifford would never have killed Oliver,' Jeannie said hotly.

'She wouldn't have had to, to sell his treasure. It could have been opportunistic. Nothing can bring Oliver back. She might have decided selling the artefacts was fairly harmless.' Though future generations would miss all those bits of history and it looked as though Nan might have started before Oliver died.

'Do you really imagine she'd have done that?' Jeannie said. 'I find it utterly incredible.'

'If it weren't for the money she's spending, and her visit to Frank Fellows in the small hours, I'd say the same,' John said. 'But you have to admit it looks odd.'

'The police haven't found any treasure at Mr Fellows' house,' Tony said. 'It's possible he was killed, and it was stolen, or that he never had any and died by accident. And everything in between.' He looked around the group. 'I don't want to get anyone overexcited, but the programme he was watching was about detectorists and treasure they've dug up.'

'He could have been comparing what he'd bought from Nan to the artefacts on TV.'

'The police put it down to interest after the prof's death and the news of his hoard.'

'Do you know what Frank was wearing?' Bella asked.

'Still in his daytime clothes, with a thick padded jacket to keep out the cold.'

'So if he was shoved into the mantelpiece—'

'It's possible he'd have escaped bruising from his attacker. Yes.'

'They'll talk to Nan Gifford?' Bella said, as Jeannie huffed. 'She might be innocent, but I'm sure she has vital information.'

'Already have, I gather. She says she was returning a scarf Mr Fellows had left here. She'd meant to do it earlier, but it had slipped her mind. She'd heard he slept badly, so she guessed he'd be awake. If he hadn't answered, she'd have put it through the letterbox.'

'Oh, come on!'

'I know. But there was a scarf just inside the front door on a chair – not on the coat stand where you'd expect it to be. She says,' he looked at his notepad again, 'that Mr Fellows invited her in for a cup of tea to thank her for her trouble.'

This was ridiculous! Dixon must have smelled a rat, surely? 'And the fact that she took her shopping trolley with her?'

'She says she always takes it after dark. If she's attacked, she can shove it at her assailant's ankles and it makes a noise, so anyone up to no good knows she's coming.' Tony looked at Bella from under his bushy eyebrows. 'That does tie in with official advice. It's more dangerous if a burglar or any other wrongdoer gets taken by surprise or cornered. Whereas if they know you're coming, they can run.'

Lucy had come into the room quietly as they talked. She was clutching an open book; Bella couldn't tell if she was listening.

Tony went on: 'Anyway, a neighbour spotted Nan return to her house around half one. They said they'd seen her out walking at night before. She says it helps clear her head.'

'And I suppose she always takes her trolley, just as she claimed?' Bella asked.

'She does, apparently.'

She sighed. Even if it *was* her habit, there was no way Nan had told the whole truth. 'She could have gone out again later, I suppose.'

'She could,' Tony said calmly. 'But you all agree she doesn't seem the sort to kill to bolster her fortunes.'

They nodded.

'Have they looked at Oliver's treasure now?'

Tony smiled. 'They have, despite the humdinger of a day they've had. Your sense of urgency must have had an effect. You won't be surprised to learn that they didn't find any of the prof's academic notes. Nor the gaps you noticed.'

'I expected it. It's a huge mess.' She should have told Dixon about the books earlier. But he was right, of course – it might have made him wonder, but he'd never have been able to recover them. 'Do they admit Nan must have been meddling now? Did Dixon ask her about the books I saw her drop into the Kite?'

Tony nodded. 'She says they were diaries, and that it was like a burial, because her uncle was fond of the river. She didn't want anyone reading his private thoughts, so she did it before she reported the hoard to the police.'

'Seriously? And he was happy with that?'

'He said he was minded not to take it further, under the circumstances.'

'Despite her disguising the gaps John and I saw?'

'It'd be your word against hers, but give him his due, he did ask her about the missing pieces. She says she was worried the prof had sold them. She didn't want people to remember him as greedy.'

'Good luck with that,' Leo said, 'considering his stash.'

'But it could be true all the same,' Jeannie said stoutly. 'Oliver could have sold them.'

'But if he did, then why?' Surely everyone could see it made no sense? 'He adored his artefacts – you can see that from the way he looked after them. And there's no sign he was short of money. Besides, if he disposed of them, then where has Nan's extra income come from?'

John told Jeannie about the MacBook Air. 'Cal didn't have it the Friday before Oliver died, Mum.'

They all looked at each other.

'I'm sorry, but Nan must be lying.' Bella felt like a vulture, her shoulders were so hunched. 'The police are refusing to see what's under their noses!'

As Jeannie protested, Leo patted Bella on the back. 'Take some deep breaths. We are where we are.'

She refrained from replying but Tony nodded and pointed a finger at Leo. 'What he says. It's a rum do, but we have to accept our limitations and move past them. If we want Dixon to act, we need to find more evidence.'

Jeannie was sitting up straight, her eyes fiery. 'We can't let this be. We need to find the real killer. And what does anyone mean by attacking poor Frank? He wouldn't hurt a fly. He was the physical embodiment of mild-mannered. A little proud perhaps, a little finickity.'

'Very exacting, our mother,' Leo said.

'Well, he was. But he was kind. He minded about people.'

Bella had thought the same. She turned to Jeannie. 'What about this story of him leaving a scarf here?'

'Perfectly possible. And Nan's the sort to take it back.'

'But after midnight?' Gareth said quietly. 'That I don't believe. Why not just leave it until today?'

Jeannie ruffled her metaphorical feathers but stayed silent this time.

'And why knock at all?' Bella added. 'The scarf and a note through the letter box would have done just as well. Does Dixon seriously believe all this?'

Tony shrugged. 'I'm sure he's got doubts, in his heart of hearts, but they're so busy. Every day is like having a metal bucket put over his head, then someone hitting it repeatedly with a hammer. The higher-ups will be strongly tempted to push the paperwork through if they're convinced the death isn't suspicious.'

'What do you think?' Bella turned to him.

'Me? I'd say it stinks to high heaven.'

TWENTY-EIGHT

NAN GIFFORD'S STORY

In Vintage Winter on Saturday morning, Bella and John updated their sheet of notes, adding the information they'd unearthed about Julia the day before.

Bella put her pen down and stood back. 'The take-home point is that she met Oliver twice shortly before his death and didn't want us to know about it.'

John stared at their notes. 'She could have been seeing him on the quiet because their relationship's secret from her new boyfriend, or because they were discussing Oliver's nighthawking.'

Bella nodded. 'Either way, she could have started the rumour to get him to the ruins.'

'The motive might be revenge because Oliver was rejecting her, or greed because she wanted some of his hoard.'

'Yes, though having talked to her, passion or fear feel more likely than greed as motives. And if he rejected her, it would explain the timing. If she killed for the treasure, then why now?'

The page of notes was getting crowded. They had Julia as the queen of hearts, who'd loved too much. That still seemed possible, though Bella wondered if it was more complicated than that. Then Alexis as the queen of spades, striving for immortality with her poetry, but the same objection remained. She hadn't known Oliver that well, as far as they were aware. And why on earth would he worry about her career?

It left Meg Jones as the enigma, with the question mark next to her name on the flyer, and Nan Gifford as the one who feared too much. Those both made more sense.

Bella went back to the front showroom. She wasn't convinced by any of it. She needed to keep tabs on Nan, Meg and Julia at the Sweet Agnes celebrations that evening. See what more she could find out.

Through the window, she spotted the woman from Back Lane who'd looked at the painted blanket chest. She was peering in again. Bella stood back so she wouldn't put her off. The woman took two paces towards the door, then bit her lip, turned and strode round the close towards the high street.

Bother.

John tapped her shoulder, making her jump. 'I've got Gareth on the phone. He wants to talk to you.'

'*I thought you should know that Jeannie's in a state.*' His quiet voice with its soft Welsh accent was calm and matter-of-fact. '*She heard Nan Gifford crying in one of the bedrooms. She's desperately upset. It could just be the shock of the latest death, but maybe it's something more. I've told Jeannie she should give her some space. She already tried to talk to her about Oliver and it didn't work. Between ourselves, I thought you might like to have a go instead. You could sneak in while I distract Jeannie with some menu planning.*'

Bella didn't need to think twice. 'Thank you. You're one in a million.' After she'd rung off, she explained the situation to John as she pulled on her coat. 'You'll be all right here?'

He put his head on one side. 'Need you ask?'

'It seemed polite to. I'll go and see what I can get out of Nan.' She might not be the killer, but Bella had a strong feeling

she'd sold Frank some treasure, which might have led to his
death. If she could prove it, Dixon would have to open a murder
investigation. How would he explain the lack of treasure in
Frank's house otherwise?

'You will pause long enough to come up with a plan, won't
you?' she heard John say, behind her. 'It'll be hard to claim you
were just passing if you have to go into one of the bedrooms to
find her.'

He had a point. The Blue Boar was just around the corner.
Walking helped with thinking, but she'd have to do the latter at
speed.

Bella crept into the inn, peering around for Jeannie, but
there was no sign of her. It looked as though Gareth had done
his stuff. Bill was serving on the front bar, but she managed to
sneak to the stairs without him spotting her.

She had a basic plan; she'd tell Nan she'd dropped in and
Jeannie had sent her upstairs to fetch something. It was the kind
of thing she'd do; she was good at employing passing labour.
'Your legs are younger than mine' was a favourite phrase.

Bella trotted up the stairs, clutching her full skirt so it didn't
rustle, her feet quiet on the thick carpet. It was essential to take
Nan by surprise. At the top, she turned left and right, listening,
hoping no one came past and struck up a conversation.

At last, a little way down the back corridor, she heard
muffled crying. She hoped to goodness it was Nan and not one
of the guests.

She knocked on the bedroom door and the crying stopped
instantly. It was half a minute before anyone answered. 'Who is
it?' The voice was Nan's, still thick with tears.

'Bella. Can I come in?' She turned the handle as she asked,
in case Nan said no. She trotted out her excuse for being
upstairs. 'I couldn't help hearing you cry. You sounded so deso-
late. Can I help?'

'No. No thank you.' Nan turned away from her, towards a

window with a cypress tree in view outside, coated in frost. 'It's just Oliver. It didn't sink in at first.'

Bella sat down on a button-backed velvet chair. 'I thought you might be upset about Frank Fellows's death.'

Nan caught her breath. 'It's very sad, of course. He was in here a lot. We passed the time of day.'

Bella thought of the trolley Nan had wheeled to his house the night before. Conversation wasn't the only thing that had passed between them. Nan had gone back to making the bed. Her cheeks were tinged pink. She looked just like one of Bella's sisters when they had something to hide. She probably wished Bella would leave.

Bella stayed put. 'I have a confession to make. I told the police I saw you visit Frank on Thursday night.'

Nan looked around at her, too surprised to hide her red-rimmed eyes. 'What were you doing there?'

Bella handed her the anonymous note she'd been sent, suggesting she follow Nan.

Nan's face puckered with worry as she read it and more tears spilled over. Whatever she'd been doing, Bella couldn't help feeling sorry for her. She looked so vulnerable.

'I— That's horrible. I don't know who would send that. But it was all perfectly innocent.'

'People can be very interfering sometimes. Perhaps someone let their imagination run wild and decided you were hiding something.'

She put a hand to her eyes. 'That's rubbish. I told the police, I was just returning Frank's scarf. I knew he'd be up. Everyone knows he suffers from insomnia. If his lights had been out, I'd have gone back home.'

'He must have appreciated it. Though I'm sure he'd have understood if you'd left it until morning.'

Nan pulled a tissue from her pocket. 'Of course he would. He was a nice man. But...'

She hesitated and Bella waited. Waiting had been her top method of getting the truth out of her sisters. It worked well when a dealer was trying to pull the wool over her eyes too.

'But?' she said at last.

'But it's claustrophobic, sometimes, just me and Cal.' Her hands twisted. 'I know he must feel it too. He likes to get out with his friends. And I— Well, my job and my lifestyle don't lend themselves to a social life. Sometimes, by the end of the day I'm wound up and itching to get away from the house. Cal's sixteen now. Old enough to stay in by himself. I left him a note saying I'd popped out and ran the errand because I wanted some space. Ten minutes outside and a job ticked off.'

Her words came across as heartfelt. Bella was sure she was describing genuine feelings, but she didn't believe it was the whole story. Not when combined with the hand wringing and the tinged cheeks.

'I thought your visit might have been to do with your uncle's nighthawking and the treasure he found. Just because you took your trolley with you. I wondered if you'd let Frank buy some.'

Nan went pale now. 'Never. I'd never have done that! You're speculating just like everyone else. Poring over the gossip in the papers. It's mean!'

'It is. I'm sorry, but I knew about the treasure before it went public, and that there were bits missing. It was a liberty, but John and I sneaked into Oliver's house after he died. John had a key so he could feed Smudge. He was worried about what Oliver might have been involved in after he gave him that coin.' She left out any mention of the playing cards. 'I thought I could set his mind at rest. Only then we discovered the artefacts.'

'So it was you,' Nan muttered. If anything, she sounded relieved. 'The key card wasn't in the desk any more. It took me hours to find it.'

'I'm sorry.'

Bella had thought she'd be angry, but her shoulders sagged. 'You told the police a lot.'

'I felt I had to.'

'What with your dad, I suppose you did. But my visit to Frank was nothing to do with the treasure. I always take my trolley with me when I walk at night. I used it once when a loose dog came at me. The owner was nowhere to be seen. I realised then that it was useful for more than just carrying things.'

Once again, she sounded honest. But that didn't mean the trolley had been empty on Thursday night. Bella couldn't see Nan killing Oliver for his house or the treasure, but his artefacts had to fit in somewhere. She wasn't getting the whole truth.

'Frank watched me and John as we left your house.'

'Really?' She looked down at her hands. 'That's odd. He must have been passing, I suppose.' Her watery eyes met Bella's. 'Was it you who saw me dump the notebooks in the Kite?'

Bella nodded. 'It was by chance, that time. After what John and I found in Oliver's house, it seemed too much of a coincidence that you'd be leaving his place in the dead of night with anything unrelated to the treasure. And we had noticed those missing pieces.'

Nan put her head in her hands. 'Oliver must have sold them. I made up a story about the notebooks when the police asked. I don't know if they believed me. I thought they might take the investigation further if they saw there were pieces missing. I've dealt with enough shame on behalf of other people. There was my husband... Well, never mind. But I already know what it's like to have the whole town talking about you, then go silent as you walk past. It's happening again, even though I've handed everything back. The gossipmongers believe I knew all about Oliver's habit when he was alive. That he might have been buying my silence by giving me bits of treasure.' She took a juddery breath. 'People look at me and nudge each other. They whisper.'

It sounded awful. 'I'm so sorry. So you noticed there were items missing and covered it up? You honestly think Oliver sold them?' She watched Nan closely. 'I'd have thought he'd be too passionate to let them go. Wouldn't he have given up his car if he'd run out of money? Saved on the repayments?' And he hadn't run short anyway, not if his wine collection was anything to go by.

Nan looked nervous. 'He must have. I wish he'd offloaded the lot, not left me to deal with it.'

Her last sentence was full of feeling, but Bella wasn't sure about the rest. 'It must have been awful to be faced with it. You knew about Oliver's nighthawking before he died, then?'

Nan looked out of the window at the wintry scene beyond. 'No. I only realised when I started going through his belongings and found the key card. I'd always wondered why part of his attic was walled off.'

It was perfectly possible, but she was looking away still, and twisting her wedding ring. Bella didn't believe her.

'So if you told the police you'd seen me at Frank's, and that I'd dumped notebooks into the river, why didn't you tell them about the anonymous note?'

'I thought it might be malicious. You've no idea who wrote it?'

She shook her head. She was pale.

Bella believed her. 'Perhaps we should tell them about it, now they know the rest.' Or Nan's version of it.

'Maybe,' Nan began. But as Bella put the printed letter back in its envelope, she gasped. Her eyes were fixed on Bella's name, written in block capitals on the front. Not enough to disguise the writing of someone she knew, Bella guessed.

It took a moment for her to speak. 'On second thoughts, don't tell the police. I'm sure whoever sent it just wants a reaction.' She blinked. Tears were welling and she couldn't stop them.

A new suspicion crept into Bella's head. Cal had seen his mother leave her cottage. How many times had he watched her from his bedroom window?

TWENTY-NINE

PLOTTING AND PLANNING

Bella managed to leave the inn without attracting attention and returned to St Giles's Close, crunching over the frosty grass outside the church.

As she neared the antiques centre, her phone went.

'Bella Winter.'

The caller was Robert Mead, one of the antiques dealers she'd contacted in Shrewsbury. At last, a lead on the precious items Sienna had spirited away from the Hearst House Museum.

'I can't get to you today,' she told him, trying not to sound too desperate, 'but I could come tomorrow.'

It was arranged.

Outside Vintage Winter, she noticed the change in the window immediately. And arranging stock was her domain, unless there was an immediate need to fill a gap. That could mean only one thing. Someone had bought the bronze lizard.

She went inside, shivering at the temperature change from freezing to warm.

'Someone bought my lizard, then?'

'I suppose it wasn't strictly speaking yours,' John said, his eye on a small wooden box he was polishing. 'And we are trying to sell stuff.'

'Who took it?'

'They paid, as a matter of fact. I made it clear they had to. It was someone from out of town. Notice anything else different?'

Bella stood back and realised. 'Oh my goodness. The woman from Back Lane came back for the blanket chest?'

'Yup.'

'That's amazing. Well done, John.'

He gave a small smile.

'You deserve tea. Well, you probably deserve champagne but that would be harder to manage.'

'Tea sounds good. And news. How did you get on with Nan Gifford?'

'Let me get the drinks and I'll fill you in.'

She set everything on a tray and opened a packet of chocolate biscuits she'd been saving for just such an occasion. 'You win employee of the month. What would I do without you?'

'What indeed?'

Bella sat on a stool and took up the tea which she'd served in a gilt-rimmed rococo set she'd bought in Shrewsbury. Perfect for people who believed teatime should be an occasion. She relayed everything Nan had said.

The lines on John's brow shifted subtly as she spoke. His eyes remained on the box.

'Do you think she was telling the truth?' he said at last, lifting his gaze for half a second.

'Frequently, yes. That's what makes it so confusing. But she's hiding something. It can't be coincidence that Frank Fellows was loitering when we left her place. Maybe he was the person who called her while we were there, and she told him about us. I think we made her nervous, and he's got a stake in whatever she's been up to. I'd say there's way more to her Thursday-night visit than she's letting on. I'd hoped she might crack. She must feel terrible if Frank was killed for treasure she sold him. He seemed like a kind soul, though buying stolen goods makes one wonder.'

'So you still think she gave in to temptation to make a limited amount of money and got caught up in something?' He was looking down, biting his lip as he performed a delicate operation.

'I can't see how else it fits. She stuck to Oliver having sold the missing pieces we spotted, but she wasn't convincing. She could have lied to protect Cal, if he was the thief, but she's the one making late-night visits, and spending money. I think she was lying when she said she didn't know about Oliver's habit until after his death. She wouldn't meet my eye.'

'And you really think it was Cal who sent you the anonymous letter?'

Bella visualised Nan's expression as she'd seen the writing on the envelope. 'I'm pretty sure. She looked crushed.'

'Why would he do that? To his own mum?'

'Anger at being kept in the dark? Jealousy that she was spending time elsewhere? I get the impression she might not have told him where she was going. My sisters were volatile at that age and it's like you said, Cal's had a difficult time. On top of that, it fits with the way he was when we visited. He implied Nan kept secrets, and drove the message home when she took that mysterious call. I'm trying to remember what he said. Something like: *Makes you wonder, doesn't it?* It was the same MO. Inviting us to think ill of Nan. Punishing her, I suspect.' Bella's second-oldest sibling had had a fine line in passive aggression as a teen and had weaponised it against Amanda. But Amanda had been nothing like Nan. It had been water off a duck's back. 'Jeannie said he was bad-mouthing Nan at the grocer's shop too. It sounds as though he's hitting out with whatever ammunition comes to hand.'

'Cal must have guessed you'd take the bait,' John said. 'He

was suspicious when we asked questions at their place. I have a nasty feeling he's worked out what we're up to.'

'I'm afraid you might be right.'

'So where does all this leave us?'

'Still without enough evidence to convince the police Frank Fellows's death was murder, but I'm not done yet. Tonight's the perfect time to make progress.'

It was Sweet Agnes's Eve. The townsfolk would meet at the Blue Boar before the torchlit procession to Agnes's Haven, the island in the centre of the River Kite. She was hoping for a good turnout, including Julia Sandford, Nan and Cal Gifford and Meg Jones. It was time to divide forces and get more information.

THIRTY

SWEET AGNES'S EVE

That night, Bella followed John into Jeannie's private sitting room at the Blue Boar, where they found Gareth, Leo, Carys, Lucy and Jeannie herself. Jeannie had brought in staff from outside Hope Eaton to run the inn that evening. She had no intention of missing out on the fun and was armed with a brimming glass of mulled wine. Bella saw Peter creep past, a book under his arm.

'Peter!' Jeannie was at the door.

'My darling. You carry on.'

She looked dramatically crestfallen.

'You're the lynchpin this evening, you know you are. You do it so well. And you'd never relax if we both abandoned the old fortress.' He patted the inn's wall.

She sighed. 'You're right.'

He kissed her on the cheek, with a look of nervous fondness, and went on his way.

'He's been with the accountants all afternoon,' Jeannie said.

He did all the ordering too. In fact, everything on the administrative side. He and Jeannie were chalk and cheese, but the partnership worked.

'Such a shame about Matt,' Jeannie said, shaking her head.

Leo shook his too.

Because he was absent? Or were they talking about something else? Bella was tempted to ask, but she didn't want to seem too interested.

An unfamiliar barman had furnished her with a hot chocolate and Baileys. It would be a good defence against the cold. The bars in the inn were thronging, as was the courtyard, bright in the winter night with its strings of lights. Jeannie's sitting room was the only place that offered some privacy.

'Thank heavens for some peace and quiet,' said Gareth.

Leo was hovering near him. 'It's a hard life, being a chef. Speaking of which, did you note down that recipe?'

Carys looked shocked. 'You've surely not got him to divulge his secrets?'

'Yes, but I've explained it's for personal use only,' Leo said hurriedly.

Gareth took a piece of paper from his pocket and Leo unfolded it eagerly the moment he'd handed it over. Bella could see the black squiggly writing, and then, as Leo held it up to the light, she saw the watermark.

Not what she'd expected, and enough to raise goosebumps.

'Gareth, why didn't you use the Blue Boar's paper?'

He frowned, his dark hairline drawing down. 'I didn't think Leo would demand the recipe on something with a crest.'

That seemed like a rash assumption. 'But that's the Alexandra Arms's notepaper.'

'Is it?' He tried to take it back, but Leo gripped it tightly.

'I haven't fought for this for nothing.'

'Desperately melodramatic,' said Carys, whipping it from his fingers and holding it up to the light. 'Bella's right. What's it doing here?'

Jeannie grabbed it now, went to the door and hailed a passing member of regular staff, her voice reverberating around the private quarters. 'Find out why we have another inn's paper, would you?'

While they waited, Bella and John updated everyone on the latest developments. There was still no reply on the notepaper when it was time to go. As they joined the procession half an hour later, everyone knew their allotted jobs. Bella was going to focus on Nan and Cal, in the hope of overhearing something that would confirm Nan had been taking treasure to Frank Fellows. That was crucial, because proving it ought to force the police to treat his death as suspicious.

Carys was going to look out for Julia and watch who she talked to. See if she made any move to quiz the history group or the Howards for information, which might betray anxiety. She'd promised to bring up Frank Fellows's death in conversation too, and watch her reaction. Bella had picked her especially for this. She and Julia had an existing relationship, and Carys was used to spotting tells, albeit with six-year-olds. Bella knew how sharp teachers were. Leo was going to help Carys – Bella didn't think she could stop him.

John, much to his chagrin, was to speak to Meg Jones again. Just like Carys, he'd discuss Frank's death and observe. Bella had drummed it into him that it was a natural topic of conversation. Meg's mysterious dislike of Oliver and the way she kept popping up was enough to keep her on the suspect list. She was well known around town. If Frank was familiar with her and had discovered something that put her in the frame, she could have killed him in desperation. Bella had liked her. She found it hard to imagine, but she couldn't rule it out.

Jeannie and Gareth had promised to keep tabs on members of the history group, whom they saw regularly at the Blue Boar, and listen for gossip.

The townsfolk carried torches and lanterns along the high street, then down one of the town's many flights of steps towards St Luke's Bridge. Jeannie had made her way to the front ('A natural born leader,' said Leo), but Bella hung back with John and Gareth. She'd done that when she'd come with her dad. It meant you were high up on the hill as the procession stretched out in front of you, a river of light, flowing down into the valley towards the intense midnight darkness of the Kite.

As she neared the bottom of the steps, the first Hope Eatoners had reached the island, spreading out between the trees. Tears were pricking her eyes, memories of her childhood and the beauty of the scene entwining.

'It gets me that way too.' Gareth's gaze was on the crowds. Maybe he'd caught her sigh. She thought about replying but she was still choked up and it didn't matter. He understood.

At last, it was Bella's turn to cross the narrow bridge onto Agnes's Haven with John and Gareth just behind her. She felt it flex as they tramped over. Visions filled her head: the people of the settlement all those centuries ago, crossing onto the island to ask for Agnes's help: nervous, hopeful, full of awe. Bella might have joked with Rupert Edgar about it, and have got to hate the candles, but she wouldn't miss this occasion. Especially not as she lived here. She wondered at Rupert and Matt, choosing to absent themselves.

As they reached the end of the bridge, edging their way through a bottleneck, she took a deep breath. It was time to get busy. She turned to John.

'Ready to split up and search for clues?'

'Your Scooby Doo methodology sounds less than professional. And no, not really. Good luck.'

He and Gareth headed towards the open end of the island and Bella went for the trees. If Cal wanted to escape his mum on Sweet Agnes's Eve he'd probably make for cover, so she would too. He seemed more likely to talk unguardedly than his mum and he'd clearly been keeping a close eye on her. If he was catching up with friends, the outlandish death of a family member less than a week earlier would be a hot topic. Eavesdropping could give Bella the leverage she needed to push Nan into being more honest.

Thoughts of the anonymous note she'd received filled her mind. She hoped Cal knew something useful about his mum, and wasn't only acting up to punish her for having a personal life. If the note he'd written stemmed from meanness rather than hurt, she wondered if he'd also be mean enough to kill his uncle for a better standard of living. Him organising the rumour still felt like a stretch, though. She pondered other options. Maybe he was in contact with one of his dad's dodgy cronies. Someone who'd spotted an opportunity when Cal talked about his uncle. Cal could have tipped them off about Nan's visit to Frank. Whereupon they'd gone in, killed, then helped themselves. If so, Cal would be way out of his depth.

But none of that fitted if her and Tony's idea about the cracked window was correct. That rested on the killer being someone Frank knew and trusted, who'd used the window as an excuse to knock on his door.

She put the thoughts to one side and focused on the shadows. She'd been right about teenagers and the woods. Unfortunately, it wasn't just Cal; there were loads of them. As she approached the trees she could hear giggling, and see dark shapes in the moonlight.

The saving grace was her black calf-length coat, dark hair and black hat. She stuck her lantern in the ground next to several others, abandoned by the teenagers. After that, she walked beyond the trees. She kept close to the edge of the wood, gathering her coat around her so it didn't catch on a hawthorn. Then at last she slipped amongst the trees, protected from sight by the trunks of willow, alder and holm oak. Luckily, the teens made a fair amount of noise. Bella moved from place to place, keeping an eye out for Oliver's great-nephew.

At last, she spotted two lads on the town side of the island, leaning against a tree. She was sure the nearest one was Cal.

She crept closer and took out her phone, so an onlooker might think she was absorbed, not eavesdropping.

'... it's weird that she's not talking about it. My mum's been going on about it all week.'

Cal shrugged. 'She's sorting out the funeral but if I ask any questions, she gets cross. Don't reckon she was that fond of him. I wasn't either. He came on all high and mighty. Always trying to teach me stuff. He was an old fraud.'

'Don't mince your words, man. He's only dead after all.'

'Doesn't make any difference. He didn't trust us. I mean, I could see it with Mum. She's been weird. Especially the last couple of months. She's always asking me where I'm going, but she clams up when I ask her.'

'Sounds bad. But your uncle didn't trust you, either?'

Cal shook his head. 'Wouldn't even let me feed his cat. Got some stranger to do it.'

'No wonder you thought he'd got something to hide.'

The shrug again. Bella hated shrugs.

'And I was right, wasn't I?'

Bella saw the friend grin now, a glint in the shadows. 'You knew, didn't you? Before he died? Bet you did. You were always dropping hints. Bet you wanted to get in there on your own and take stuff. But you couldn't manage it. He'd locked up good and proper. Bet you never got in there.'

'Oh, didn't I? You don't know—'

But at that moment Nan Gifford appeared, weaving through the trees. Bella wondered how much she'd heard. 'There you are! Come and talk to Miss Turner.'

Cal swore.

'Callum!'

'Well, who wants to talk to their teacher on Sweet Agnes's Eve?' He shoved his hands into his pockets and stormed off through the trees towards the end of the island.

His friend looked at Nan, shrugged (naturally) and wandered off in the opposite direction.

Bella's gaze followed Cal's mother. Her voice had been raw. It sounded as though she was fighting tears again.

Bella followed, wondering what was afoot, creeping carefully between the trees. If she could hear Nan speak to Cal she might get what she needed. If she'd overheard his conversation, she'd be even more worried about the rumours circulating. But when Bella caught up with the pair they weren't talking. Cal was chucking the largest stones he could find into the Kite. Hurling them, making the water splash up violently. And Nan was watching him, tears streaming down her cheeks.

After a moment, Cal said, 'Why'd you have to go and tell the cops about Oliver's treasure? We could have been set for life.'

Nan gulped. 'I was always going to confess. How can you possibly imagine I'd do otherwise? And you'd have forced my hand anyway, with your "hints" and your boasting. Now I've got the entire town pointing fingers at me, saying I must have known. How do you think that makes me feel? Do you have any idea of how hard life's been?'

Her voice had risen in volume and pitch, but there was no one close enough to hear except Bella and Cal.

For a second Cal looked up, startled, a look of uncertainty in his eyes. Bella guessed Nan didn't often share her feelings. But then the shutters came down again. 'Well, we both know you've been getting money from somewhere. And I knew Oliver better than the people in town. *I* know he wouldn't have given you any of his treasure.'

THIRTY-ONE

CLUES ON AGNES'S HAVEN

Bella walked back to the main clearing. She had her proof that Cal had known about the treasure. And it was as she'd thought before: if he'd been hinting about it to his friends he was probably innocent of killing for it. He might speak without thinking, but she guessed he had some sense of self-preservation. It didn't prove he hadn't stolen some, though. He could have accused his mother of that to convince her *he* hadn't taken any. Bella felt it should be him, but it was no good. It was Nan who'd come into money.

Most unsatisfactory. And Bella hadn't got the material she needed to push Nan into confessing the truth about her visit to Frank Fellows either. She kicked a stone to relieve her frustration, then checked she hadn't scuffed her boot.

She found Carys and Lucy eating toasted marshmallows.

'Would you like some?' Lucy speared her one and they moved closer to the fire, sparks shooting up, logs crackling.

'Thanks.' She glanced at Carys. 'Any luck with Julia?'

'She didn't come up in bumps when I mentioned Frank Fellows. Just said the standard things about how sad it was. She'd met him a couple of times at history talks, apparently.

Oliver introduced him. She's spent some time talking to the history group though. Jeannie and Gareth listened in. They caught her asking if anyone knew Oliver had been interested in the ruins.'

That might mean something. Bella suspected Oliver's interest hadn't come as a surprise to Julia. She'd met him two nights running before his death, including in the pub where the rumour had started. So maybe she was gauging what the history group knew.

'We've been chatting to Lucy's form teacher since we left Julia,' Carys said, keeping her voice low.

'Who also happens to be Cal's,' Lucy added, in an undertone.

'What do you think of him?' Bella asked, after flicking a glance over her shoulder.

'A pain. But I only see him for ten minutes in registration. Miss Turner knows more. She collates our reports.'

'Nan Gifford was talking with her just before us, so we heard more than we might have.' Carys bit into her marshmallow. 'Poor Nan. I've heard four people muckraking about Oliver's treasure and what she might have known. They hardly bothered to lower their voices. As for Miss Turner, I think she's got reservations about Cal. "Independently minded" translates as "stroppy". I use euphemisms in social situations too. Nan dashed off after they'd spoken. Miss Turner said how protective she is.'

It fitted with Bella's impression. It made her habit of sneaking out at night all the odder. Bella believed in her need to get out of the house, but something must have persuaded her to do it in the small hours.

John appeared at her side. 'I've talked to Meg.' He gave a small shudder at the memory. 'I could hear myself putting on my telephone voice. It felt so unnatural. I'm sure she'll have noticed.'

'Yes, yes, but what did she say?'

'She cried over Frank Fellows. She'd met him a few times at the history group.'

'She's clearly emotionally involved, then.'

'It could be remorse.' Leo had appeared in time to hear their exchange.

'Can you honestly see her ramming his head into a mantelpiece?' John asked.

Bella could see his point. 'Only if she was desperate. If Frank somehow knew she was guilty. And just possibly if she was badly in need of money and knew Frank had a houseful of treasure. But that seems less likely.'

'A *lot* less likely,' John said.

Gareth joined them. 'Most of the history society are standing over there, tucking into the mulled wine. I've listened in but there's been nothing soul-shaking. I thought you might like to join them.'

'You thought right.' Bella strolled over and introduced herself, though she already knew Harvey Howard, of course. Meg Jones wasn't with them.

'I can't believe Frank's gone as well,' said a man with an extravagant moustache.

Harvey closed his eyes. 'It's a crying shame.'

'You never know what's coming next.'

'I'd heard he was unhappy,' Harvey replied. 'I'd wondered if there was something we could do but I never got round to asking. And now it's too late. I feel terrible.'

'I think he was lonely,' a woman with cropped grey hair said, 'but he loved our group. Let's not forget that. He wrote so many notes at the meetings. And investigated further in his own time. I saw him after the one about nighthawks, up by the standing stones, pacing about, staring at the ground.'

'Yes, that's true.' The man with the moustache patted Harvey on the arm. 'He was a genuine enthusiast. We all should have done more, but it's good that he was in the group.'

When the members went their separate ways, John turned to Bella.

'Mum listened to the lecture about nighthawking. She said the speaker talked about illicit detectorists targeting scheduled monuments like the stone circle.'

'And the Raven Hall ruins.'

'Exactly.'

'Maybe Frank was pacing around, imagining the possibilities.'

'He could have been interested like Oliver was, for the wonder of owning something like that. And it's the same as it was for Nan. It might have seemed like a victimless crime.'

As Bella scanned the sea of faces, lit by flickering firelight, she saw Julia Sandford. She noticed her gloves. This season's; she'd seen and coveted them in the window of Birdwell's on the high street. Anyone might need new ones of course, but mid-season? They looked pristine. Was there any chance she'd bought them after losing a glove outside the ruins on Sunday?

More interestingly still, she was chatting with Meg Jones. Julia started as she spotted Bella, but then nodded and smiled rather stiffly. As she left Meg, Bella heard Julia say, 'See you at work.'

Her eyes met John's. 'What? Meg works at Acton Thorpe University? I'm going to ask Julia about it. You ask Meg.'

She saw John's chest rise and fall. 'I can't. I've already talked to her once.'

'You can. Truly. You're the soul of tact.'

She turned to follow Julia. 'Hello again. Sorry, I just spotted you talking to Meg Jones. A friend was saying they were interested in hiring her, but I guess if she works at Raven House and Acton Thorpe she probably won't have time.'

Julia frowned, pushing her long hair out of her eyes as the

wind caught it. 'You could ask her. She only works a couple of days a week at the university I think.'

'Ah. Though that's still quite a lot if she's there all day.'

Julia put her head on one side. 'I think she just works mornings. I've never seen her there after lunch. She does the bathrooms and common ways, so we bump into each other.'

'Oh, it might work then. Thanks.'

A minute later she was joined by John. 'She must know I'm up to something now. I asked where she was working on the back of wanting to know how many free slots she has. She says she didn't mention her shifts at the university because it's ad hoc, early in the morning – nothing where she and Oliver might overlap.'

'Interesting, and rather creative, because it's not what Julia said.'

By half past eleven, they were back in Jeannie's private sitting room, burning down a Sweet Agnes candle. Bella had found it exciting and magical as a child, sitting up late with her father. Now, she wouldn't care if she never saw another.

Traditions were weird. They were lovely, but hard when things changed. People went. Time moved on.

'So, where are we at?' Leo asked.

'Cal and his friend were talking about Cal breaking into his great-uncle's house. Cal hinted he'd got in, but it could have been bravado. His friend was goading him. And he challenged Nan about where she'd got her money from, as though he thought Oliver's treasure was the source. That fits with Nan being the thief, but I'll bet Cal would have taken some too, if he'd had the chance. I keep remembering the look in his eye when he saw your coin, John. I think he wanted it very badly.'

John frowned. 'I suspect you're right.'

'And Julia Sandford has new gloves,' Bella went on.

'Entirely circumstantial, but maybe she lost one of her old ones. And she asked if any of the history group knew Oliver was interested in the Raven Hall ruins. It's probably nothing, but if she and Oliver had discussed them together, she might have wondered if Oliver had mentioned her interest to anyone. There's no way he'd have told the society he was planning to dig there, but he could have asked them what they knew of the site.'

'The history society were discussing how fascinated Frank was with nighthawking,' John put in. 'As for Meg Jones, she's been cagey about working at Acton Thorpe University.'

'But I doubt she's guilty,' Jeannie put in. 'Her mother was such a nice woman.'

Leo grinned.

'If Meg and Oliver were lovers, she could be hushing it up,' Bella said. 'There's a fair age gap between them, but not much more than between him and Julia. Maybe Meg's secrecy has a bog-standard explanation, if she's cheating on a boyfriend.' It overlapped with her thoughts on Julia. 'Meg was widowed last year but Alexis Howard mentioned she's dating their gardener. But if Meg and Oliver had a relationship, I'd guess it went sour. Her mood shot downhill when we first asked about him.'

'The threatening note to Oliver was on Alexandra Arms paper,' John added. 'And Meg's cousin works there. That makes her seem suspicious.'

'Oh!' Jeannie tapped her forehead. 'I meant to say. Linda found someone who knew about the headed paper Gareth used. Apparently, a whole boxful of the stuff was delivered here by accident. Someone offered to return it, but the company said it wasn't worth the cost and we could use it as scrap.'

'So the sender could be anyone with access to paper here or at the Alexandra Arms,' Bella said. It didn't rule Meg out, but Nan Gifford was in the frame too.

THIRTY-TWO

THE PLOT THICKENS

On Sunday morning, before the shop was due to open, Bella drove Thomasina to Shrewsbury to keep her appointment with Robert Mead.

She couldn't resist detouring past her childhood home. She, Amanda and her dad had lived in the lower floor of a Georgian townhouse until she was six. St Mary's opposite had stopped being a parish church when she was three years old, but she was convinced she could remember hearing the bells. Her father had joked that her mother used to complain about them when they rang, and then at the lack of them when they stopped.

Bella found the building. It was much smarter now, the sash window frames painted cream, the door a glossy navy blue. The tarnished knocker she remembered, in the shape of an owl, was absent – replaced by a too-shiny lion's head.

It didn't do to look back.

Ten minutes later she'd parked on a side road and walked through to Fish Street, where she found Robert Mead's place.

He was around ten years her senior, with a friendly smile and twinkling brown eyes.

They chatted about business, and Bella's Shrewsbury roots. He was easy to talk to.

'So,' he said at last, 'you're interested in the items from the Hearst House Museum. I bought them from the new owner last week. It's sad that the old lady's dead.'

'Very.' Bella injected the word with plenty of feeling.

He gave her a meaningful look. 'It was... interesting to meet her niece. A different sort entirely, I felt.'

Bella nodded. 'You used to visit the museum?'

'At least once a year. And old Mrs Hearst bought the odd item from me for her collection, though most of her treasures were donated by the locals.'

'My colleague used to work there. He said everyone loved her. She was like a universal grandmother.'

Mead grinned. 'Would your colleague be John Jenks?'

'That's him.' Bella hadn't told John about her errand. He'd only tell her that it didn't matter, when it most certainly did. She explained the background to Mead.

'So I'm afraid Sienna's not my number one fan,' she finished. 'I wanted to buy the items back for John. He's so fond of them.'

'He should definitely have them. I'd love to give you them cut price but I'm afraid Sienna drove a hard bargain. I can only manage the standard discount.'

'That's still brilliant.' It was so good of him not to take advantage.

Robert Mead told Bella the price for the candlesticks and the medicine cabinet. Slightly breath-taking, but infinitely worth it.

He wrapped them. 'I almost disliked Ms Hearst enough to refuse them, but they're such beautiful pieces. It'll give me pleasure to know they've gone to John. He's as nice as the old lady.'

He was right.

'By the way,' Bella said as she settled up, 'you haven't heard of any iffy goods changing hands here in Shrewsbury, have you? Things that might be undeclared treasure trove?'

His brow furrowed. 'No. What makes you ask?'

'Just a rumour I heard. I've been keeping an eye out.'

'Thanks for the tip. I'll put the word around. Don't be a stranger.'

On her way home, she passed a gleaming 1970s Jaguar E-Type convertible. It was Tyler Smith at the wheel, the woman she'd seen previously in the passenger seat.

He really was taking the mick. She wondered if she should tell Harvey Howard, but she baulked at the idea of losing Tyler his job. He'd seemed very young for his age when they'd dropped in. All the same, the salesroom was meant to be open on Sundays. She shook her head. Harvey was bound to notice himself, sooner or later.

As Bella walked through the rear entrance of the Antiques Centre, one of her fellow shop owners wished her a happy Sweet Agnes. The day of the festival was always a lot quieter than the eve.

She was on her own on Sundays and would be for a while. She had to build up the business and until then, she'd be the anchor for the shop. If she had an auction or fair to attend, John was good enough to swap days. She didn't want to risk closing when visitors came to town. They shut on Mondays instead.

Currently, she was glad to be on her own. She was dying to unpack the items from Robert Mead and work out where to put them so that John would see them when he returned on Tuesday.

Inside, in the warm, she put the coffee on, then approached the unboxing, taking the two pieces from their shredded paper nests and putting them on the table. She visualised the office. She could put them on the shelves, in amongst the stationery and bits of stock waiting for repair. Then she'd take John in there and at some point he'd look up and notice—

The shop bell jangled, making her jump.

It was a woman with curly chestnut hair and big teardrop earrings. Bella knew her by sight. A Hope Eaton local.

She bustled over to the Sweet Agnes candles. 'Are these on special offer now?'

Bella hadn't had the chance to mark their price down yet. 'Yes. Thirty pence each.'

The woman smiled and took six. She couldn't possibly want that many for herself. Maybe she'd distribute them around her neighbours and the meagre takings would drop further next year.

Bella pasted on a smile as she put the purchase into the till.

The shop kept her busy, but half her mind was always on her plans for that afternoon. Vintage Winter closed early on Sundays, and she was intending to mix business with pleasure afterwards. A health-giving walk in the bracing winter air would allow her to deliver more leaflets and follow up on a hunch she'd had.

It was quiet after three and Bella prepared to leave the shop the moment she'd closed, exchanging her shoes for her calf-length lace-up boots. There was a touch of the Victorian about them but they still went perfectly with her coat. At one minute past four, she was locking up, armed with a bag stuffed with Vintage Winter leaflets, bound for Oliver Barton's road. She had questions she wanted answering on Old Percy's Lane.

It was dark by the time she got there. Sunday was a good day to choose. Many of the cottages that had looked unoccupied when she and John visited Oliver's house were cheerfully lit now: a rosy glow behind red curtains here, views into a front room with an open fire there. She peered at the rows of books, a

TV flickering and a cat curled up on a sofa. Everything told a story, just like the pieces she sold.

Bella paused. She'd want to leaflet the whole road, of course, but a targeted approach made sense initially. Tony's words were in her head, echoed by her father's long ago. If you wanted to catch a crook, you had to act fast. The police weren't paying attention; she needed to move quickly in their stead.

She knocked on the door of Oliver's immediate next-door neighbour to the left.

The woman who answered had a baby on her hip. In the background, Bella could hear the sound of at least two more children.

'I'm sorry.' She smiled and raised an eyebrow. 'Possibly not a good time.'

The woman jiggled the baby, who looked ready to start grizzling.

But Bella had anticipated that sort of situation. And no one wanted to keep their door open on a night like this. She had a two-sentence pitch and an advantage: everyone would be relieved she wasn't selling door-to-door.

As she talked, she caught the baby's eye and started to make one of her leaflets into a fan. Unexpected activity had often worked to distract Jemima, Suki and Thea when they were small. Bella could see it was distracting the mother too, but it couldn't be helped.

'So, it's lovely to meet you,' she added. 'As a new neighbour as much as anything else. And if we can help you find things that you or your friends will love then that will be my pleasure. Have you been here long? I'm still finding my feet.'

The baby had quietened, and the woman looked less stressed. 'Seven years now. It's a friendly place. You'll soon settle in.'

Bella nodded. 'I'm sure you're right. Before I go, on a much more personal level, you haven't had a leaflet from someone called Meg Jones, have you? I got one the other day, advertising her Busy Bee cleaning service. Very eye-catching: red, with bees doing household chores. Only I'm after a cleaner and I wondered if you'd heard of her and if she's any good.'

The woman's attention was back with her. 'No, I haven't. But I'm after one as well.' She gave a slightly ragged grin in the baby's direction. 'I work full-time and I've got three under five, with a childminder who comes in. Someone to help with the chaos would be great. Would you let me know what she's like if you try her?'

Bella agreed and they said goodbye.

Interesting. She moved beyond Oliver's place to his other immediate neighbour. The door was answered by a middle-aged man in an apron, covered with more than the usual amount of flour.

'I'm sorry. Bad time?' Once again, Bella delivered her two-sentence pitch, along with her new-neighbour introduction and popped her leaflet on the man's hall table. It wouldn't look great, covered in flour.

'If you've got anything you'd like to sell, please feel free to pop in too.' The table was delightful. Bella tried not to look covetous.

She repeated her enquiry about Meg Jones and left two minutes later, feeling thoughtful.

THIRTY-THREE

AN UNEXPECTED LINK

Bella was going to be just as targeted as Meg Jones had been. Rather than leafleting the rest of Old Percy's Lane, she made a note to revisit it later and headed up Raven Climb instead, the steep lane that led out of the valley towards Raven Edge and the houses closest to the ruins.

As she walked up the deserted path that ran next to the lane, high banks of sandstone rock to her left and right, she called John.

'Sorry to bother you on your day off. It's not work.' She explained what she'd found by visiting Oliver's neighbours.

'*Meg Jones targeted him?*'

'It's hard to imagine otherwise. As soon as we found out she worked at Acton Thorpe – and that she was lying about how much she saw of the academics – it made me wonder. One neighbour might have forgotten her leaflet, but I doubt both would have. The design was memorable. I'd say she zoned in on him for a reason. At first, I wondered if they'd had an affair, but that doesn't fit with the way she leafleted him, and only him, like that. What was she up to?'

Meg hadn't liked Oliver, but it appeared she'd tried to get

close to him all the same. Considering his death, that was worrying.

'*Gareth's got the evening off. We were about to play chess. Maybe we can play guess Meg Jones's secret instead. I'll call you if I think of anything.*'

'Thanks.'

The houses on Raven Edge were different from those in the town. Larger, detached, and with porches that meant they could close an inner door and chat without letting the cold air in.

Handy.

Bella kept to her speedy pitch when handing over the leaflets, but then moved on to her new-neighbour status, asking questions about the best shops, the market, book groups and the church. She picked her topic according to her impressions of the householder. People were happy to talk.

'I've been here six months already,' Bella said to a woman who'd come to the door of a double-fronted Victorian villa. 'But I've been so busy at the shop that I haven't got involved in town life yet. I went to Alexis Howard's poetry recital on Thursday, though. And they very kindly put me up last Sunday too, after a boiler disaster. I was the one who discovered poor Oliver Barton's body.'

The woman put a hand to her mouth. 'Oh dear, that must have been awful.'

'It's been haunting me, rather. Such a horrible thing to happen. And so odd, the way he was behaving.'

'Well, I know.' The woman put Bella's leaflet in her pocket and folded her arms. 'Of course, it all makes sense now. I was astounded when the paper reported his hoard. You never know, do you? And it's been a week of shocking news with the other man who was found dead too.'

'Very sad. Did you know him?'

'By sight. I'd seen him around here, in fact.' She leaned forward. 'Not to speak ill of the dead, but he was a bit of a nosy parker. He'd peer at the Raven Hall ruins. All very well, but the house is only just beyond. You can't see much at that distance, but it still seemed intrusive.'

'Goodness.' Bella nodded, as though this was nothing more than idle gossip. 'If he was around at the right time, he might have seen Professor Barton's accident.'

'He could have. But he'd have told someone I suppose. I didn't see him on Sunday. He's up and down though, patrolling the town. The newspaper said he was an insomniac. Perhaps that's why. He's been up here on and off for at least the last year.'

Bella had hoped she might find someone who'd seen something, but she hadn't expected this. A direct link between Frank Fellows and the place where Oliver had died.

She paused at the gateway to the house she'd just left, thinking. Different ideas pooled in her head. The possibility that Nan Gifford had sold treasure to Frank. The chance that Frank had seen something the night Oliver died. The thought that Cal might have got into his great-uncle's place. Found the treasure maybe. Taken some too.

It fitted with Cal's fury at Nan for telling the police. From what he'd said, he'd obviously thought it would be quite legitimate to carry on selling off the hoard to fund a nice new life. If he realised Nan was selling a subset of the artefacts, he'd regard it as the height of hypocrisy. It might explain the note he'd written to Bella. Or maybe Frank had killed Oliver and then been killed. But why would he? And having met him, it was very hard to imagine.

Bella trailed around the other houses dotted about Raven Edge until it got close to suppertime and she knew she'd no longer be welcomed.

By the time she walked back into the valley, she'd been

invited to join (and give a talk at) the local WI, as well as being plied with information on the flower club, the Hope Eaton Society, bell ringers, church choir and much more besides. Oliver's neighbour had been right. The locals were friendly. Mostly.

The image of the man who'd shouted at her to go away from an upper-floor window flashed in her mind.

But it was people's comments on the two deaths that filled her head as she made her way towards St Luke's Bridge.

She walked midway and paused to watch the thickly moving water below, so dark in the lamplight. Mesmeric.

Several people she'd spoken to had known or recognised Frank Fellows.

'A real busybody.'

'A nice old gentleman.'

'A neighbourhood-watch type.'

And then she'd struck gold. Though she was uncertain it meant anything. 'Yes, I did see him on Sunday. But only from behind. He was bustling off down the hill towards low town as I came home from book club. It must have been latish. Half ten, quarter to eleven? I normally say hello, but he was hurrying.'

Too early to have witnessed the murder. But surely his death, combined with his presence on Raven Edge the night Oliver was killed, couldn't be a coincidence. Perhaps he wasn't killed for treasure after all, but because he'd seen something. Either way, the murderer would have removed any artefacts. Because they wanted them, or to stop the police making the link with Oliver.

Bella had also spoken to one person who'd seen a woman with long hair that evening. Julia Sandford? Nan Gifford? Or Meg Jones? It would fit any of them. But Julia Sandford had the new gloves, and she'd been the one who met with Oliver on Sunday evening...

THIRTY-FOUR

A MIRROR AND A PLAN

Bella was in the bathroom well before dawn on Monday morning when she heard Matt's flat door close. She glanced at her watch. Quarter to five. What was he up to this time? Or was it a girlfriend leaving early?

It was none of her business, of course. She had no excuse to sidle through to her living room, leaving the light off, and peer from behind the curtains.

It had been Matt. He was heading up the river, towards Boatman's Walk and St Giles's Steps. Her feet felt chilly. What was she doing, standing in the cold? As she crossed the hall, returning to her bedroom, she heard a yowl outside her front door.

Cuthbert. *Honestly.*

She opened up, eyes still half closed. 'All right. You can come in. But only if you keep quiet. My alarm's not set for hours yet.'

Although Bella had decided to close Vintage Winter on Mondays, mirroring the other outlets in the centre, she spent

most of them at the shop unless she was due at a sale. She
thought of the previous week, when she'd discovered Oliver's
body. How shocking it had seemed then, and what an immov-
able part of reality it was now.

Today, Bella wanted to work on certificates to go with some
of the items that were still in the office. Where possible, she
included not just their provenance, but the more personal back-
story that went with them.

Before she started, she went to the office and added the
latest information about the key players to the drawing board,
from Frank Fellows's presence on Raven Edge on Sunday night
and his neighbourhood watch-like activities, to Julia's new
gloves and Meg's targeted leafleting.

She was all the more convinced she'd allocated the Queen
of Diamonds – the enigma – correctly. She doubted Oliver had
ever planned to hire Meg Jones as a cleaner. He had far too
many secrets to let an outsider in. So the question mark on
Meg's leaflet meant she'd puzzled him.

She could still imagine Nan being spades too, full of fear.
She'd shied away from her and John when they'd showed her
Oliver's coin. She already had one family member in prison,
and Oliver, imperfect though he was, was their only familial
support. She might have dreaded him being caught and prosecuted. And of course, her fear would have intensified if she'd
stolen from him. She'd never have killed to hide that, though. It
wasn't as though Oliver could have reported her for it.

Bella looked at the last two cards, hearts and clubs. The
woman who loved too much and the one who'd wanted immortality. Julia had to be a strong candidate for the former. Her feelings for Oliver dated back years. But what about immortality?
Had he really meant Alexis? She still couldn't imagine why her
passion for poetry would worry him. It made no sense.

What to do next? That was the question. Julia Sandford
was a top priority. It would be good to talk to her again. If she

was guilty, Bella persistently popping up might make her nervous enough to let something slip. Catching her at the university could be best, if Bella could swing it.

She wondered how to set the visit up. Carys might help. Bella texted to ask. After that, she sat at her laptop at the refectory table so that she could peer out of the window. On previous Mondays, she'd opened the door to anyone who seemed interested and offered them a private viewing. It had worked well, that feeling of exclusivity. She'd sold several items.

Her plan that day was the same. The first nibble on the line was a young woman with a pushchair who spent some time looking at the window display. When she'd been there for five minutes, Bella opened the door a crack.

'We're not officially open, but if you'd like a closer look, I'd be delighted to show you.'

The woman blushed and smiled. 'I'll come back tomorrow. I'll be passing again.'

Bella nodded and gave her a wave as she trundled the buggy towards the high street.

It was enough. A friendly interaction. No pressure.

Bella wrote up details of a Poole Pottery deco vase, green and teal with leaf patterns. They had a nice history for this one. It had been given as a wedding present in 1930 to the grandmother of the seller. She'd taken it with her to Italy, where she and her husband had lived in Verona and then on to Bloomsbury in London. Their marriage had lasted seventy years until the grandmother died at ninety-five. Bella added snippets of information about the pottery, and events in 1930 and in 1995, where that bit of the vase's story ended. She then added the vase's move to the granddaughter in Hope Eaton.

Her attention was dragged from her work by the sight of Alexis Howard hovering outside.

Bella went to open the door. 'Please. Feel free to come and have a look if you like. I'm just catching up on paperwork.'

Alexis took up her offer. 'I'm sorry. I didn't know you closed on Mondays.'

'Of course. Please don't worry.'

'You have a lovely collection.' Alexis sounded overly bright. Bella wondered what feelings she was battening down. She made self-conscious small talk, asking Bella about sales and her flat and mentioned Frank Fellows too.

'I can't believe he and Oliver died in the same week.' She closed her eyes for a moment. 'And for both to go so suddenly like that, in such untoward ways.'

'Did you know Frank?' Bella asked.

She shook her head. 'Not really. Just to say good morning.'

Bella remembered Frank staring at Alexis during the drinks reception after the poetry recital. She wished she knew what he'd been thinking.

'Is there any news about the ruins?' Bella followed her around the shop. 'Have the people from Historic England been?'

'They're due tomorrow.' She sighed. 'I shall be glad when they've reviewed the site. It's too much responsibility, having it on our land without knowing how to deal with it and make sure it's safe. It feels like poor Oliver's death was our fault.' A tear trickled down her cheek and Bella put an arm around her shoulder.

'You couldn't possibly have known.' But she could understand her anguish.

She let Alexis circle the shop again to regain her composure and take in what was on offer.

It wasn't long before her eyes lit on a beautiful mirror, its oak frame carved to represent grapes on a twisting vine. Bella loved it too, but Alexis's choice still struck her as odd. She'd picked it the instant she saw it. Most people toured the shop several times, spotting treasures here and there. Things they'd like in their own home. Then they kept circling as they debated inwardly whether they wanted to spend the money, and which piece they liked best. She'd see them gradually give in to the fact that they'd fallen for something. Or if it was love at first sight, then it was obvious. They'd rush over to an item and pick it up or walk round it to examine it from all angles. Their eyes would light up. But Alexis showed no particular emotion. And the mirror was one of the most expensive items in the shop. Large and heavy.

'I'd like that please. Only I can't take it with me. I'm not in the car. Is there any chance you could deliver it? I'll pay, of course. I'd ask Harvey to come for it, only he's away for the day.'

'There's no charge. I can bring it up later this afternoon if that suits you.'

The poet nodded as she produced her credit card. 'Lovely, thank you.'

She hesitated, close to Vintage Winter's doorway. It was only when Bella's mobile rang that she finally left.

It was Carys on the line. *'Thank you for making me your accomplice. I told Leo you wanted me to help you meet Julia again and he was horribly jealous. I've got tomorrow morning free and an old friend who works at the uni's come to our aid. She can meet us for coffee, dish any dirt, then we'll drop in on Julia. I can pick you up at ten. That suit you?'*

'Perfect.' Julia hadn't sent her memories of Oliver for the fake memorial yet. Bella could say she happened to be on campus and was chasing for them. She was looking forward to it.

THIRTY-FIVE

A MOMENTOUS DISCOVERY

That afternoon's work took longer than Bella thought, and it was dark by the time she packed Alexis's mirror, lugged it outside and stowed it safely in Thomasina's boot.

It wasn't her only cargo. In the passenger area of the taxi, she'd put the shop's folding steps. She wasn't planning to use them. Or probably not. The risk of being spotted was too great. But if she decided to explore the ruins they'd be necessary. Oliver had used a ladder and she still wanted to know why.

The thought of the potential escapade made her stomach twitch with nervous excitement. It was nine tenths pleasurable, but she must only use the steps if she could do it safely. It would be counterproductive otherwise. She focused on the mirror instead.

It shouldn't matter why a client bought something. It was the mark-up and the contribution to the shop's success that counted. But Alexis's detachment as she'd chosen the mirror occupied Bella's mind as she drove over the river and up the steep hill to Raven Edge. She *wanted* her to feel passionate about it. Bella had, when she'd found it at a sale four weeks earlier. Her heart had lifted at the sight of it. She'd had to stop herself rushing over and alerting rival buyers.

She shook her head as she drove through the open gate to the ruins and Raven House. The income would come in handy. And maybe Alexis thought Harvey would love it.

Her gaze slid left as she drove past the point where she'd found Oliver's body. The mesh barriers were still up and tomorrow, Historic England would be there to assess the site. Bella's chances of a closer, private look were closing fast. The folding steps were at the forefront of her mind again.

The Howards' garage door was open, the building empty. Harvey must still be out.

Bella parked and heaved the large mirror in its protective packaging to the front door, setting it down as she rang the bell. She heard approaching footsteps and Alexis opened up.

'Thank you for bringing it.'

'Where would you like it?'

'Just against the wall here. Harvey will help me with it later. He's been out all day, catching up with an old school friend.'

Bella put it gently into position. The regret at letting it go was sharpened by the feeling that Alexis might not appreciate it properly.

'Would you like a drink?'

The chance to talk could be useful. Some bit of local knowledge might come out or something related to the site or to Oliver. Alexis might know something crucial without realising it. But time was of the essence. What Bella really wanted was a closer look at the spot where Oliver had died.

'Thank you, but I'd better be getting back. I expect you'll have Harvey home soon.'

Alexis laughed. 'Probably not for hours, in fact.' There was a slight catch in her voice. 'But I understand. I expect you've had a busy day.'

Suddenly, Bella wondered if Alexis had bought the mirror

solely to build their friendship. She might want someone to confide in. It would be a wildly expensive approach, but she and Harvey didn't lack money.

For a second, she hesitated. If Alexis was upset, maybe she should stay. Leo had said he thought her and Harvey's marriage might be in trouble.

But she also remembered her godfather's words. Had Oliver used the Howards' ladder to look at something on top of one of the walls? She wasn't sure she'd be able to see anything with the barriers in place, but she wanted to try.

'Things should get easier once the business is established. It would be lovely to meet up more regularly then, if you've got time.' Bella stepped back into the night and Alexis waved her off.

She drove back beyond the trellis that marked the boundary between the Howards' garden and the ruins. Glancing over her shoulder, she could see light in the upper floor of Raven House, but it was just one narrow window. There was no one to be seen.

She paused Thomasina at the side of the driveway, close to where Oliver had died. She only hoped Alexis was right about Harvey not being back for hours. At least he was in his car. She could listen for an engine. She took the folding steps and tucked them under her arm.

As ever, she was glad of her black coat and hat, but the metal steps glinted in the moonlight. She looked ahead and over her shoulder. Anyone could be watching from the shadows, over the perimeter wall or through one of the gateways. She listened, but all was quiet.

The area where Oliver had been killed was fenced off, but not the wider ruins. She pictured Harvey picking up the ladder from the frosty grass. It had been between where Oliver had died and the house, close to the ironwork trellis with its young clematis.

She found the spot. If Oliver had been climbing there, there was an obvious bit of wall he could have been exploring. The outer boundary of the old hall.

Taking a deep breath, with quick glances left and right, she climbed the steps to look.

There was nothing on top of the wall except lichen and patches of moss, glinting as another frost formed.

She took the steps to another nearby bit of wall, but drew a blank again. She couldn't get close enough to the damaged wall to see it in detail, but it couldn't be relevant anyway. Even with the topmost stone which had crushed poor Oliver, it had never been high.

Could Oliver have been told to collect something from the top of one of the walls? If so, it would naturally be gone. Tony hadn't mentioned the police finding anything unexpected or valuable on his body, but his killer could have taken it.

She put the steps back inside Thomasina. Discovery was an embarrassment to be avoided, and if the Howards gossiped about her explorations then everyone would know. But she went back to have one last look at the place where Oliver had died.

She approached the fencing and peered through, still imagining him slumped there. As before, the height of the wall convinced her any of the key players could have pushed the stone. She imagined Julia, standing there with malice in her eyes.

The moonlight had been making Bella feel vulnerable. Creeping around the ruins was like crossing a stage without knowing if anyone was in the audience. But the level of illumination was helpful too. Beyond the chicken wire, she could see the holes Oliver had dug.

Once again, she puzzled over the set-up. Oliver had heard the rumour about treasure and was here digging the very next night. His killer could have predicted his sense of urgency, come along to look for him, brought a blunt instrument but used the stone instead to fake an accident.

But Oliver didn't seem the sort to fall for a hoax. He was an expert and he'd believed the story of treasure. What had convinced him?

She peered more closely at the bit of wall where he'd been digging. It was covered with lichen from near the ground to the top. He'd dug a hole close to the wall's base, but in several other places too.

She moved her gaze from one hole to the next, looking at Oliver's neat work. And then she stopped, her focus on one hole, just inside the mesh panel.

It was then that she heard the growl of an engine behind her. Turned to see the headlights of Harvey's Jaguar, lighting up Thomasina's bonnet and windscreen. Heard the engine still, a door open and bang shut again.

There was nothing she could do. Thank goodness she'd put the stepladder away. She silently pleaded with Harvey not to look inside the cab. She had no right to be on his private land. She didn't think he could be guilty, but...

He'd located her now, his eyes fixed on hers, his hand raised in a wave.

'I'm so sorry,' she said, walking to meet him. 'I was up at the house, delivering a mirror to Alexis. She dropped in to buy it earlier. But driving off again brought the death back. I stopped and came over to try to lay the ghost. Only I don't think it'll work. I can still see Professor Barton slumped there.'

Harvey looked pale in the moonlight. 'I've been doing exactly the same thing.' He put his hand over his face. 'Poor Oliver. He was a good friend. Why in the world did he have to come here? The danger notices are everywhere. I had no idea he had a secret life. The whole thing's so hard to get used to.'

Bella breathed again. He got it. And she'd told a part-truth.

She *had* gone back because of the memories. But she'd spotted something too. Its importance set her mind whirring.

But she was distracted from the thought by crunching gravel. Alexis was coming down the drive. Maybe she'd been listening out for Harvey's return. She glanced at them, then padded across the hard ground.

Bella explained again and Alexis's eyes glinted in the moonlight. 'Of course. I understand.'

THIRTY-SIX

TELLING ALL AT THE STEPS

Bella called John and found he was at the Steps with Leo and Carys. She went to join them for a hot chocolate. Her hands had got steadily more numb as she'd stood in the eerie moonlight by the ruins, talking to the Howards.

She was still feeling waves of relief at them not finding her halfway up the folding steps. After telling Alexis she needed to get home, being found out would have felt especially awkward.

Leo bounded over to her the moment she got through the door. 'John says you've discovered something interesting. I've texted Lucy, Mum and Gareth and promised them updates.'

'Lucy's with a friend.' Bernadette had gone home and Carys was wiping a vacated table. 'Come and sit down.'

John was the only one who hadn't bounded, but she knew he was interested. He was in a window seat, apparently scanning a second-hand book, but she'd seen him glance up at her.

The café was almost empty now – it was near closing time – and Leo and Carys joined them. Through the window, the lights of the valley glinted back at them. In the centre of it all sat the dark mass of trees on Agnes's Haven, the Kite flowing round it.

'So?' Leo leaned forward. 'Out with it!'

Even John put his book down.

'Oliver wasn't the only digger at the ruins, the night he died.'

'What?' John blinked. 'How can you tell?'

'The holes he dug are neat. Professional-looking, as you'd expect. We know he must have done it many times before. But there was one hole that looked different.'

'Couldn't it have been the last one he started before he was killed?' Leo said.

'No. It was in the wrong place. He was digging up against the wall when the stone landed on his head. And there's more.' Leo was busy texting. 'There were little half-moon marks around the messy hole. Someone had jabbed the earth repeatedly. Looking for softer ground, or maybe out of sheer frustration. It must have been hard-going. Oliver was sufficiently determined to put in the effort, but it looks like the other person wasn't.'

'I wish we knew why he was so convinced there was something to find.' John sat back in his chair.

'I've been thinking the same thing. I'm sure he'd have done his own research.'

'So he was with someone who lacked patience,' Carys said. 'Maybe someone who hadn't done it before or who wasn't as keen as he was.'

'Of course, the presence of a second digger might be unrelated to Oliver's death,' said John, ever cautious. 'Maybe the killer simply hung around and waited for them to go.'

Bella nodded. 'Not impossible. But we need to identify them, regardless. There's a hint Julia Sandford might have been on Raven Edge that night. Someone saw a woman with long hair, and Meg Jones says she found a glove. Julia's got new ones, though that's hardly compelling evidence. Either way, I can't see her being the second digger. She might not be an archaeologist but she'd know what was involved; she'd have been prepared if she went with him.'

'Lucy agrees with you,' Leo said a moment later, peering at his phone. 'The moment I described the hole she replied saying, "not Julia".'

Bella wasn't surprised. Lucy was like John: one for details. She went on: 'I've found someone who saw Frank Fellows up on the Edge that night.'

Everyone started, except John, whom she'd updated by text the previous night.

'But,' Bella held up a hand, 'they saw him scuttling down the hill, as though he was in a hurry, between half past ten and a quarter to eleven. Whereas Alexis heard the ladder fall after half past midnight.'

'Maybe he came back,' Leo said.

Bella visualised the retired history teacher. 'He could have, but I don't buy him as the second digger. He walked quite stiffly. I can't imagine him on his hands and knees in the freezing cold. Someone described him as a neighbourhood-watch type.'

'A dangerous hobby, if there's a murderer in town.' Carys sipped her tea. 'If he did return, perhaps he saw the killer.'

'I wondered the same.' Bella savoured her hot chocolate. 'It feels like too much of a coincidence that he was there, and now he's dead too. Though his death might relate to the artefacts Nan Gifford sold him – if that's what she did. The person I spoke to on Raven Edge says they had the impression he didn't want to stop and talk. I wonder if he'd seen something that both-ered him.'

'You'd think a neighbourhood-watch type would go to the police,' John said.

'You would.' Bella had been musing on that point. 'Perhaps he'd bought stolen artefacts before, and was too scared to talk. Maybe he goes out looking for youths, up to no good, but thinks nothing of his own illegal purchases.' But that was all speculation, and she wasn't sure it fitted his character.

'So who else might be the second digger?' Leo still clutched his phone.

'Nan or Cal Gifford, Meg Jones or the Howards,' John said.

'I think we can discount the Howards.' Bella pictured them. 'They could go and dig their own grounds any time. It wouldn't be legal, given it's a scheduled monument, but they had no reason to get Oliver involved.'

'Unless they wanted his expertise,' John said.

Bella frowned. 'It's possible. But if they'd arranged to dig with Oliver, then where does the rumour at the Black Swan fit in? And why not cancel when I turned up? If you're going to do something criminal, it makes no sense to do it with a guest on site.'

'You have a point,' Leo said, tapping away.

'And I don't think Nan's the second digger either. She seems genuinely horrified at what Oliver got up to,' Bella went on. 'Even selling the odd bit feels like a stretch for her.'

'Agreed. So that leaves Meg and Cal.'

Bella's hunch was high in her mind, but she'd work through both options. Her dad would have. 'If Meg and Oliver were in a relationship then I suppose I could see him inviting her along like a big kid, imagining it was the most exciting evening he could possibly offer. And her being unconvinced.'

John nodded slowly. 'Though we don't have a motive for her. Other than a feeling she didn't like him, which makes a relationship seem less likely.'

'True. But she might have wooed Oliver for her own reasons. We know she leafleted him individually about her cleaning services.'

'We do?' Leo said.

'Neither of his immediate neighbours got one.'

Everyone looked at each other and Leo pinged off another message.

'I assume she lied about not seeing him at Acton Thorpe too. And she joined his history group. I think she wanted to get close to him, but I don't know why.'

'So Meg's a possible for the second digger?' Leo asked.

'I'd say so,' Carys said. 'If she was plotting something.'

'I agree.' Bella took out her beautiful notebook and wrote the conclusion down.

'If it was her,' John said, 'maybe Julia Sandford could have killed Oliver out of jealousy, once Meg left.'

Bella was ready to produce her theory. 'I reckon Cal is even more likely for second digger. He told his friend that Oliver was always trying to teach him stuff, but also that he didn't trust him. What if Oliver took Cal under his wing, and introduced him to his passion?' She reviewed her notes. 'His mum says he and Oliver were out for a bat walk, the night Oliver died. But maybe that's rubbish. Perhaps he was at the ruins, learning the ropes.'

Leo's eyes widened; he was busy with his phone. 'Lucy says the bat walk sounds highly unlikely,' he reported, moments later. 'She's used rather colourful language. I must remind her not to.'

Her comments on the bat walk figured. It had started to seem questionable to Bella too. 'Cal has a temper. He was angry on Saturday night and chucking stones into the river to relieve his feelings. I could imagine him jabbing at the earth out of frustration while Oliver lost himself in his work.' She went back to her notebook. 'Oliver called Cal at eleven thirty that night. I suppose we can assume they weren't together then.'

'Unless Oliver was already dead, and Cal had both phones.' John's eyes met Bella's.

'Except Alexis Howard heard the ladder crash down sometime after twelve thirty, when she went to sleep.'

'True.'

'But Cal could have gone back after getting the call.'

'And killed him?'

Bella frowned. 'It's not impossible. And it could have happened just because he lost his temper. Shoved at the stone not thinking it would shift much, but it did. I don't buy him as a criminal mastermind, with plans to sell the hoard, but I think he was resentful towards Oliver. Being able to get his hands on the odd piece after his death might have been a bonus. Maybe he stole the ring and the brooch.'

'Perhaps he and his mum both dipped into the hoard. Nan must have got her extra income from somewhere.'

Bella nodded. 'And Frank links them together. He was visited by Nan before he was killed and he was there the night Oliver died. He dashed off, earlier than the accident, but he could have seen Cal and Oliver together, if they arrived at the site early enough.'

John leaned forward. 'Maybe he warned Nan that Cal was getting into trouble, but kept quiet more generally if he was buying part of Oliver's hoard.'

Bella mulled the idea over. 'It would involve some double standards, but plenty of people have them.' She thought of Nan, sobbing at the Blue Boar. Suddenly, she felt the ground give way under her feet. She couldn't see her as a murderer before, but now... 'She could have killed Frank to keep him quiet. Tried to bribe him with treasure maybe, but found him incorruptible. Gone back to take the next step. And she might have killed Oliver too, to protect her son.' Maybe she'd written Oliver the threatening note on the Alexandra Arms paper. Bella could see it all. If she knew Oliver was leading Cal astray, turning him from your average bolshy teenager into a criminal who could end up in jail like his dad... She'd been one of the least likely suspects in Bella's eyes. Now, she was top of the list.

'I've texted that idea to Mum,' Leo said.

'What does she think?' Bella imagined her furious reaction.

'She hasn't replied.'

The fact chilled Bella more than anything else. It sounded as though Jeannie was starting to have doubts.

'What next?' said Leo.

'Nan's just overtaken Julia at the top of my list. I need to talk to her again.' Bella drained her chocolate and stood up.

THIRTY-SEVEN

MORE PART-TRUTHS

Bella had managed to lure Nan out by telling her she was worried about Cal. They were sitting in the back bar of the Blue Boar; Gareth had earmarked a secluded table the moment he knew what was going on.

'Nan, I've been delivering leaflets and chatting to the locals. Including up on Raven Edge.' She let the words sink in. If she knew Cal had been there with Oliver – or if she'd been there herself – it ought to strike home.

Bella could see Nan's mind working. Her eyes widened. She was fiddling with the sleeve of her blouse.

'I think Cal was at the ruins, the night Oliver died.'

The woman opened her mouth but closed it again. She wouldn't know what she was dealing with. Whether there'd been a witness.

'He sent me the anonymous note, didn't he? But he's not the only one who's been writing secret letters. You wrote to Oliver, threatening him if he didn't stop nighthawking. You used the Alexandra Arms's watermarked paper. The office here is full of it; it was delivered to the wrong inn and everyone's been using it as scrap. You must have been terrified for Cal.'

It was too much. Nan put her hands over her face and leaned forward on the table.

'You told Oliver you'd make him stop if he didn't do it of his own accord. I can understand how desperate you must have felt.'

When Nan removed her hands, her eyes were bleak. 'It's like I told you. Oliver wrote to me when my parents died and my husband was away. He said he wanted to help. He knew that my husband— He knew our situation. And yet the moment Cal was old enough, Oliver decided to introduce him to his hobby. Of all the stupid, selfish—'

No wonder Nan had disposed of Oliver's notebooks. Leaving aside the question of who had stolen what, they probably gave away Cal's involvement in the digs.

Gareth had emerged from the kitchen. He passed the table like a ghost, deposited a brandy in front of Nan and disappeared again. She picked it up a second later, as though it had been there all the time.

'I was so angry when I guessed what was going on. Cal is, well, he's easily led. Life's been difficult for him. He needs strong role models. Not some stupid arrogant thief.' She shook her head sharply. 'It felt like I'd caused Oliver's death just by wishing it. I hoped he'd think the letter was from some thug who could beat him up.' She looked down at her hands. 'I'm not much of a threat.'

But she could have pushed the stone. She loved Cal so much. Was desperately anxious for his future. Nan looked up and caught her expression.

'You think someone killed him?' Her jaw went slack. 'It wasn't me! When Cal told me they were going for a bat walk, I didn't believe a word of it. I followed him, ready to have it out with Oliver. For once they were somewhere local. They'd gone off before, but in Oliver's car and I don't drive so I couldn't follow. I had a good idea what was going on, but I couldn't prove it. They denied everything. Made me out as paranoid.'

It must have been so frustrating. And hugely worrying. All the more reason for Nan to get violent this time.

'Finally, I had the chance to see what they were up to with my own eyes. But when I got to the ruins, intending to have it out with them, I could see a figure,' she paused and swallowed, 'watching them over the wall. I was scared they might be recognised and the police would get involved.'

'What did you do?'

Her shoulders sagged. 'I ducked out of sight and called to warn them, but they both had their phones on silent. In the end, I had to give up. I decided I'd talk to them later and left. If I'd joined them with someone watching it was more likely we'd be identified. Three members of the same family, all together.' The last sentence came in a whisper.

Bella leaned forward, though the inn was noisy enough to cover their conversation. 'Could it have been Frank Fellows watching?'

Her jaw went slack. 'Why do you think that?'

'I heard he'd been up there too.'

'I think it might have been.' Her words were almost inaudible.

'Did you recognise him? Did he approach you about Oliver's artefacts after Oliver died? Or to tell you he'd recognised Cal?'

Nan's brow furrowed. 'Why would he approach me about Oliver's artefacts?'

'Isn't that what you took him, the night of his death? I can imagine you might have offered him something. You must have wanted him to keep quiet about what he'd seen.'

'No! I told you—'

'I know, but delivering a scarf after midnight makes no

sense. And if he took delivery of something valuable, it might explain why he was killed.'

'You think his death was murder too?' Nan's shock morphed into a violent shake of her head. 'That's not why I was there.'

Bella was reminded of conversations with her younger siblings. The gradual chipping away at their fibs. The bit-by-bit confessions. She knew she was on the verge of getting something. 'But nor was delivering the scarf.'

Nan closed her eyes. 'He gave it to me. We had an agreement that if I ever needed an excuse for visiting, we'd use the scarf in winter, or his sunhat in summer.'

'Why all the secrecy?'

Nan leaned forward, her eyes full of tears and Bella knew she was finally going to get her answer.

THIRTY-EIGHT

NAN OPENS UP

Nan sipped her brandy. 'Frank Fellows was a kind man. It all started when I found him here, in the Blue Room. He was staring into space and he looked so lost. It was the end of my shift and I asked if he'd like a game of dominos. I don't know what made me do it. The moment I said it I felt ridiculous, but his face lit up. I'll always remember it. He said he'd like that and I sat down and we played. It was quiet. There was no one else in there.' She shook her head, smiling through her tears. 'It happened a few times after that. I got to know him, and heard about his insomnia and how alone he felt. He said the nights seemed endless sometimes.'

Nan had been generous. Bella wondered if she'd have done the same and decided not to examine the question too closely.

Nan went on: 'We became friends and one day, on the spur of the moment, I offered to visit him a few nights a week, to play board games and chat. He was the perfect gentleman. Always. But he...' She hesitated. 'He gave me money. I didn't want him to at first. I would have visited just to see him happier, but he knew I had debts and he insisted. He got me to do errands. Bring him shopping, and so on. He said he was paying me for that, not for my company, but it was over the odds for such small tasks. We both knew it.'

The expensive purchases from the delicatessen were for Frank! It all made sense now – Bella was buzzing. 'So that's why you took the shopping trolley.' For shopping. Go figure. She imagined John slapping the side of his face when she told him.

Nan nodded. 'But the whole arrangement was secret. Frank was a proud man. And old-fashioned. Any hint around the town that he was paying for company would have been unbearable for him.'

It made so much sense. No one would relish something like that getting out.

'I know he felt guilty too, for keeping me away from home late at night,' Nan went on, 'but I've never needed much sleep. The truth is, I've been lonely too.' She sighed. 'I think Frank fell a little bit in love with me. He hinted occasionally that he'd be happy to remarry. I think he wanted me to know, in case I was keen, but it wasn't... well, it wasn't what I was after. My husband and I haven't divorced. And Frank was a lot older than me. But it made no odds to the way he behaved. He was endlessly selfless and generous.'

Bella visualised Cal, hunched over his laptop. 'He bought you presents?'

She nodded. 'Ridiculous things I didn't really need.' Tears filled her eyes. 'The most recent was a crazily expensive laptop for Cal. The old one we had kept crashing and Frank had picked up on my worries about his schoolwork. He didn't realise the trouble it would cause. Cal knew it was an expensive model the moment he saw it. He wanted to know where I'd got the money and I couldn't tell him without breaking Frank's confidence.' She bit her lip. 'I said I'd got a bonus from work.'

How ironic and sad that thoughtfulness for Cal's welfare had led to a row. Cal might have believed the same as Bella: that his mother had found Oliver's treasure and was selling it off. Or that Oliver favoured her above him and had given her money. It would have added to his bitterness. And his anger. She'd relegated Cal on her list of suspects because he'd gossiped about treasure before his uncle died. She hadn't thought he'd be so unguarded. But faced with this new information, she revised her opinion. He might be guilty.

It made him sending the anonymous note about Nan all the more believable too. He was hurt. Felt he'd been shut out.

'I was so fond of Frank.' Nan gave a helpless shrug as tears came again. She was looking at her hands. 'In truth, I knew for certain it was him, watching Oliver and Cal at the ruins. The idea of him knowing that my son and my uncle were involved in something so wrong was awful. If he'd thought I knew about it, that would have been even worse.'

'Do you think he realised it was them?'

Nan sniffed and pulled a tissue from her pocket. 'He never mentioned it.'

But if he'd identified Cal, he might have wanted to protect Nan from the knowledge. And Cal from the police, because he loved Nan. It would explain him keeping silent. Just how much had he seen? Cal nighthawking? Or had he returned much later, and seen him kill his great-uncle?

'When did you see Frank next?'

'That night. I was back at home when Cal came in at eleven. Then over at Frank's by midnight.'

Well before the falling ladder Alexis had heard. Nan wouldn't know if Cal had left the house later. But it made it unlikely that Frank had seen Cal kill Oliver.

'Cal and I had a massive row when he got in,' Nan added. 'I let rip at him for going digging. Then he asked again about the nice new things we had, and I gave the same explanation. He didn't believe me. He said my new stuff was the reason Oliver didn't trust us any more. Him not trusting us! What a joke.'

'Oliver never gave you a key to his house? I know he asked John to feed Smudge.'

She nodded. 'He admitted he didn't want Cal tramping around and so it was best if neither of us did. So Cal didn't feel singled out. He talked about bad influences at school. But what could be worse than what he was doing?'

'But you guessed about his hobby before he died? You knew about the hidden room?'

She frowned. 'I had no proof. I kept the note I wrote him vague. But I suspected. I worked out that part of his attic was walled off. When we visited, he got twitchy if we went upstairs. And his excuses for going off with Cal weren't believable. Then I overheard Cal talking to a friend about sneaking onto private land. He mentioned something being "worth a packet". I got more and more scared. When Oliver died, I got hold of a key as his executor and searched his house in earnest.'

Cal could have followed her. Or discovered the room sooner if he'd managed to get into the house before Oliver died. 'Have you seen Cal with anything that might have been Oliver's? An ancient brooch or a ring?'

'Were those the bits that were missing? I didn't read the labels.' She shook her head and closed her eyes for a moment. 'Cal couldn't have taken them. He didn't have a key.'

But that didn't stop burglars. Bella could see Nan was worried. Besides, he could have pinched her key after Oliver's death and copied it.

Bella leaned forward. 'It must have been so hard, grieving for Frank and not being able to say anything. You could tell people now.'

But Nan shook her head. 'It's not just Frank who was proud. What woman would accept money for keeping a neighbour company?'

But Bella could see exactly how it had come about; it had

been rooted in generosity on both sides. Nan had done nothing wrong.

'I slipped into his house over the weekend,' Nan went on. 'I always knocked if Frank was home, but he'd given me a key. I needed to visit one last time, to come to terms with what's happened. The whole place smelled of him: the cologne he wore and the pipe smoke.' Her shoulders slumped forward and she seemed to crumple.

Poor Nan. Her grief was sharp, and she must feel so lonely. She was still suffering whispers and gossip from the townsfolk in return for her honesty in reporting Oliver's hoard. And all the time she'd been guilty of nothing but a kind heart and striking up an unconventional friendship. Bella felt terrible for doubting her. She must find out the truth. Set things right. She hoped to goodness Cal wasn't guilty. How would Nan cope? At last, she asked: 'How did things look, when you slipped in? Did anything strike you as off?'

Nan's gaze met Bella's and she hesitated. 'He had a notebook, bound in leather. He kept it on a shelf in the TV room, amongst his other books. He was secretive about it: shoved it back on the shelf if it was out when I turned up. That always made me wonder, and I'm afraid I looked for it.' She blushed but Bella thought it was perfectly natural. 'It was gone. I suppose the police might have taken it, but why would they, if they think Frank's death was accidental?'

'His family could have picked it up.'

Nan frowned. 'Perhaps. But I'd swear the other books on the shelf are still there.'

So why home in on that one?

Nan took a tissue from her pocket and blew her nose. 'Frank was anxious when I visited him the night Oliver died. I'm worried he'd recognised him and Cal at the ruins. And after Oliver's death his anxiety got worse.' She was twisting her hands. 'Maybe he thought Cal was involved. If we'd talked openly, I could have told him he was home by eleven.'

It didn't seem to occur to her that he could have gone back out. His uncle had called him. Cal claimed it was about homework, but that seemed less and less likely.

'Frank was anxious like that before, too,' Nan was saying, 'a month or so back. I kept catching him muttering. Something about: "right under his nose". But who was doing what under whose nose, I never found out.'

THIRTY-NINE

AN ANSWER AND A FRESH MYSTERY

Late that evening, Bella, John, Gareth, Carys, Leo and Jeannie were drinking winter warmers in the snug in the Blue Boar. Through an internal window, Bella could see the hubbub beyond. People milling and lights gleaming behind the bar.

Tony was with them. He'd spent some time talking to Peter, which raised some eyebrows. It looked as though he might turn into one of the few visitors Jeannie's husband genuinely welcomed. Bella felt faintly put out at not having the same effect.

Now, Tony sat between Bella and John. 'The missing note-book's a worry,' he said. 'Barry Dixon ought to hear about that.'

'I told Nan to tell him. She doesn't have to come clean about her and Frank's arrangement. And we mustn't tell either.' She was confident they wouldn't. Even Leo. He was excitable but not unkind. Poor Nan. 'I wonder if it was a diary. He could have recorded his feelings about Nan and what he saw at the ruins too. If so, the killer was lucky to find it. From what Nan says, Frank kept it tucked away. But maybe he had it out when they knocked on his door.'

Tony sipped his drink. 'If Frank's visit to the ruins cost him his life, either the killer thought he'd stayed longer than he did, or something he spotted earlier was damning. Unless he did go back later and Nan's covering for him. She could have invented the missing notebook to make him look like a victim.'

'But she wouldn't protect him now he's dead, surely?' Jeannie looked incredulous.

'It's amazing what people will do for love. Do you think she was in love with him, Bella?'

She shook her head. 'Not "in love", but I think she loved him. She's devastated by his death. I'm pretty sure she was with him that night. It rang true when she said how anxious he was. So I think she's out of it, either as the murderer or an accessory.' She savoured the warmth of the rum in Gareth's recipe. 'I reckon it's as we guessed before: the killer wasn't sure if Frank was a threat. They cracked a pane of glass to get an excuse for knocking on the door, so they could test the water.'

'Even if Frank didn't witness the murder, Cal could still have killed him if Frank admitted to seeing him with Oliver.' Carys's brow was knotted. 'It would have panicked him if he was guilty.'

'True.'

'You think Frank would have invited Cal in?' John sounded sceptical.

Bella nodded. 'Nan said how kind-hearted he was and that he'd hinted he'd like to marry her. He was up for the role of stepfather. He might not have believed Cal was capable of anything truly horrific. He could have seen it as his chance to offer him a listening ear. Try to steer him in the right direction, for Nan's sake.'

'Sounds possible,' Tony said. 'And if it wasn't Cal who killed him?'

'Then we have to look again at who killed Oliver. Julia Sandford out of hurt or because they'd dug together before and he'd refused to share his finds? She was in the right place to spread rumours about the treasure and discover Oliver's plans. She still seems the most likely to me, joint with Cal.

'And Meg Jones continues to bother me, but she's even more of a mystery. We need to know why she didn't like Oliver and what drove her to get close to him.

'Whoever's guilty, it could have played out the same way. Anyone might have given themselves away as they talked to Frank. Then smashed his head against the mantelpiece in desperation. He didn't look physically strong. And the attack was probably out of the blue.'

'It's a bold way to kill someone,' Tony said. 'It would take nerve. Hard to get it exactly right so it would look like an accident. That rule anyone out?'

Bella pictured the key players. 'I think Julia could have managed it. She's mature and reasonably cool headed. She didn't crack when I said she'd been seen at the Black Swan. And even Cal would be capable, I think. He's angry. I could see him losing it and managing it by sheer luck. He might have needed to kill Frank for practical reasons, but I expect he resented him too, if he'd worked out where his mum was going several nights a week. And then there's Meg—'

'Don't look now,' John said, 'but she's just walked in with her boyfriend.' They all looked up at once and he sighed heavily. 'It might be interesting to watch them. Subtly.'

'I'll go and check everything's all right at the bar.' Jeannie pushed herself to her feet.

'Bang goes your hope for subtlety,' Leo said, to a sharp look from his mother.

They watched as Jeannie strode towards the bartender closest to Meg.

Meg's boyfriend had his arm round her waist as they waited for their drinks.

Bella followed them with her eyes as they found a table near the window. Jeannie followed them with her legs, stopping to talk to a patron close by.

Next to Meg and her boyfriend, Bill the barman who'd played poker at Oliver's was clearly off duty. He sat with a friend, playing cards.

Bella watched as Meg's boyfriend peered at the game. Meg touched his hand and he laughed and shook his head.

Then Meg said something, her hand on his arm now, and the boyfriend shook her off. An irritable movement.

A moment later, Meg got up, leaving her drink, and walked out of the inn, not looking back.

Her boyfriend half stood, frowning – part-injured, part-annoyed. After another moment he downed his pint in double-quick time, then stomped off after her. Bella gave him minus points for prioritising his drink.

Jeannie rejoined them and squeezed past Leo and Carys so she could retake her seat next to Bella. 'Well, that was interesting. All the boyfriend said was, "It's years since I played cards." She said "good", quite firmly, and took his hand. She wanted him to look at her, not the card game. But he was still glancing at the next table. He said he fancied a game, she grabbed his arm and said no, then he shook her off and off she stormed.'

And now, Bella remembered. She took her notebook from her bag and turned back the pages. 'The one thing Meg Jones admitted knowing about Oliver was that he gambled. Which is interesting when you come to think of it, because you never let him play for money in here, did you Jeannie?'

'I did not. I had an old friend who got addicted. It only brought him misery.'

'So how did Meg know Oliver gambled?' Carys asked.

'Good question. Maybe she played with Oliver and got hooked. He might have recognised her name on her flyer, hence the question mark. Or perhaps it was someone close to her. We don't know much about the husband that died.'

'Other than that he was ill for a while beforehand,' said John. 'And his name: Joe Jones. We were introduced once.'

Joe. That rang bells, now he mentioned it. Bella had overheard Alexis mention him by name.

'Would anyone like another drink?' Tony got up.

'I'd better come with you.' Gareth rose hastily. Bella doubted he'd trust anyone else to prepare his winter warmer. She could understand it. She found delegation hard too.

She followed them. She had a mission.

While Gareth got busy and Tony got his wallet out, Bella went to the table where Bill and his friend were playing cards.

'Sorry to interrupt.' She focused on Bill, who instinctively covered his hand. 'You mentioned you used to play poker with Oliver Barton. Did you ever come across the woman who left suddenly? The one who was sitting at the next table?'

The young man frowned. 'No. Never.'

'And what about a man called Joe Jones?'

The barman blinked. 'Yes. I told you about him.'

'Remind me?'

He lowered his voice. 'He was the one Oliver took pity on. He was betting way too much. Oliver could see it would all come crashing down, so he let him win and didn't invite him again.'

Bill *had* mentioned his name, but she'd forgotten. It hadn't seemed to matter at the time. The connection sent a tingle through her. It must be significant. But if Oliver was kind to Meg's husband – had wanted to save him from himself – then what was Meg's grievance?

FORTY

HIDING IN PLAIN SIGHT

Bella was walking through the mist the following morning, en route to Vintage Winter, when she saw Alexis Howard.

She was sitting on a bench to one side of Kite Walk in the cold and damp, staring at the river.

Bella left the path and went to the bench. 'Good morning. Everything okay? I was just on my way to work.'

Alexis blinked at her, taking a moment to come to. 'Oh, good morning. Yes, I'm fine.'

I'm fine. So easy to say. Bella should have stayed for that drink the day before. Though if she had, she'd never have realised there'd been a second digger at the ruins.

'What did Harvey think of the mirror?'

'Oh.' Her look was hazy, almost as though she'd forgotten about it. 'Yes, he thought it was nice.'

Nice? It was gorgeous. She swallowed her feelings.

'I meant to ask, Meg Jones cleans for you, doesn't she?' Bella tucked her coat under her as she sat down too. She wanted as much faux astrakhan between her and the bench as possible. No one would sit out on a day like this unless they were trou-

bled. That, or up to something. It made her think of Julia Sandford and Oliver Barton, sitting outside the Blue Boar.

'That's right; she's wonderful.' Alexis sounded as though
she was dragging her mind back to the present.

'I saw her in the Blue Boar last night and she seemed upset.
Did you know her husband? The one that died?'

'Not really. They'd separated, but I could see she still loved
him.' She frowned. 'Relationships can be so complicated. I
know she instigated the split.'

'I wasn't sure how he'd died.' Bella looked out at the water
sweeping past. Thea had always shared more when she wasn't
staring at her.

'Between ourselves, I heard he'd drunk himself to death.
Poor Meg. I think she carries a lot of guilt over it, but you can't
always mend the person you love.'

She sounded as though she was talking from experience. It
made Bella wonder what problems Harvey had, beneath the
successful-businessman veneer. But maybe she wasn't talking
about him. Bella remembered the young man who'd paid her so
much attention at the recital. The one who'd been on the same
lecture tour as her.

'I heard he gambled too,' Bella said. That or the drinking
might have led to the separation. But could Meg have blamed
Oliver, even though he'd seen the danger and stopped playing
with Joe?

'She's never mentioned it,' Alexis said, 'but now you say it, it
makes sense. Harvey was talking about the owners of Raven
Hall gambling it away. He laughed over it, and I'm afraid I did
too. Meg was there, polishing the silver in the background, and
she said it was no laughing matter. I could tell she was upset.'
There was a long pause, then Alexis sighed. 'Addiction's an
awful thing. I shouldn't have made light of it.'

Again, she sounded as though she was speaking from experience. That it had affected someone she loved. Harvey? Or her son, away at school? Or...

Bella looked at her.

She was wearing the same gold scarf ring she'd had on at the recital, with the peacock-blue silk square. And the brooch she'd worn then too, on her lapel. It had glimmered in the lights of the Howards' reception room, but it looked old and less glitzy in the cold, misty light of day.

Old. The cold was filtering through Bella's coat, making her numb, but her shiver wasn't caused by the frigid weather.

She looked at the scarf ring. Gold, with a depiction of something. It was hard to see properly. A man? Stepping out of something? It looked like a cave.

Bella's hairs stood on end as the labels for Oliver's missing artefacts came back to her. A medieval gold iconographic finger-ring with a depiction of the resurrection. And a medieval flower-shaped gold and diamond brooch. And she'd been wondering if the diamonds were genuine at the recital. To be fair, she hadn't got a good look.

'You're wearing some of Oliver's finds.'

Alexis went absolutely still. From seeming dreamy and far away, she was alert as a mouse in the path of a fox.

'What do you mean?' she said at last.

Bella explained about John, the house key, and seeing Oliver's artefacts.

Alexis put her hands over her eyes, as though blocking her view of the world would make it go away.

If she'd taken the treasures, she'd taken them to wear. Could she have killed Oliver to avoid discovery? No. That made no sense. He couldn't report her, and there was no way she'd wear her spoils at a public event. She'd only do that if they mattered to her so much she felt she must keep them on.

'He gave them to you?' Bella had been convinced Alexis

was involved with the young poet from her lecture tour. But perhaps he was driving that connection. And after all, Alexis liked older men, if Harvey was anything to go by. 'You were lovers?'

How could Bella have missed the artefacts when Alexis wore them before? They'd been hiding in plain sight. What would her father say?

Alexis didn't speak but Bella was sure she was right now. And this linked Oliver to the very people on whose grounds he'd died. She needed to tread carefully.

'When you talked about addiction, you sounded pained. As though someone you loved was affected that way. Were you thinking of Oliver and his hobby? Not the gambling, but the nighthawking?'

At last, Alexis nodded, very slowly. 'When he gave me the ring and the brooch I told him I didn't want them, but he just smiled, put them into my hand and closed my fingers over them.'

He must have loved her very dearly. Bella was sure he'd never have sold his treasure but bestowing it with his heart was a different matter. Looking at the gaps in his collection he'd have felt warmth, not regret. He'd given John the coin, too.

'When he died,' Alexis went on, 'I wondered about taking them to the police. Telling them what I knew. But I couldn't bear to. Even when Nan did the decent thing and reported his hoard, I didn't want to give them up. They're all I've got left of him. And I was worried it might get out. I don't want to hurt Harvey. He's so good to me. We lean on each other, and it provides a sort of comfort. He spends all his time fishing and visiting friends, and I – I can get on with my poetry, and travel when I want to. We both love the house and the ruins. It ought to be enough, but I'm not sure it is any more. It might be time to face facts.'

Bella thought of the contrast between Harvey and Oliver. Oliver had been sparky, mischievous and full of ideas, albeit reckless ones. He'd given Alexis some fun.

But staid, needy Harvey, with his adoration for keeping up appearances, was newly interesting. If he'd discovered the affair, he had a first-class motive for murder.

'Didn't Harvey ever ask about the jewellery?'

'He's not the noticing type.' She shook her head. 'I told him I'd treated myself to some upmarket costume items. He said, "very nice", without actually looking. Oliver gave our son that book on archaeology your friend's daughter was reading too. He was delighted when I told him Barney was interested. He even wrote to him at his school. I was terrified Harvey would find out – it seemed such a risk. But he never asks about my life, or about Barney's. We don't talk. Not about anything meaningful.'

'Did you know Oliver was planning to visit the ruins the night he died? Did Harvey know?'

Alexis looked at her quickly. 'No, I had no idea. And I don't see how Harvey could have.'

'Weren't you hurt that he came to dig on your land without telling you?'

She shook her head. 'He wouldn't have seen it that way. Even I don't. It would be different if he'd dug in our garden, but the ruins aren't really ours.'

'It seems weird that a professor would find treasure belonging to the nation and keep it for himself.'

Alexis stared at the water. 'We talked about that. He said, what good were any of these artefacts if they remained undiscovered underground? And when he died, he was sure Nan would hand over his collection. He'd made lots of notes. It made him gleeful, anticipating people's reaction.'

Bella thought of all that precious historical data at the bottom of the Kite, and Nan's shame. The gossip she'd had to endure. It had been selfish and cavalier of Oliver to assume so much.

Alexis turned to Bella. 'Please be discreet about this.'

'I will.' She was confident John wouldn't tell if she asked him not to. 'But might Harvey know about the affair already?'

'No, I'm sure not. Oliver came and found me at the ruins not so long ago, but I told him never to do it again. Although I panicked, Harvey was away at the time, and it was dark. Besides, I'd know if he knew. His behaviour would change. If I've upset him, he becomes stilted, monosyllabic. He'd never be able to hide it.'

'You're sure? Because Oliver died on your land. It looked like an accident but—'

Alexis's eyes opened wide. 'You think he'd have killed him? Out of passion for me? Or from humiliation?' She shook her head. 'He couldn't have. When the sound of the ladder crashing down woke me, Harvey was lying there in bed, sound asleep. I had to wake him. And although he turned over and nodded off again, I stayed awake for hours. He never left the room.'

Bella visualised the scene. Unless a third party had sent the ladder crashing down after Oliver had used it – and after he'd been killed – for some unrelated reason, then Alexis was right. And that set-up would be crazy. She remembered the way Harvey had talked about Oliver at the recital too. She was sure he'd been genuinely fond of him.

'Do you really think someone killed Oliver?' Alexis's eyes were hollow.

'I think it's very likely.' Why lure him out with talk of treasure otherwise? But then why had Oliver fallen for the rumour? 'I'd love to know what he was doing with your ladder.'

Alexis nodded. 'So would I.'

They walked up the hill towards high town together.

A minute after they'd parted, Bella looked over her shoulder. The man who'd been on the same lecture tour as Alexis had joined her.

Maybe she didn't exclusively prefer older men – just anyone who loved her for herself and had time to talk.

John pressed a cup of coffee into Bella's hands at the shop.

He looked as inscrutable as ever, but as he turned away, she caught the flicker of a smile. He sat down to polish a silver candlestick and didn't look up as he spoke. 'Did you travel the length and breadth of Shropshire to find the pieces from the Hearst House?'

Again, his lips curved upwards for a second.

'Absolutely. On my hands and knees. Anything for you.' She sipped her coffee. 'The internet and modern communications may have played a part.'

He looked up, his hands still for a moment. 'Thank you.'

'It's my pleasure. Please take them home so Gareth can enjoy them too.'

He nodded.

As he worked and she drank her coffee, she explained what Alexis had told her. 'I promised I'd be discreet, so this had better be between us. Unless anything changes and we need to tell my godfather or Barry Dixon.'

'Agreed. So, you think she's right? Harvey really doesn't know about her affair?'

Bella nodded. 'He looked genuinely devastated about Oliver's death. I can't imagine he'd hide his feelings so successfully if he was aware. I think Alexis is being honest too. About the affair, and the crash in the night.'

'So neither Meg nor Julia were Oliver's current lover.'

'Not unless he was more than usually energetic.'

John gave her a quelling look.

'But Meg was homing in on him. And I suspect it's connected with her late husband. We need to talk to her again. As for Julia, if she was still in love, we've identified the object of her jealousy. I'm glad Carys has arranged for me to visit her.'

'Where are we with the playing cards?'

There was no one in the shop, so they went to the office and looked at the drawing board.

Queen of hearts, spades, clubs and diamonds – 'Three passionate women. One who loves too much, one who's full of fear, and one who's striving for immortality. And then the fourth. An enigma, but one who worries me.'

'Alexis has to be a contender for the queen of hearts now. The one who loved too much. My impression is that she adored Oliver, but his nighthawking made her miserable, as did her betrayal of Harvey. But it could also be Julia Sandford, who maybe never stopped loving Oliver after they split up. She drank with him the night he died, tracked him to the Black Swan, and it might be her glove Meg Jones found, close to the ruins.'

John nodded. 'And Meg still fits for queen of diamonds: the enigma. She kept popping up. Though her working at Raven House might be a coincidence.'

'I think you're right. She said she got the job through a friend.' Bella moved on to the other queens. 'Nan fits spades all the more convincingly now – full of fear. She was terrified about Oliver involving Cal in his addiction.'

'So who's striving for immortality?'

'Good question.'

At ten o'clock, Carys swept in. 'I'm meant to be lesson planning, so I'm high on freedom. Ready? Leo's still feeling jealous, but I know John's more mature.'

John didn't rise to the bait.

'You don't mind me pressing on without you?'

'I see myself as your enabler. That's good enough for me.'

She smiled. 'Well, hold yourself in readiness. We need to seek out Meg Jones over lunch, assuming I don't find her at Acton Thorpe as well.'

John grimaced. 'If we must.'

Carys and Bella sat in a café on the Acton Thorpe campus. Steam clouded the windows and the place smelled of coffee and pastries, sweet and enticing.

Bella had chosen a pain au chocolat but Carys had stuck with coffee. Her old university friend, Samira, had an almond twist and Bella wondered if she should have gone for that instead. It looked gloriously sticky.

They'd already covered the latest developments in Samira and Carys's lives. Bella had listened patiently, but was pleased to see Carys frown and lean forward. *Down to business.*

'So, how do you find Julia Sandford these days? We bumped into her on Sweet Agnes's Eve. I thought she seemed a bit fed up.'

'She's sad about Oliver Barton's death.' Samira sighed and stirred her drink. 'We all are of course, but they went out ages ago. Just after I started my lectureship here.' She raised an eyebrow. 'There was a lot of talk about it at the time. He was quite a bit older than her, and you know how people are. Gossip spices up the workplace.'

'Were they still close?' Carys asked.

Bella adopted a look of casual interest as Samira frowned. 'I think he'd moved on more than she had. It was weird when they split up. I know she broke it off, but she seemed just as upset as he was. The atmosphere was terrible for a few weeks. He kept trying to talk to her and she wasn't having any of it. I'd come into a room and they'd clam up.'

'I'd have told them off,' Carys said.

Samira grinned. 'I know you would. It was difficult, but I felt sorry for them. I wondered if he'd two-timed her, though she was more upset than angry.' She shook her head. 'Recently, I had the impression Julia regretted the break-up. Or at least, that she was talking to Oliver as a friend again. She looked excited. As though things had taken a turn for the better.'

'I'd heard she was seeing someone new.'

Samira looked surprised. 'That's news to me. But of course, she could be keeping it quiet if she wants privacy.'

Perhaps she'd lied to disguise the way she felt about Oliver.

'I can't believe she's not a professor yet,' Carys said. 'Surely her work's good enough.'

Samira nodded. 'Some loudmouth got the promotion instead. Julia's worked her fingers to the bone, spoken at umpteen conferences, written papers that get published in the top journals. But the new professor went to the right cocktail parties. I wonder if she'll ever get the recognition she deserves.'

Carys shuddered. 'I'm so glad I didn't go into academia.'

'Oh my!' Samira glanced at her watch. 'I've got a lecture in two minutes. I'll have to love you and leave you.'

Carys turned to Bella. 'Time to track Julia down? Follow me.'

They left the café and crossed a quad to a building marked 'History'.

Carys marched up a set of stairs, entered a corridor that smelled of new paint and pushed open some swing doors. On the other side she darted through an open door, knocking as she went.

Bella followed her. The office had four workstations, but they were all deserted. Carys looked around as though she could make Julia appear through sheer force of will. It didn't work.

'I'm sorry. Samira checked her timetable. She should be here. This is her desk.'

Bella walked closer. Her papers were neatly stacked. Not like the chaos she'd seen in Oliver's house.

In a desk organiser that rose behind Julia's computer, there was an array of ring binders and lever-arch files. Bella eyed the one labelled 'special projects'. The shelves were tight for space and that ring binder wasn't quite flush with the rest – as though Julia had jammed it in recently.

She glanced at her watch. Ten past eleven. If the room's other occupants were in lectures they probably wouldn't reappear until twelve. But were they? And where was Julia?

Carys glanced at her. 'If there's something you want to look at, I can keep watch in the corridor. Create a diversion if anyone appears.'

'Yes please.' It would give her time to put the special projects file back and get out.

'Of course.' Carys didn't bat an eyelid, making Bella wonder what sort of person it took to be a teacher.

The moment Carys left, she eased the file from the shelf. The folder was crammed with information about some newly discovered historical records, dating back to the 1500s, found in a Tudor house just outside Hope Eaton. The facsimiles were hard to decipher, but from what Bella could tell, they revealed interesting details of social history. But in amongst this work, which fitted with Julia's research interests, was an aerial photo which looked familiar. Anyone glancing casually might not recognise it, but Bella had seen it before.

It was the Raven Hall site. A more up-to-date version of the one in the local history book Bella had bought from Bernadette.

Suddenly, she heard Carys's voice outside. She needed to put the file back, but the photo might differ from the one she had access to. She laid the file on Julia's desk and grappled with her phone, accessing the camera app. A moment later she had a record.

She could hear Carys saying, 'So down this corridor, then where again?'

That wouldn't hold for long.

She took a breath and pushed the file home, turning towards the office door as Carys's 'Thank you' rang out.

There was no way she could make it out of the office in time.

The door opened.

It was Carys. 'Turned out the guy was just passing, not coming in here. He'll think I'm as thick as two short planks. The directions to the bathroom really weren't that complicated.'

Before they left Acton Thorpe, Bella stopped at reception. First, she asked for Julia Sandford's whereabouts, in case they could still catch her.

The woman behind the counter referred to her computer. 'There's nothing in her calendar.' She shook her head despairingly. 'Ah, but there's a meeting of a committee she sits on. She's probably in there.'

'Thank you. Not to worry. And is Meg Jones in?'

The woman inputted her name and scanned her machine again. 'You've just missed her, I'm afraid,' she said at last.

'Thanks anyway.' Maybe she and John would find her at home.

On the way back to Hope Eaton, Carys got onto family chat. When she mentioned Matt, Bella turned to her.

'Why didn't he come to Sweet Agnes's Eve? Jeannie said what a shame it was.'

Carys sucked in a breath. 'People don't talk about it much. You mustn't let on I've told you.'

'Deal.'

'It's a bit of a sad cliché, to be honest. Seven years back, he was engaged to a girl he'd known since school. She'd left the valley but come back again and they fell in love. It was all wonderful, until it wasn't.' She'd had her eyes on the road but glanced at Bella for a moment. 'She went off with his best friend. Left him a note on Sweet Agnes's Eve and ran away. They haven't been in the valley since. It caused a lot of drama at the time. Matt never joins the festivities. Can't take the sympathetic glances, I guess. It's the downside of Hope Eaton. People have long memories.'

FORTY-TWO

ON MEG JONES'S TRAIL

Back at the shop, Bella closed for lunch, ready to look for Meg Jones. She hurried around the close with John in her wake. The weather was perishing again.

'How was Acton Thorpe?'

'Interesting.' She told him what Samira had said. 'So perhaps Julia hoped to patch things up with Oliver. She told us she was seeing someone else, but Samira didn't know about that. Either way, I doubt it was solely a romantic liaison she had in mind.'

'What makes you say that?'

Bella explained about the aerial photo.

'I can't believe you went through her stuff.'

'It's not like I read her private diary. It was just sitting there in her office. I wouldn't have recognised the photo unless I'd already seen an aerial view of the ruins. Anyway,' she went on, 'it suggests she might have been talking to Oliver about the site, not affairs of the heart. They were definitely secretive about it. She could have started the rumour about the treasure, or heard it the same time Oliver did.'

On the high street they were overtaken by Jeannie, hurtling along on a bicycle that looked too small for her.

John winced. 'I do wish she wouldn't ride that thing. She doesn't look where she's going. At least I fixed the brakes.' He and Gareth were keen cyclists. Bella had decided Hope Eaton was too hilly for that.

'Hello, you two!' Jeannie skidded to a halt, forcing another cyclist behind her to perform an emergency stop.

'Close one that, Jeannie,' the grey-haired woman said, with admirable restraint.

'Was it?' Jeannie clearly had no idea what she was referring to. 'Jolly good.'

The woman rode on, shaking her head.

'Where are you off to?' Jeannie asked. 'It's almost time for a spot of lunch. Gareth's got venison casserole.'

'It sounds wonderful,' John said.

Bella knew how much he'd prefer to sit in the warm inn than have awkward conversations with his old school friend. 'It does. But we can't. We need to talk to Meg Jones.'

'Oh well!' Jeannie made a spinning motion with her right hand. 'Turn around! I saw her just a moment ago, heading up St Giles's Lane from Uppergate. If you hurry, you might catch her.'

John gave a resigned sigh. 'Any chance Bella could borrow your bike?'

That wasn't happening. Bella hadn't been on one since she was a child.

'Of course!' Jeannie dismounted. John was already rushing towards a second bicycle, parked by the Blue Boar. He fished out a bunch of keys.

'Tell Gareth his hasn't been stolen, will you?'

Jeannie waved a vague hand.

'Come on then,' said John to Bella. 'If we have to do this,

let's make sure we catch her. I can't go through the anticipation more than once.'

'We'll probably miss her when I fall off and bring the high street to a grinding halt,' Bella muttered.

As she gathered her coat around her, mentally thanking whoever had fitted Jeannie's bike with a skirt guard, she spotted Matt approaching the inn. He waved to John, then double took as he saw Bella.

'I hadn't got you down as a cyclist,' he said.

Bella bristled. She wasn't one. It wasn't her thing. But why would he think that?

'No time to lose, Bella,' John called from up ahead. She ignored Matt and set off, pushing down hard on the pedals. It was the one thing she remembered from when her dad had taught her. Don't lose momentum.

They arrived on St Giles's Lane intact, though Bella's nerves were jangling.

'You're a natural,' said John.

'Yeah. Right.' There was no sign of Meg up ahead but they cycled round the close. It was much more relaxed there than on the high street.

John slowed. 'Maybe she's gone down the steps.'

'And a fat lot of good bikes will be for that.'

But at that moment Bella caught movement, close to the church, amongst the tombstones.

She caught John's eye. 'Maybe she's visiting a grave. It could be Joe's.'

He nodded. 'Let's wait.'

FORTY-THREE

MEG'S SIDE OF THE STORY

Meg Jones's eyes were glistening as Bella and John approached. She was walking away from the grave she'd been tending, towards St Giles's Steps.

'Hello.' Bella had the urge to pat her shoulder but it was John who knew her well enough to do that and it wasn't his way. 'We're just out for a lunchtime stroll.' They'd propped their bikes out of sight.

'I've been walking round the churchyard.' She sniffed.

'Your husband's grave?' Bella said gently.

She nodded. 'People think of him as my ex, because we'd separated, but I still loved him. I'd hoped the split would be temporary. Until things came right.'

It was a horrible, unfinished way to lose a partner.

'I met someone recently who knew him,' Bella said. 'One of the bartenders at the Blue Boar. He said your husband and Oliver were friends.'

'Friends!' The word came out like the crack of a whip. She took a deep breath. 'They knew each other.'

'The bartender said Oliver was kind to him.'

Meg folded her arms. 'Kind how?'

'They were playing cards. Maybe Joe was new to it. The bartender said he got a bit out of his depth and Oliver let him win, then sent him home.'

Meg Jones was shaking. 'That's right,' she said at last. 'Joe admitted he'd been reckless that night. Told me he'd almost lost everything. But it had all been all right in the end. He'd won that last hand. He was so good that Oliver Barton never invited him back.'

Bella went cold to her very core. 'Oliver's actions encouraged him?'

She nodded. 'He was already getting hooked, but Oliver was renowned as an excellent poker player. When Joe beat him – or so he thought – he got even more delusional. Someone else mentioned Oliver had let him win as a kindness! I ask you. And I was supposed to be grateful. What did he mean by playing for money with people he barely knew? Couldn't he see Joe was vulnerable?' She turned away, her shoulders rigid. 'It took a long time for him to go downhill, but the fall was inevitable. I knew I'd lost him. He was out of reach. I told him he'd have to leave if he carried on. The drink and the debt were impossible. And finally, I threw him out. I couldn't take it any more, but I never stopped loving him.'

Nor hating Oliver. 'You wanted to get close to the professor.'

She hesitated, then nodded. 'I needed to understand him. To figure out how someone who's supposed to be so clever could be so stupid. I'm not sorry he's dead.'

'Did you know he'd be at Raven Hall the night he died?'

Meg seemed thrown, her brow furrowed. 'No. How could I?'

'You were a member of the history society. And you both worked at Acton Thorpe. You said you never overlapped, but Julia Sandford knows you. I imagine Oliver did too.'

She gave a sharp sigh. 'All right, yes, he did. But although he talked to me – chatted even – we never spoke about the ruins. I had no idea he trespassed as well as gambled. Why do you want to know?' As she watched their faces, shock spread over hers. 'You think his death wasn't an accident?'

Her horror looked genuine. 'We suspect not,' Bella said. 'I don't suppose he ever realised the harm he caused your husband, but I can see that doesn't make it any better.'

'He had a blind spot,' John added. 'He never realised how harmful his passions could be.'

It was true. He'd worried his great-nephew was on the wrong track, without seeming to consider his own part in that.

'Having a blind spot's a poor excuse!' Meg's cheeks were tinged pink.

'Did you bring up his gambling when you talked to him?'

She nodded. 'I said I'd heard about it and he laughed. Said it was a bit of fun. So I spat in his tea when he was out of the room and wrote anonymously to the university authorities. I've got no idea whether they spoke to him.'

'And you hoped he'd hire you as a cleaner.'

'I wanted to find his cards and burn them. Graffiti his house with warnings. Make him see what he'd done.'

Bella thought of the question mark Oliver had written on her flyer and wondered if he'd had any idea why she kept crossing his path. He'd meant to help, but his role in Joe's addiction had become all-consuming in Meg's mind.

As Meg walked towards the steps, John and Bella went back to the bikes.

'Angry but not murderously so?' John said. 'And surprised at the idea of Oliver being killed.'

Bella nodded. 'And it's true she'd be unlikely to know Oliver was at the ruins unless she followed him on a regular basis. And that would have been a challenge. He lived in high town and she's on the other side of the river in the valley. Poor

Meg. But I can't help feeling sorry for Oliver as well. He messed up but he didn't mean any harm.'

Fifteen minutes later, Bella and John had returned the bikes and were at the Steps. They'd found Lucy, back from school for lunch, as well as Leo. They huddled briefly at a corner table, looking over the valley, still shrouded in mist, the tops of trees just showing on the hills beyond.

Bella told them about her trip to the university.

'Judging by the map and Julia's recent contact with Oliver, I'd say they were both interested in what they might find at the ruins. Unless Julia started the rumour to get Oliver there. She might have used the aerial photo as a map, so she'd know her way around. Either way, she could have killed him – out of passion or from greed.'

'She could have turned up to dig at the site herself, on the back of the rumour, and seen Oliver discover something interesting,' John said. 'I know the police didn't find anything valuable but maybe he struck lucky just before he was killed and she took that one standout discovery.'

Bella frowned. 'But do you see Julia crushing the head of a man she'd loved to steal a single ancient artefact, even if she could retrieve it?' She thought of Julia's struggle for promotion at the university. 'It's not as though she could trumpet the discovery to get recognition.' She shook her head. 'We need to talk to her again. Ask some direct questions and watch her reaction.'

John winced.

'The interesting thing is, if Julia was also investigating the site on the back of the rumours, why did both she and Oliver take them so seriously? They were experts, and they expected to find something.'

'The aerial photo might help.' Lucy's gaze was still on the book she'd been reading. She was so like her uncle.

'In what way?'

'I read that you can tell a lot from them. See patterns that hint at old Roman camps and Iron-Age settlements. Crop marks, changes in the colour of grasses showing archaeology underneath the soil.' She turned the page of her book. 'They show up especially well when it's dry.'

Bella looked at the picture she'd taken of Julia's aerial photo. It seemed to her that there were some ridges in the field beyond the fallen stone walls of Raven Hall.

She handed it over, hoping Lucy would take one look and shout, aha! But she shrugged, pointed to the ridges Bella had noticed and said: 'Could be.'

'So maybe the killer knew Oliver would be tempted because Raven Edge has some interesting history, but it's not something a layperson would be aware of.'

'That would point to Julia,' John said. 'She's got the expertise.'

Bella had the feeling she was missing something. That they had almost enough to piece everything together if only they could work out how. But it was time to get back to Vintage Winter.

As they opened the shop, John turned to her. 'What's next?'

'Cal Gifford. He could have gone back to the ruins and

killed his great-uncle. Nan was with Frank, so she can't vouch for him.'

'He didn't steal the brooch or the ring.'

'No, but maybe he took something. And he was resentful of Oliver. I doubt Cal would have planned the killing in advance. The rumour would have to be coincidence, unless he had help. But it's still possible.'

John nodded. 'Fair enough.'

'If we're not too busy, I'll follow him after school. See what he gets up to.'

Bella kept tabs on Cal from the moment he left the high school. His first port of call after slouching out of the gates was the newsagents, with its familiar smell of sweets and newsprint. The woman at the counter cast her eyes over the rear of the shop where Cal stood, apparently aimlessly. Bella kept behind him. She was sure he hadn't seen her.

And then, as a couple of customers came in and went straight to the counter, she saw him pick up a chocolate bar and stuff it in his pocket.

Oh, the sweetness of being in the right place at the right time. 'Hello, Cal.'

He jumped, and Bella smiled.

'I'll make you a deal. If you put that chocolate bar back, and tell me exactly what happened when you met your great-uncle at the Raven Hall ruins, I'll consider not telling the shopkeeper you're a thief.'

At first, he gaped. Bella supposed Nan hadn't told him she'd guessed. But it wasn't long before shock turned to anger and his fists clenched.

'Take it or leave it,' Bella said. 'It's not a bad offer.'

For a moment she thought he'd shove past her and walk out. He seemed torn between pride and practicality.

'How do you know I was there?'

'I guessed and someone confirmed it. What happened? I was staying at Raven House and I'd like to know. It wasn't the only time you'd gone digging with your great-uncle, was it?'

He shifted his weight from foot to foot. At last, he shook his head. 'Oliver first took me with him a couple of years ago. It was to places outside Hope Eaton. He'd tell Mum we were camping or doing bat walks. She liked it at first. She thinks I need a father figure. Seems to forget I already have one. I don't know when she got suspicious, but she asked a lot of questions in the last six months.'

'So you and Oliver were close. It must have been hard when he died.' She hadn't seen Cal look upset.

'I liked him at first. And the trips. He said he wanted to show me the secrets hidden in the earth, and the beauty of what was out there. But he got angry when I suggested he could sell some of it. I wanted a new bike. Just one of his precious bits of treasure would have paid for ten of the most expensive ones, from what he said. And I'd helped him dig. It was so unfair. He ignored me. He said it wasn't about the money.'

'Why wouldn't he let you in his house?'

'How did you—'

'I heard.'

'He was just mean.'

'There must have been a reason.'

Cal shrugged. 'He found me upstairs one day. I'd gone to the bathroom and then up another floor to explore. I was just interested. Bored. He said I'd got no business going up there without permission. Talk about a control freak.' He sighed. 'After that, he still took me digging, but he was more like a teacher, less like a friend.'

It was ironic that he seemed to have regarded his time spent with Cal as an attempt to keep him on the straight and narrow.

'Did he show you his secret room where he hid the treasure he stole?'

Cal frowned. 'No. But I knew he must keep it somewhere. He held out on me.'

'I suppose you never managed to find it yourself?' She made it sound like an insult. In similar circumstances, goading had worked excellently on her sisters.

She could see the internal battle on Cal's face. At last, he sighed. 'All right. No, I didn't. But now it's made the papers, you can see how well hidden it was.'

She believed him. 'And what happened, the night he died?'

The boy scuffed his trainer on the shop's carpet. 'It was harder than usual. The ground was like rock and he hadn't found anything good. I was still on my first hole. It was freezing and I got bored. And then I saw this figure, outside the stone walls around the ruin. Thin. Tallish. Wearing a cap. He was keeping back like he didn't want to be seen. I warned Oliver but he didn't take me seriously. He had a quick look, but the guy had stepped into the shadows. He told me I was imagining things. I didn't want to stay after that. Mum would have killed me if someone reported us. I told Oliver I was going and as I went, I saw the same person ahead of me. Running almost, down into the valley.'

Poor Frank Fellows.

Cal shuddered. 'I was sure someone would dob us in. And then I heard Oliver was dead... I couldn't work out what had happened.'

'What was the real reason Oliver called you, later that night? And don't tell me it was about homework,' she added as he opened his mouth.

'He said I should come back. That I might learn something.'

What, exactly, if he hadn't dug up any treasure? Endurance? But he'd written that exclamation mark in his notes. What did it mean?

'Did you go?'

'No way. I didn't want to go back into the cold for another one of Oliver's lessons.'

At that moment she heard a female voice, greeting another customer.

'It's my mum.' Cal sounded weary.

'Here, let me have the chocolate bar.' Bella walked briskly to the counter, paid for it and gave it to him.

'What's that for?'

'Don't take this the wrong way, but you suddenly reminded me of one of my sisters. They were always in trouble, but they came good in the end. Sort of.'

FORTY-FIVE

A TRIP TO THE RUINS

Back at Vintage Winter, Bella told John what she'd found out from Cal.

'He seemed different when I put him on the back foot. Less worldly-wise. I think it's a hard-man act and he's still a big kid. I suspect he genuinely got bored, cold and fed-up that Sunday night. And was spooked by the figure too, though it was probably poor old Frank Fellows, doing his neighbourhood watch bit. Cal's bitter that Oliver started to treat him like a child, but I can't see him going back out to kill over it. Nor masterminding an effort to steal his treasure, as we said before. He's no angel, but it feels beyond his level. But Oliver did invite him back.' She explained the phone call. 'I'd love to know what had interested him.'

'Maybe it was something on top of the wall. Something the killer took.'

She bit her lip. 'Could be. But what would that teach Cal? Either way I'd like to head up to the ruins after we close. Historic England were visiting today. I presume they'll have finished.' The sun had already set. 'Maybe the Howards can tell us about it.'

.   .   .

As Bella and John approached the ruins, they found someone still on site, standing on the drive, talking to Alexis and Harvey Howard.

And there, looking on, just outside the stone-wall boundary, was Julia Sandford.

Bella turned to John. 'Just the opportunity we needed.'

'Hurrah.'

'Sarky.' Bella strode towards Julia. 'Hello. We were just wondering about Historic England's visit. Is that why you're here too? It's your subject, isn't it? Or at least, I suppose history and archaeology connect.'

Julia nodded. 'They do, especially in this case.'

Her eyes looked red and sore. It was bitterly cold, but Bella knew upset when she saw it.

'The experts are convinced the site is Roman. Just as I thought.' Julia's knuckles were white.

Roman? Wow... 'You thought? You and Oliver had discussed it, then?'

She turned her gaze on Bella, her eyes widening.

'Someone found your glove here the morning after he died.' It was worth chancing her arm. 'And you were together before he came here too. I wondered if you'd arranged to meet.' She said it quietly. Almost as though she was talking to the night, not to Julia.

Julia shook her head. 'No. No we hadn't.' Her voice was clipped. Barely controlled. 'Oliver and I didn't operate in the same way. And he... he lied to me.'

'What about?'

'I need to start at the beginning. His nighthawking was the reason we broke up. Back when we were together, he took me on one of his expeditions. I was blinded by excitement. And by my feelings for him. But the moment we arrived and stole onto someone else's land I knew I couldn't do it.' She shook her head as though trying to rid herself of the memory. 'Oliver was everything that I wanted – or so I thought. But his hobby went against every principle I had. Despite all that, I carried on missing him after we split. As time went on, I hoped he'd left nighthawking behind. I knew where to find him, so recently I'd been turning up at the Black Swan, hoping to talk. It's no use at work. Gossip is rife.'

'You said you weren't with him there. And that you were seeing someone else.'

She sighed. 'I didn't want to admit that I still missed him. What's happened is too humiliating.'

Bella hated showing her weaknesses too, but she couldn't let it rest. 'He didn't want to get back together?'

'I don't think he did. But it wasn't that. I made the mistake of sharing some information with him and once he'd got it, he betrayed me.' Her voice was shaking.

'You sound furious.'

'It's sorrow as much as anger. You'll understand if I explain. I thought he'd got over his addiction, and I wanted to be close to him again, so I shared an important discovery I'd made. I've been working on some records, found in a Tudor house nearby.'

The subject of her special projects folder. 'Go on.'

'I worked my way through the documents and found a reference to an old song, all about Romans marching to a camp on Raven Edge.' She shivered. 'I've found no other reference to the song. It's been lost in the mists of time. But it was enough to make me wonder. I started to study the area. When I looked at aerial photographs, I concluded the Raven Hall ruins were the most likely site.'

'You told Oliver that, even though you knew he'd been a nighthawker?'

Julia put her hands over her face. 'I knew how excited he'd be. It was a chance to connect with him again. And he swore he wouldn't go exploring. We were going to do more research together. It would have meant our names associated with the discovery forever. Historic England would have got there eventually, but we'd have beaten them to it. Made them bump Raven Hall up their agenda.'

'But he went behind your back.'

'I was scared he would, the moment whispers about treasure surfaced.' She confirmed what they'd heard at the Black Swan. 'It was one thing agreeing not to dig when it was our secret, but quite another when someone might get there first. The desperate excitement was there in his eyes. He was like an alcoholic with his next drink just out of reach. That's why I asked to meet him at the Blue Boar.'

'To try to talk him out of it?'

She nodded. 'And he agreed. We said we'd go public with our findings early the following week instead.' She closed her eyes. 'It wouldn't have done my career any harm.'

Bella thought of Samira's comments about Julia's elusive professorship. 'Did you consider publicising your discovery anyway, after Oliver died?'

Julia shook her head. 'I was too upset, and I worried people would think I'd tipped Oliver off so he could dig. We used to be lovers after all.' She sighed. 'The way he was at the Blue Boar rang alarm bells. He kept looking at his watch. Jiggling his leg. He was on edge and I just didn't trust him. Then later that night I came here and saw him. I was devastated.'

She must have been livid too. If she'd still loved him, the betrayal would have felt all the sharper. She could have killed him.

'What did you do?'

'I wanted to have it out with him, but I'd started to cry. Couldn't stop. It wasn't upset, so much as frustration and fury. How could he? I couldn't let him see me like that. Didn't want to give him the satisfaction. I was tempted to report him to the university. I took a photo, though it was grainy. But I was over-taken by events.' She turned to Bella. 'It's possible to hate someone and love them at the same time. And now I can't even have it out with him. It's a huge irony that the thing he loved so much killed him in the end.'

Bella let her recover for a moment. At last, she spoke again. 'Was he on his own when you saw him?'

Julia frowned. 'Yes. Why wouldn't he be?'

As she walked off, Bella could still see Alexis and Harvey talking to the expert from Historic England. She turned to John. 'I think Julia was angry enough to have done it. But would she admit how furious she was if she'd killed him?' She thought of the playing cards. 'I think she's the queen of clubs, striving for immortality. She wants recognition and she finally thought she might get it. Oliver let her down badly, but I think we can cross her off the list. She still believes the death was an accident.'

John nodded. 'So we've identified all our queens. Alexis who loved too much, Meg the enigma, Nan who was full of fear and now Julia. I'm not sure any of them seem likely murderers.'

'I'm with you.' Bella glanced over her shoulder. The Howards were still safely involved in their conversation. 'Alexis could have killed Oliver, set up the ladder scene then shaken Harvey awake later in the night. We've only her word about it crashing down. If Oliver wanted more than she was prepared to give, it's a possible motive. But it wouldn't account for the rumour at the Black Swan. And if she'd felt threatened by him, she'd hardly wear the treasure he gave her.'

'Perhaps Oliver and Frank's deaths weren't murder at all,' John said.

'Yes, you're probably right. Let's go home.'

'How I wish you were serious.'

'The answer is, we've missed something.'

John was gesturing over her shoulder. She turned.

Alexis and Harvey were approaching with the woman from Historic England.

When the trio got near, Bella explained they were interested in the archaeology.

Alexis looked slightly feverish. 'Please, come in for a drink. We can tell you all about it.'

Harvey looked less keen, his jaw tight.

Bella spotted Julia, still sitting in her car at the side of the lane. 'Would you mind if we invited Julia Sandford too?' She pointed. 'She's an academic who worked with Oliver. She came to find out more. I know she'd be fascinated.'

Safety in numbers.

Harvey turned his back, but Alexis sounded eager. 'Of course. She must come. Let's fetch her now.'

FORTY-SIX

A GLIMMER OF LIGHT

The gathering over drinks was awkward. Harvey was monosyllabic. He might not have known about Oliver, but Bella wondered if he'd heard rumours about Alexis and the young poet who'd toured America with her. He was behaving just as Alexis said he did when he was upset.

She couldn't help feeling Alexis had wanted her and John there as a buffer. It was a role Bella had performed as a child when there were tensions at her mother's place. Not her favourite pastime. As for Julia, she looked as though she'd been crying in the car.

Alexis explained what the team from Historic England had said, her words pouring out.

'Isn't it extraordinary? It seems we've been living on a Roman site all this time and we never realised. They've done a geophysical survey and they'll find out lots more. They looked at what Professor Barton had dug up and were surprised at the number of things he'd found, though of course it was all modern and worthless.'

She'd flushed as she'd mentioned Oliver.

'A fork, bottle tops, a metal mug. Maybe someone camped there once. Maybe—'

Harvey got up and left the room.

'I'm sorry,' Alexis said. 'He's tired. He was out until recently. Long day.'

'Did they say why they thought Professor Barton hadn't found anything Roman?' Bella asked.

'They said there might have been almost nothing left. Though there's usually something, even if it's just something tiny. But someone could have dug everything up long ago, so that's a possibility.' She was still talking at speed. 'It's hard to tell because Ol— Professor Barton dug quite extensively, they said, so any signs that someone got there first would be hard to detect. And if it was years ago, centuries even, then they probably couldn't tell anyway. If it's more recent, it changes how densely packed the soil is, apparently. Someone might arrange a proper dig. It was all so interesting.'

She looked at Julia, who was staring into the fire as though she hardly saw it.

Alexis caught Bella glancing at the clock.

'Please, have another drink.' But her voice slowed, as though she knew she couldn't keep them there forever. She and Harvey needed to have it out.

'Thanks, but I'd better be off,' Julia said, and Bella and John echoed her.

It was grim for Alexis, but she and Harvey would have to talk sooner or later. It sounded as though their marriage was on borrowed time.

Alexis waved them off and Bella watched as the heavy oak door closed, her flushed face disappearing behind it.

Julia strode towards her car. She looked like she'd had enough. Bella could well understand that. Though she might have known Oliver would go behind her back, with his track record. He'd behaved appallingly, but she'd been distressingly naive.

'I think we got out of there just in time,' John said, as he and Bella paused near where Harvey had found the ladder. 'There's definitely a row brewing.'

Bella nodded. 'There's a lot to glue Alexis and Harvey together: their son, and their settled family life. And he supports her loyally in her work.' She shook her head. 'But she doesn't love him any more. I'd say she's looking to that younger guy for comfort in the wake of Oliver's death. I doubt she wants to hurt Harvey, but perhaps they've been seen together and word's got back. I think she knows the marriage has reached the point of no return.'

John sighed. 'I feel for them. But where does that leave us? Can we go home now?'

Bella looked at the ironwork trellis that marked the beginning of the Howards' garden, then at the ruins beyond.

'Soon.' *Well, soon-ish. Perhaps.* She paced. 'We should go over what Alexis told us just now. What struck you?'

John followed her, his brow furrowed as she glanced at him. 'The amount of modern stuff Oliver dug up. The experts commented on that.'

'Yes.' Bella walked on, coming to the spot where she'd found his body. 'That was odd.' She peered at the holes he'd dug. The people from Historic England had fenced them off again. 'But the absence of any Roman stuff wasn't so unexpected. It could have been dug up decades or even centuries ago. Only there's no way of knowing. Any changes to the soil compaction won't be detectable, now Oliver's dug over—'

She stopped mid-sentence, the ghost of an idea flitting through her mind.

'What is it?'

'I'm not sure. But what if that's the point?'

'I don't want to sound insulting, but you're not making sense.'

'I wonder.' She took out her phone and googled Howard's Classic Cars. A couple of reviews, both five-star. Not many, if it was well established. She racked her brain. How to get more information? After a moment, she clicked on Google Maps, entered the salesroom's address, then used Street View to look at the premises. In a rural place like that, the images wouldn't be updated often.

She zoomed in.

'What are you doing?' John whispered over her shoulder.

'Looking at the cars on display in Street View.' She showed him. 'Now look at the photos I took when we visited.'

John let out a sigh. 'They're almost identical.'

She nodded. 'I'd say Tyler Smith talked the place up. In reality, sales are few and far between. And Harvey hardly ever goes there. Alexis said he's always off fishing or seeing old friends. He told me he's passionate about his business but there's no evidence he is. It explains why Tyler's so relaxed about driving his girlfriend round in the merchandise. I was wondering how he could get away with haring off when the showroom was meant to be open.'

'And so?'

'What if Howard's Classic Cars is a front? Harvey's first business folded, and his second doesn't make money either. He found wealth another way. And there's plenty of it. Enough to keep up their house and a lavish lifestyle. To support Alexis handsomely and send his son to boarding school in the family tradition.'

'And it can't be family money,' John put in. 'Carys said his father left him the house, but almost nothing else. The brigadier bequeathed the rest to set up a school somewhere abroad.'

'That's right.' Bella remembered the tale. 'He thought Harvey should make his own way. And Harvey's the sort to want money. A lot of it. Not out of greed but from a deep-seated lack of confidence, to hang on to the things he holds dear: Alexis, his family home and his reputation. He'd want to live up to the ideal.' He'd struck her as needy. Always trying to bolster himself up. Putting a hand on Alexis's arm. Leaving his garage door open to show off his smart car. Talking about his businesses and his time in the cadets.

'He doesn't support his wife emotionally, but he lavishes money on her. In the desperate hope it'll keep her with him, I imagine.'

John faced Bella, his breath fogging in the freezing air. 'So, what are you thinking?'

The answer to that was so many thoughts that Bella could barely order them.

FORTY-SEVEN

A CREEPY POSSIBILITY

Bella took a deep breath in an attempt to steady her heart rate. 'I think Harvey worked out there might be valuable treasure here and went digging in the ruins.'

'What? How? And when?'

Bella reviewed what they knew. 'Lucy said she'd read that you can see evidence of ancient sites by looking at aerial photos. And when we came for the poetry recital, she was looking at Harvey's son's book on archaeology. Perhaps that's where she got her information.

'I think maybe Harvey read it and looked at the aerial photo we've seen of the ruins. Maybe he researched some more online.' She imagined him poring over the information, wondering, getting excited. Half his mind on his business, which was failing.

'As for when, while Alexis was away in America.' He'd have been desperate by then. Carys said he'd got to the point of selling furniture to make ends meet. 'Alexis said she was gone for months and while she was away, he sacked their gardener. He'd have needed to. He couldn't dig openly. It's not just that anything he found would be treasure trove. It's a scheduled site, so digging would be illegal. Once the coast was clear, I think he bought a metal detector and started to explore.'

'And struck gold?'

'Literally. That's my hunch. He must have found unscrupulous buyers who'd take the pieces off his hands and suddenly he was made for life. He could offer Alexis every luxury. I imagine he told everyone the car business had taken off and everything in the garden was rosy.'

'And it was, until he heard that Historic England was finally coming to assess the site?'

Bella nodded. 'I think so. After all, they'd write to him first. We've only his word for it that he had no idea. I think he got the letter and was terrified they'd discover he'd been digging. Maybe he googled and found the soil would be less compacted where he'd been at it. And he messed up when he planted the modern objects where he'd dug. The experts found that odd.'

'Why would he do that?'

Why indeed? 'My guess is as insurance, in case anyone had used a metal detector there before and recorded the results. It would look suspicious if someone from Historic England came back and found nothing. But he went about it in a blunt way.'

'So it was Harvey who spread the rumour about the treasure?'

Bella nodded. 'I think so. Not personally, of course. I imagine he paid someone to put the word out at the Black Swan, which seems to be known for its nighthawking community.'

'And it didn't matter who turned up? Oliver wasn't the target after all?'

The fact made her chest feel heavy. 'That's right. I think Harvey vandalised the security lights, then waited for someone to come and dig where he'd dug, to cover his tracks. Because if they didn't, Historic England and the police might start to look at *him*. He might claim an intruder was responsible, but they'd wonder why he hadn't noticed the digging and reported it. And everyone knows the place has good security lighting. They'd ask themselves how someone managed it under his nose.'

John was nodding. 'So what happened that Sunday night?'

'I imagine Harvey was anxious. Nipping outside to see if anyone had taken the bait. It was too late to backtrack, even though I'd turned up unexpectedly. But why kill? That's the question. He was probably shocked when Oliver turned up. He might not have realised he was a Black Swan regular. But he'd get the job done. Harvey could report the illegal digging the next day and protect himself, just as he'd planned.'

But then suddenly she had it. 'No. Wait! The exclamation mark in Oliver's notebook. And what he said to Cal on the phone. "Come back. You might learn something." That's it, John!'

John raised an eyebrow. 'What's it?'

'Harvey wanted any old nighthawker to get him out of trouble, but what he got was an expert. An academic with years of digging experience. Oliver knew! He knew someone had been there before him. Noticed the changes in the soil and the oddness of the modern-day objects he found.' She drew in a deep breath and felt the shock of the ice-cold air. 'Maybe he was muttering to himself. And then calling Cal. To any other onlooker it would have meant nothing but to Harvey, with his guilty conscience, it would have been terrifying.

'I think Oliver bent down to dig again and Harvey crept forward, wondering how on earth he could save himself. And then he saw his chance and crossed that terrible line. He liked Oliver. Never expected to find him here. His shock and sorrow when he talked about it was genuine.' She remembered his words. *Why in the world did he have to come here?* 'He can't have had any idea Oliver had been sleeping with Alexis. But when faced with shame, prison, his son being pulled out of boarding school – all the things that would go with his downfall

– he pushed the stone. He seems pompous, but he's crushed inside.'

'Excellent work, Sherlock. Except for one thing. If Harvey killed Oliver just after he'd called Cal, that puts his death at what hour?'

Bella checked her notes. 'Eleven thirty.'

John nodded. 'But Alexis swears she heard the ladder crash down sometime after...'

'Half twelve.'

'And at that point, she insists Harvey was sound asleep next to her. You think she lied to protect him? That they're in it together? Or she heard something else fall?'

Bella hadn't seen anything else that could have caused a similar sound. The crash of a ladder coming down would be distinctive.

Walking back to where Harvey had found it, she looked at the ironwork trellis ahead of her, and then at the wall behind. The ladder had been just in front of it.

John was right. If Bella was correct, the ladder had fallen at least an hour after Oliver had died. Without any conceivable human intervention at the time it fell.

'We've got the new time of death right. I'm sure of it. It's the ladder that's wrong, John! We never found any reason for Oliver to need it. It has to be a prop.'

She took it in stages, as her father had taught her.

'If the falling ladder was rigged, it was made to stand upright first. Harvey could have balanced it leaning away from the trellis, if he'd tied it to the top of the ironwork. He might have used string, or a length of washing line or...' She blinked and shook her head. 'I'm barking up the wrong tree. He's a keen fisherman.'

John nodded. 'He'd have used fishing line.'

'I reckon. So the ladder would be pointing away from the trellis, towards this wall. But it couldn't fall, because of the line.'

'So how did Harvey make it crash down later in the night?'

A very good question. For a moment her mind was blank, but then the heat of realisation crept over her. The gradual dawning of how it could have worked and how the time could be controlled quite precisely.

The answer had been staring her in the face, day-in, day-out at Vintage Winter.

FORTY-EIGHT

LATERAL THINKING

John was waiting for Bella's solution. How could Harvey have rigged the ladder to come crashing down at least an hour after Oliver had died? Bella thought she knew but she needed to check something first. She glanced at the house but there was no sign of anyone watching.

The prickling sensation on her skin intensified as she dashed towards the trellis.

Could it really be true? She crouched down and found it. Tiny traces of wax to the far side of the ironwork. For a second, she thought of her father, smiling.

'A Sweet Agnes candle.'

'I beg your pardon?'

'I think Harvey was terrified after the murder. He was desperate to create the impression that Oliver had been drunk and out of control. And active after he and Alexis were in bed. It would make it easier to write his death off as an accident. So he levered the shed lock off and took out the ladder. He must have wrapped Oliver's hands around it.' It was a grim thought. 'The police noticed fragments of rust on his fingers. And if they'd bothered to take prints, I'm guessing they'd have found those, too. Harvey was careful. He thought there might be a proper investigation.

'Then all he needed was a couple of bits of kit. Everyone's got Sweet Agnes candles this time of year, and they have hour markings on them. The gaps in the trellis are only four inches or so wide. He braced a nine-inch Sweet Agnes candle sideways against the far side of the trellis, tied fishing line around the middle and fed that through one of the gaps. Then he tied the other end to the ladder, holding it upright. After that he lit the candle. It was a bitterly cold night, but it was still. I remember noting it. He knew that once the candle burned down suffi-ciently it would slip through the gap, the fishing line would go slack and the ladder would crash down.'

'Waking Alexis when he was safely tucked up in bed.'

Bella nodded. 'She said she's a light sleeper. He would have guessed she'd wake up. I doubt he was really asleep. He'd have been too tense. If she hadn't stirred, I expect he'd have woken her instead and told her about the crash, but in the end it all worked a treat.'

'If this is right, what was Alexis doing when he was outside killing Oliver?'

Bella thought back. 'Watching an Agatha Christie on TV. She told me she was a superfan when I visited, but that Harvey isn't keen. Both Bernadette and your mum mentioned there was a new adaptation on that night. Bernadette said it was very dark, so she wasn't surprised it aired so late. We know the TV's in a room at the back of the house, thanks to Leo's nosiness, and I heard it playing after I went to bed. I doubt she'd have heard a thing.'

'He'd have needed to get rid of the fishing line and leftover candle, even if he missed some of the wax.'

'True.' And Alexis said she'd barely slept after being woken. He couldn't have sneaked out during the night. 'I'd guess he tidied up while she was showering the following morning. I remember hearing her singing and there was movement down-stairs. It wouldn't have taken him more than a couple of minutes.'

'So you think Harvey killed Frank too?'

It was an especially grim thought, that someone who'd stolen but never set out to kill had wiped two people off the face of the earth. She reassessed her thoughts, with Harvey in the role of murderer, and shivered. 'I'm afraid so. It was the same night as the recital. Frank had been talking to Harvey. Perhaps that made him nervous. And when he walked in on him watching a TV programme about detectorists, that must have been the final straw. He'd have been sure Oliver's dig and his death were on Frank's mind.

'I bumped into Alexis the morning after. Neither of us knew Frank was dead at that point. She told me she'd had her first proper night's sleep since Oliver died.' She shivered. 'Now I'm wondering if Harvey gave her something to make sure that was the case.'

She imagined him knocking on Frank's door. Making an excuse for his late-night walk. Expressing concern over the window which he'd deliberately cracked. Then attacking him. Managing to kill him so skilfully. Maybe it hadn't been luck after all...

'Do you remember Tony implied the murderer must have been knowledgeable or lucky?'

John nodded.

'Harvey's father was in the army. His dad could have told him tales of derring-do. He sounds like the sort to wish Harvey might follow in his footsteps. Harvey could have known enough to look it up beforehand. Work out a plan. And he was in the cadets. He talked about it at the recital.'

'I don't think they teach the cadets how to kill people,' John said drily.

'No, but I'll bet he and his friends watched films and read

up on close combat. As it happens, I don't think Frank saw
Harvey at the ruins. He, Julia and Nan were all gone by the
time Oliver called Cal. But Harvey must have made Frank
suspicious. I'd guess he realised he'd given himself away.'

'So he attacked him in a panic, and took his diary?'

'Yes. I assume Frank had it out and Harvey realised what it
was before he left. Frank was clearly obsessing over what he'd
seen: watching the TV programme. Rereading his journal entry
perhaps.' And then Bella went cold all over. 'Oh no, John, I've
just remembered. Nan Gifford said Frank was worried about
something a few weeks ago. Before all this business with Oliver.
He kept muttering to himself. Talking about someone doing
something under someone's nose. And Alexis said Oliver came
to meet her at the ruins once. She told him never to do it again.
But what if that's what Frank saw, and it was in his diary?' It
seemed to fit. 'Frank wanted to talk to Alexis at the recital.
Perhaps he hoped to warn her. Maybe he spoke to Harvey in an
effort to find out if he knew. To see if he'd had a motive to kill
Oliver. He'd have been reassured when Harvey laughed about
the lipstick on Oliver's collar. No husband would be so relaxed
if they knew it came from their wife. His guard would have
been down when Harvey knocked on his door.'

John shuddered. 'You think Harvey might know the truth
now, if he's read the diary?'

Her heart had gone into overdrive. 'It would explain how
angry he seemed, and Alexis not wanting us to leave her.'

'You think she could be in danger? But he did all this to
keep her. The theft of priceless artefacts and two murders. And
her lover's dead now.'

'That particular lover. But I think Alexis was finally making
up her mind to leave Harvey when I saw her by the river. And
as soon as she tells him, he'll have nothing left to lose.'

At that moment, they heard a scream from the house.

FORTY-NINE

WALKING INTO DANGER

Bella and John's eyes met.

'I'll call 999.' John had his phone out.

But would the police be in time? As he spoke into his mobile, she strode towards the house, crunching up the gravel. Nearing the building, she heard a roar. Harvey sounded like a wild animal.

John looked at her, his eyes wide, as he hung up. 'They're on their way.'

A howl. Harvey again.

'He'll kill her before they get here.' He sounded utterly out of control. Bella looked about her. She wanted a stone. A good large one. At last, she saw what she was after. 'We've got to distract him. Make him realise they're not alone.' She lobbed the stone through a window but the breaking glass sounded quiet in comparison to the row going on inside.

'Stop!' Bella yelled through the window, but there was no sign he or Alexis had heard.

'We have to get inside.' She looked for something larger, to take out more of the glass.

John grabbed a terracotta pot and smashed at the pane. How could Harvey not hear? But the yelling would drown it out. John took off his coat and padded the bottom of the window frame to protect them from the jagged shards.

'At least with us and Alexis he's outnumbered,' Bella said, as she clambered inside.

John looked less certain as he scrambled in after her. 'I think they're upstairs.'

'I'm going to go up there and shout. He won't do anything if he knows he's got company. And he doesn't know we've guessed about Oliver and Frank.'

She took the sweeping stairs two at a time, up to the galleried landing, her coat swishing around her.

'Hello?' Her voice wasn't as loud as she wanted it to be. What should she say? For a second, she felt uncertain. Maybe she'd just broken a window so she could walk in on a common-or-garden row. Harvey might not mean Alexis any harm. Maybe she was wrong about him. But then she heard his voice.

'I did it all for you! Don't you see? For you and for Barney. I couldn't lose you. I won't lose you.'

'Harvey! No!' Alexis's voice pushed all doubts out. It shook with horror and fear.

Bella hammered on the door of the room they occupied.

Silence fell. Then Harvey wrenched the door open. He was holding a gun.

Bella darted towards the rear of the house, John towards the stairs. No. She couldn't bear it. John was the threat and Harvey could see it. Bella was cut off but if he let John run, he could leave the house and call for help. Harvey didn't know they'd already dialled 999.

'The police are on their way!' Bella yelled. 'It's too late, Harvey. Put the gun down.'

'I don't believe you!' Harvey was running at John, approaching him from behind. A split second later she heard the bang. So loud. So horrifying. Her breath went out of her as she saw John stumble and fall. The awful sound of him thumping down the stairs.

'John!'

And now, Harvey turned towards her.

FIFTY

A LIFE OR DEATH DECISION

Harvey was entirely focused on Bella. He stood between her and the stairs. There was no way she could get past him.

She stood her ground, staring at him, as tears for John coursed down her cheeks. She had no idea what to do.

He walked towards her, the gun pointed at her chest. His eyes on hers. And hers fixed on his. Yet still he didn't fire. Bella tried to keep hold of rational thought. Maybe it was psychologically harder to shoot someone when they weren't running. But there was no way he'd let her go.

'The police are on their way,' she said again quietly. 'You'll hear the sirens in a minute.'

Behind him, she glimpsed Alexis creeping across the landing. Heard her tiptoe down the stairs.

She'd have to climb over John's body. Agonising sorrow did battle with utter fury. Bella took a juddering breath.

Harvey had got so close now she could touch him.

She could lash out, he would shoot, and it would all be over in a moment. 'Is that your dad's gun? What would he think of the way you're behaving now?'

'I don't have any choice.'

Dimly, an idea came. She paused for one long moment, then ducked suddenly to one side.

Harvey fired a shot. It sounded like an explosion, echoing in Bella's ears. But he'd missed. He swung the gun up at her head instead to hit her with it. On the temple. The weak spot he'd found in Frank's skull.

He missed again as Bella ducked away once more, shrugging in her coat as she did so.

He grabbed for her, clutching at the faux fur, and she slid out of it like a lizard shedding its tail. Clutching at something fluid threw him. He stumbled and fell but he still had the gun.

He raised it unsteadily as she looked desperately for a weapon. Gritting her teeth, she hurled an antique vase at his head, and he howled in pain. He was struggling. He'd dropped the gun but it was beyond Bella's reach. He'd have it again within seconds.

She was frantic. He could aim and fire if she chose the route to the lower floor. But the attic felt just as risky.

At last, she ran along the corridor, her feet thudding on the dark red carpet, making for the room she'd stayed in. She turned a corner.

In her mind's eye she could see the extension jutting out below the bedroom. Its sloping roof.

Harvey was up. She could hear his thudding feet. She'd be in his sights in moments.

She hurled herself through the wooden door and slammed it shut, dragging the dressing table to barricade herself in. She flung open the window.

Harvey was rattling at the door. There was no time.

She was through and onto the roof, slipping down the slope in the frost. Behind her she heard the door give way, the dressing table scrape across the floor.

But at last came the sound of sirens. And down below, Alexis held out her arms, ready to help her down.

Harvey didn't appear at the window.

'He'll try to run!' Bella said. 'The police aren't here yet. And what about John?' The floods of tears were back.

'I'm so sorry, Bella,' Alexis said. 'He was just lying there. He looked so pale.'

'He was shot?'

'I didn't see any blood but I think the fall...' She shook her head.

But at that moment they heard a howl of rage. Harvey. What was happening?

Bella and Alexis rushed to the front of the house. The door was open from when Alexis had run, swinging on its hinges.

There in front of them at the bottom of the stairs was Harvey, sprawled and writhing in pain. The gun was under the telephone table.

And to one side was John, slumped against the hall wall, looking white and sick. But alive.

'John!' Bella forgot his dislike of overly demonstrative behaviour and hugged him for all she was worth. 'We thought you were dead.'

'So did I for a moment.'

Bella glanced up at the stairs. 'You genius!' He'd removed the stair rods that held the Howards' carpet in place. 'You tugged the runner upwards as he came down?'

'He was in a bit of a hurry. I sprang out when he was on the top stair and gave the carpet a yank.'

'I always knew you weren't just a pretty face.'

John winced.

Alexis went to pick up the gun.

'Not without gloves!' Some things her father had taught her were more straightforward than others.

At that moment, the police arrived. Uniformed officers were taking control of Harvey and his weapon. Then Barry Dixon and his colleagues came. For once, Dixon looked one hundred per cent awake, despite the bird seed in his hair.

FIFTY-ONE

AFTERMATH

John went to hospital to be checked for concussion. They kept him in overnight. When Bella visited the next day, he was surrounded by well-wishers and enduring the noise.

After ten minutes, he looked at her pleadingly.

'Do you want us to go?' Bella whispered. 'Leave you and Gareth to it?'

'It's not that I don't love you all.'

'I know.'

Bella encouraged the family to join her for hot chocolate at the Steps. She'd closed Vintage Winter for the morning. Everyone knew what had happened; they would understand.

When they reached the café, it was Matt who stepped in to help Poppy behind the counter.

'He works here?' Bella said to Leo.

'Only when I can get him. He rivals me when it comes to cooking, but he's annoyingly elusive.'

She turned to her new friends, who'd already become family, and explained what had happened the previous night. It was only after she'd relayed the main drama that she told them the other, lesser details she'd discovered the previous day. When she got to the bit about Cal shoplifting, Jeannie's brow furrowed.

'He needs some direction,' she said. 'I should have thought to organise it before. You should offer him some Saturday work here, Leo.'

'Not likely!'

She raised her eyebrows. 'Honestly! We'll have him at the Blue Boar then. A kitchen porter. Boxer will keep an eye on him.'

Boxer was Gareth's sous chef, musclebound, hence the nickname.

'I'm sure Gareth will be delighted,' Leo said. 'And you normally have to offer people jobs, rather than just allocating them.'

'Leave it with me,' Jeannie said firmly.

While John recovered, Bella received a series of well-wishers at Vintage Winter who wanted to know how he was. She converted several of them into customers and delivered their grapes and flowers to John at regular intervals.

Nan Gifford came in and had a good cry over a cup of tea. It was bad enough to lose Frank. Far more harrowing now she knew for sure that he and Oliver had been killed. She and Cal had had a heart to heart. She knew he'd been feeling claustrophobic, just like her. He'd agreed to take a shift at the Blue Boar. That was Jeannie for you. Bella felt a wave of sympathy for Gareth, but it sounded as though Boxer would be used as a human shield. As for Nan, she planned to take up dancing. She said she'd loved it as a teenager.

Barney had come home to be with Alexis, who was going to move out of Raven House. Get a divorce. She and her son looked close. There was talk of him starting school locally.

Harvey was in custody, of course. His business would be

sold. Tyler might have to rethink his work ethic if the new owner kept him on.

Museums were assessing Oliver's treasure, trying to work out where each piece had come from. It was the largest collection of recovered goods in living memory. Alexis had added the ring and brooch to the haul. She said she'd go and view them once they were on display; it was enough to know that Oliver had meant her to have them. John had handed his coin in, too.

As for Julia Sandford, Carys said she was applying for a professorship down south.

On Friday, John was back.

'How are you feeling?'

'Better. Have you looked at the drawing board?'

Bella had, of course, though she'd resolved not to finish it without him.

She rearranged the playing cards.

Queen of hearts, who loved too much: Alexis. *In* love with Oliver, but attached to her old life too.

Queen of spades, who was full of fear: Nan, who was terrified Cal would end up like his dad.

Queen of clubs, striving for immortality: Julia, who'd wanted to make her mark. Discover the Roman ruins with Oliver. Get the recognition she deserved.

Queen of diamonds: Meg. The enigma who popped up in Oliver's life, furious at an act which he saw as a kindness.

'It's ironic that they all ended up being irrelevant in the end,' John said.

'True, but the pursuit of them gave us enough evidence to solve the mystery.'

That night, it was finally time for Bella's date with Rupert Edgar. She opted for full-on vintage elegance in a figure-hugging dress, her hair up.

The evening was awful. Rupert treated the whole Oliver Barton affair as a joke and was incredulous when he discovered her policeman father and Oliver had been friends.

'Do you think he knew Oliver was a common thief?'

He'd struck Bella as an exceptional one, which made her think of *Die Hard*, but she didn't mention that. 'I suspect he might have. And that he was probably preparing to talk him into giving up his "hobby". His next move would have been to persuade him to take his finds to the coroner.'

'Why not just arrest him?'

'He worked to get the community's trust. Doing things by force would have been a last resort, but he was a kind and clever man. He didn't often get to that stage.'

Rupert snorted. It was the snort that did it.

She did a Meg Jones and walked out, striding back to Southwell Hall, her coat swishing. She slammed the door as she re-entered the flat. After that, she had a long hot shower and tried to calm down.

The next morning, she bumped into Matt and Cuthbert in the shared hall. The last thing she needed.

'Sorry your date didn't work out,' Matt said, stroking the cat.

She sniffed. 'How do you know I went on a date? And what makes you think it didn't work out?'

'You left looking like a million dollars. As for the end result, you came back early, slammed the door, and sang "moronic" to Blondie's "Atomic".'

'I did?'

He nodded.

He could hear what she sang in the shower? It was a horrible thought.

'I was at school with Rupert.' He must have seen him waiting, out in the lane. 'He always was an idiot. All smart trousers and no substance.'

Bella glanced at Matt's scruffy jeans and donkey jacket.

At that moment a brunette arrived, gave Bella an unfriendly glance, then kissed Matt on the lips. 'Ready?'

He nodded. 'See you around, Bella.'

She was left with Cuthbert, who planted himself firmly on her doormat, waiting to be let in. 'No. Some of us have got jobs to go to.' But she bent to make a fuss of him all the same.

As she walked up St Giles's Steps, a text arrived from Tony.

What about a nice drink at the Mitre this evening? There's an interesting little case I'd like to run past you.

A LETTER FROM CLARE

Thank you so much for reading *The Antique Store Detective*. I do hope you had fun trying to identify the killer! If you'd like to keep up to date with all my latest releases, you can sign up at the following link. Your email address will never be shared, and you can unsubscribe at any time. You'll also receive an exclusive short story, 'Mystery at Monty's Teashop'. I hope you enjoy it!

www.bookouture.com/clare-chase

The Antique Store Detective is exciting for me, as it's the start of a new series! The setting is fictional, but elements of Hope Eaton are inspired by the beautiful town of Bridgnorth, where my uncle and aunt live. It's close to my heart.

The idea for the plot came to me one hot summer when strange patterns on drought-stricken grass were reported in the news. It was fascinating to read about how these markings act as clues to the past.

If you have time, I'd love it if you were able to write a review of *The Antique Store Detective*. Feedback is really valuable, and it also makes a huge difference in helping new readers discover my books. Alternatively, if you'd like to contact me personally, you can reach me via my website, Facebook page, X or Instagram. It's always great to hear from readers.

Again, thank you so much for deciding to spend some time reading *The Antique Store Detective*. I'm looking forward to sharing my next book with you very soon.

With all best wishes,

Clare x

www.clarechase.com

 facebook.com/ClareChaseAuthor
 x.com/ClareChase_
 instagram.com/clarechaseauthor

ACKNOWLEDGEMENTS

Much love and thanks to Charlie, George and Ros for the feedback and cheerleading!

And more than ever, a huge thank you to my wonderful editor Ruth Tross, who made embarking on this new series possible. As always, her insights and ideas have made a massive difference. I'm also very grateful to Noelle Holten for her fantastic promo work and to Hannah Snetsinger, Fraser Crichton and Liz Hatherell for their expertise. Sending thanks too to Debbie Clement for her excellent cover design, as well as to Peta Nightingale, Kim Nash and everyone involved in editing, book production and sales at Bookouture. It's a genuine privilege to be published and promoted by such a competent, creative and friendly team.

Love and thanks also to Mum and Dad, Phil and Jenny, David and Pat, Warty, Andrea, Jen, the Westfield gang, Margaret, Shelly, Mark, my Andrewes relations and a whole bunch of family and friends.

Thanks also to the wonderful Bookouture authors and other writers for their friendship and support. And a massive, heartfelt thank you to the generous book bloggers and reviewers who pass on their thoughts about my work. Their support is invaluable.

And finally, but importantly, thanks to you, the reader, for buying or borrowing this book!

PUBLISHING TEAM

Turning a manuscript into a book requires the efforts of many people. The publishing team at Bookouture would like to acknowledge everyone who contributed to this publication.

Audio
Alba Proko
Sinead O'Connor
Melissa Tran

Commercial
Lauren Morrissette
Jil Thielen
Imogen Allport

Cover design
Debbie Clement

Data and analysis
Mark Alder
Mohamed Bussuri

Editorial
Ruth Tross
Melissa Tran

Copyeditor
Fraser Crichton

Proofreader
Liz Hatherell

Marketing
Alex Crow
Melanie Price
Occy Carr
Ciara Rosney

Operations and distribution
Marina Valles
Stephanie Straub

Production
Hannah Snetsinger
Mandy Kullar
Jen Shannon

Publicity
Kim Nash
Noelle Holten
Myrto Kalavrezou
Jess Readett
Sarah Hardy

Rights and contracts
Peta Nightingale
Richard King
Saidah Graham

Printed in Great Britain
by Amazon